Who, or what, is WHOM? W[...] [...] dominates the White House. Nobody is quite sur[...] [...] for, although it is generally assumed that WH stand for White House. It is a system that takes the humdrum worries of global politics off the President's shoulders, organises his love-life and calculates the probability of Armageddon; a system so complex that the only man who understands it can't explain it.

Like WHOM, *WHOM* is cunningly constructed and full of surprises. Its 'datastreams' tell stories that are apparently unrelated. White House Aide (and Pillowtalk monitor) Alb Telemann becomes obsessed by President Pike's saintly but sinister mistress, who may or may not be manipulated by his Spiritual Advisor for born-again ends. A real saint, Paul, is shipwrecked on the Mediterranean island of Lazar. In modern Lazar a young Englishwoman is caught up in a hijack with bizarre consequences for her marital status, and a young Englishman, his passport confiscated by a one-eyed ten-year-old, is stranded in the middle of a civil war. Gradually these small stories add up to one big one, the biggest of them all . . .

WHOM, Matthew Francis's first novel, is a surreal, chilling comedy for the age of the electronic office. It is also a murder mystery, a Biblical fantasy, and a hilarious satire on the lunacies of religious fundamentalism and American foreign policy. Like all the best satires, it's probably true.

Matthew Francis was born in 1956 and educated at the Universities of Cambridge and Sussex. Three of his stories have appeared in *First Fictions: Introduction 10*. He works as a freelance writer of computer manuals and lives in Winchester.

WHOM

MATTHEW FRANCIS

BLOOMSBURY

First published 1989
This paperback edition published 1990

Bloomsbury Publishing Ltd, 2 Soho Square, London W1V 5DE
Francis, Matthew
Whom
I. Title
823'.914[F]

ISBN 0-7475-0596-9

10 9 8 7 6 5 4 3 2 1

Typeset by Hewer Text Composition Services, Edinburgh
Printed in Great Britain by Collins, Glasgow

FOR CREINA

*And the kings of the earth who have committed
fornication and lived deliciously with her,
shall bewail her, and lament for her, when
they shall see the smoke of her burning,
standing afar off from the fear of her
torment, saying, Alas, alas, that great city
Babylon, that mighty city! for in one hour is
thy judgment come.*

Revelation 18, 9–10

Datastream 1; Telemann, Alb

You had to know WHOM, Jimmy Ruggins discovered. Ruggins was new to the White House in those days. He was a man in an alarmingly white suit fresh from Muscle Shoals, Alabama, where he had been making blues records and desalinating his personality, using the southern sunshine to remove the salt of Portland, Maine, from it. ('No American will ever take seriously a preacher who comes from Portland,' Jimmy Ruggins once said in a Press conference.) At any rate, even a desalinated Ruggins in white suit and sideburns did not have the *nous*, the *savvy*, the *wherewithal*, or any of the other fashionable White House terms for a grasp of the internal situation. Politics, he realized, is a game you have to know how to play if you play at all.

The first thing Ruggins discovered about the White House is that it is dominated by a computer, namely an IBM #000 (pronounced hash thousand) Series, with 1,500 local terminals and network links to the Pentagon. That was the first, and the least important: when he started realizing the subsequent things, he revised this initial statement and understood instead that the White House is dominated, not by a computer, but by a computer system. The system is called WHOM, and, you can say, simplistically and in non-technical language, that it does everything. That explanation should suffice for user-level readers. Jimmy Ruggins, in common with most aides who join the White House with no previous data processing experience, probably began by seeing WHOM anthropomorphically as an enormous brain which understood everything, organized everything, and would, if left to itself, happily take over the world, thus making theology redundant. He must quickly have found out that whatever WHOM actually is, it is a lot more like a place than a person. Really, it ought to be called WHERE.

They told Ruggins that the essence of the system was security. Ernest Hellbaum, the system manager of WHOM, explained that it was like a huge, labyrinthine office building, a little like the White House itself. Each user has his/her own small room, known as a virtual office, which contains only the data that the individual occupant might need, but no more. (*Virtual* is a word much used by Ernest Hellbaum to express the inadequate mapping of the world on to the computer. It is used in such phrases as virtual storage, virtual memory, even virtual machine; a virtual machine is something which behaves as if it were a machine when it isn't.) At this point, the analogy, like all analogies by which Ernest Hellbaum tries to explain his job, breaks down: WHOM is not like any ordinary building because some people can see into the rooms of other occupants. For example, it may well be that the Secretary of State has a security agent assigned to keep an eye on all his digital machinations, because a man in his position must not be allowed to make mistakes. This agent, if there is one, can actually intervene in the case of secretarial error and correct the undiplomatic memo or whatever. Therefore the system can't even be compared to a building in which some of the rooms are bugged. 'No,' Hellbaum concluded, shrugging his shoulders, 'it isn't really like anything much. You can't actually explain it.' Hellbaum's eyes filled with helpless tears behind his glasses.

'What does WHOM stand for?' Ruggins asked.

'What does what?' Hellbaum said nervously.

'The initials WHOM. What do they stand for?'

'I don't know. The WH is White House, I guess.'

Even allowing for the white suit and sideburns, after a few months in the White House, Ruggins began to understand. Everything that happens is known to someone and monitored by someone. Nobody knows everything; not even Ernest Hellbaum (for much of the data is encrypted); not even – or possibly least of all – the President himself. Ruggins got used, as we all do, to the small, private office with personal coffee machine and en suite bathroom (restocked every morning with lemon soap, towels and a band of inviolate paper around the toilet seat). He got used to the silence, the fact that no one ever visited him; the corridors were almost always empty, and people he met in them, or in the elevators, or in the underground parking lot, did not speak. Ruggins never even got to see the man he was supposed to advise, after the initial welcoming cocktail party at which both he and the President drank club soda and all the other guests were silent men in identical suits who drank nothing at all. Ruggins got used, finally, to the presence of the terminal on his desk. He stopped being frightened of it, the way it said WHOM in giant eyeball letters, each being composed of dozens of smaller letters, the way it said *Please Enter Identity*. Ruggins had received an identity from Ernest Hellbaum during his induction. He had entered it, and sent his nervous electronic memos about the seventh commandment and 1 Thessalonians. The President never bothered to reply.

WHOM is good to new staff. Unlike most other White House employees, it introduces itself on your first day.

> Welcome to WHOM. You have at your disposal the processing power of an IBM #000 (pronounced hash thousand) Series computer and the world's largest online relational database. You are one of the 1,500 users at your site uniquely privileged to have access to this splendid resource. Once you have mastered the computer, the whole harvest of human knowledge will be yours for the reaping, provided you are authorized to reap it. Enjoy!

> But remember – using a computer may be like a game, but it's a game you have to know how to play if you are to play at all. Please read your WHOM Users' Handbook before attempting to go further, paying special attention to Chapters 1, 3, 8 and 9. Once you have read this, you can explore the user interface of this system in the confidence that nothing will go wrong. And just in case anything does, you will need to know the name and phone number of your System Manager:

> NAME: Ernest Hellbaum. PHONE: 68392

> Now press F1 for further information.

If you're lucky, you only get this spiel on your first day as a WHOM user. In my own case, there was a problem which caused it to flash up on my screen at random intervals for the first month or so, until I finally reported it, via the telephone, to Ernest Hellbaum. 'It looks as if you have an incident,' Hellbaum said, and went on to fix it while I was hanging on to the receiver. In those days, you could still reach Hellbaum over the telephone, and he was pretty sharp.

In his first month as a White House aide, Jimmy Ruggins read the latest news from the Wocaluha Inquiry chaired by Senator Florian, in which a witness told how he personally observed the dill pickle factory conflagration at first hand. The time of day was nearly morning; he could tell this without a watch because the sky was lightening in the east. It looked as if the fire was only a couple of streets away, a thick cloud of smoke, lit from underneath by an artificial strawberry glow. The scent of dill, intensified a thousand times, seemed to be coming from inside his own head; the witness now regularly suffered chest pains and migraine headaches. His ability to work had been affected by persistent trembling of the hands (he was a lathe operator), and he was considering private legal action against the Company (the Snakattak Company of Honolulu).

Shortly afterwards, Ruggins himself was featuring in the news digest, when, in a keynote speech, he heralded the pickle holocaust as the first disaster of the Last Days, and warned of others to follow. He commented on the prevalence of violence in the modern world.

'It is evidence of the continuing decline of modern morality that people attempt to resolve their problems by the use of force.' God would not stand idly by, Ruggins argued, while mankind continued to brawl and bicker. The bloodshed and brutality in places like Lazar, Afghanistan and Northern Ireland were just one additional symptom of the great and terrible crisis towards which the world was inexorably heading, as were the famines in Ethiopia and the Sudan, and the spread of AIDS among Western nations.

'AIDS is a punishment from God for sexual immorality and the promiscuity of the modern world,' he added. 'In the same way, war, such as we have in Lazar and other troublespots, is God's punishment for man's love of killing and violence. I hear approaching hoofbeats.'

4

Even though he was not averse to making politico-apocalyptic comments of this kind, Ruggins saw his main duty in those days as an ethico-sexual one. He was naive enough to imagine that President Pike had appointed a religious adviser to advise him to be religious; he knew, as everyone else in the White House knew, as indeed everyone in the world who wanted to know knew, that the President, to use St Paul's words (1 Thessalonians) possessed his vessel in the lust of concupiscence. Even in the very week of the Inauguration, there had been a shock revelation in the *Potomac Inquirer*.

Else Vorbeam, a Washington DC social worker, claimed that she had had 'a romantic encounter' with incoming US President Warren Pike. 'It was wonderful,' she declared. 'I think he's the most attractive man. No, neither of us has any guilty feelings on the subject whatsoever. I would do it again tomorrow.' The newspapers described it as Pike's Struggle With Beautiful Women, and compared it to his wife's struggle against alcoholism.

I dare say Jimmy Ruggins, in the days before that first and only club soda cocktail party, had hoped that he would be perpetually in and out of the Oval Office with words of wisdom and support, helping Pike with his struggle, perhaps even helping the First Lady with hers, 'Courage, Warren, remember the words of St Paul; courage, Mary Beth, you don't need Jack Daniels when you have Jesus.' It must have been a bitter moment when he found himself alone in his office with coffee machine, lemon soap etc, and realized that the screen and keyboard on his desk, soulless artefacts of glass, plastic and silicon, were now his only route to the President's conscience, and the hope of a celibate America.

Ruggins sent off electronic memos, of course, but received no answer. From time to time, the memos were deleted from Pike's electronic mailbox and archived on to tape. Ernest Hellbaum carried them to a fireproof vault underneath the White House lawn, where they sat in rows with other reels of unwanted data, pleading for chastity with ineffectual magnetism. For all Ruggins knew, the President never even read them. Maybe somebody was preventing him from doing so; maybe there were people in high places who couldn't cope with a non-promiscuous President.

This is mere speculation – I mean that I am speculating on what Ruggins may have been speculating on. Who knows what Ruggins may have guessed, as he sat in front of his terminal, grinding his fingernails into the palms of his hands? He knew that Pike's sexual habits were immoral; had it occurred to him that they were also dangerous? Did he think one day as he sat in front of the green eyeball letters about the security risk of all these one-to-one personal encounters? The whole of WHOM was designed to preserve data integrity and to prevent any leakage through unnecessary interfaces. The White House itself was run on the same basis, hence its silent corridors, elevators and parking lots, the private coffee machines and en suite bathrooms. Surely, Ruggins must have reflected, the system would not allow its informational nexus, its central nervous system (the President), to exchange intimacies on a random basis with every nurse and secretary, every would-be actress and model who happened to have a ninety-five centimeter bust and a sincere personality? WHOM was too smart for that. If it guarded against logical leaks, the electronic transfer of data to unauthorized persons, there had to be safeguards against the physical variety. There must be some kind of screening mechanism, a means of weeding out the subversives, the assassins, the Soviet agents, the newspaper reporters. More than that, once the President was actually interfacing with the duly screened and selected partner, there had to be a bugging system, just to make sure their romantic encounter didn't go beyond the intimate to the confidential.

Glad to know you. My name is Alb Telemann. I am in charge of Sleeping Partner and Pillowtalk.

SUBJECT:	That's very interesting, Cissie, why are you doing that?
PARTNER:	I thought you might like it, Sir, a lot of guys do.
SUBJECT:	Really? Like that? I don't believe I've come across that one before. It's certainly unusual.
PARTNER:	Sir?
SUBJECT:	Yes?
PARTNER:	Do you like it, Sir? Like this?
SUBJECT:	It's intriguing. It's certainly different. I guess maybe it's an acquired taste or something. [PAUSE] It's not dangerous, is it?
PARTNER:	Dangerous, no, of course not, Sir, I do this all the time.

SUBJECT:	Well that's good. I guess that's OK then. It isn't perverted, or anything like that, is it? [PAUSE] What do you mean, all the time? I hope you don't do this too often.
PARTNER:	Don't you like it, Sir?
SUBJECT:	It's really very pleasant. I guess I'm just an old fogey, aren't I?
PARTNER:	You're supposed to lie back and enjoy it. Sir?
SUBJECT:	I see, lie back and enjoy it. You mean maybe words kind of get in the way of the experience? I never thought of it that way. Are you sure this isn't an unnatural vice, or something like that?
PARTNER:	It's the most natural thing in the world. Enjoy.
SUBJECT:	The most natural thing in the world, eh? That's very interesting. Enjoy? Yes, OK. You're not the first woman I've ever . . . you know, Cissie. I mean, I guess you knew that anyway because my wife . . . but she and I . . . not that much any more. I was quite late getting started with this sort of thing, Cissie, I guess I didn't know I was supposed to be doing it, not really. Do you have to turn round, or is that optional? The thing was, Cissie, I had a very sheltered Baptist upbringing.
PARTNER:	Sir . . . Sir . . . Sir . . .

*** DIALOGUE ENDS. SLEEP ASSUMED ***

When I took this job, I was not used to computers, any more than Jimmy Ruggins was. As a private detective, I was more used to following people, on foot or in cars, or in cabs. Like Ruggins, I found my job lonely and rather frightening at first; then, as he did, I grasped the principle and became a real user. With the aid of the Pillowtalk tapes, which did at least provide some of the authentic sound effects of passion, the wow and flutter of actual intercourse, I became aware that data is more than letters and numbers on a screen or in a vault under the White House lawn. That it has a human reality. Or, to put it another way, that what we think of as our human realities, are, in fact, reducible to data.

7

Sleeping Partner is not just a screening system. There is a maxim shared by me and my colleague, Fred Zolph, whom I've never met, and by our immediate superior Roly Entwhistle, whom neither of us have ever met (except electronically):

Sleeping Partner active, subject passive.
Sleeping Partner passive, subject active.

Essentially, this means that while Warren Pike is engaged in his struggle with beautiful women, he isn't intervening in the Lazari Civil War, or in Senator Florian's Commission of Inquiry into the Wocaluha disaster. Since the Sleeping Partner database, about which he knows nothing, has been in existence, Pike has led a happy, fulfilled and largely nonpolitical existence. Only when AIDS hit the headlines did he begin to worry a little, and then Fred Zolph's problem was to reassure without letting him know that the system that was taking care of that was taking care of everything else as well: making sure he didn't get involved with Communists, Socialists, foreign nationals, anarchists, Moslems, civil rights activists . . . Technically, AIDS was no problem at all. It was just a question of adding one more flag to the prospective partner file:

AIDS = N

or

AIDS = Y

In any case, no woman is ever admitted into the database unless every single one of her sexual partners has been thoroughly checked out, a difficult task and one which requires overnight processing even on a computer as powerful as the #000 Series mainframe. The important thing is to take all precautions necessary for national security, while preserving the freshness and spontaneity of the experience. I wonder sometimes why the whole business doesn't either put me off sex for good or drive me wild with desire. But then I have been well chosen, somewhat on the principle of the eunuch in the harem, as a man whose obsessional neurosis forces me to worry and panic instead. Ten thousand different community workers, nurses and secretaries, all prepared to give up their honor for the honor of their country, to become a database of:

Name

Age

Bust measurement

Address

Phone number

Previous lovers (repeating group)

Political affiliation (Democrat, Republican, Other, Don't Know)

Consummation Flag (Y/N)

Referee (1)

Referee (2)

It's beautiful, when you think about it. But I worry too much to think about it.

When Jimmy Ruggins made his speech about Wocaluha, in the wintry spring following the President's inauguration, he was already a spiritual force in the land as well as a musical one. The speech was well-received, especially the cryptic remark about approaching hoofbeats. It was his first reference to the apocalypse in his new capacity, and was taken by many as an indication of an official government eschatology.

Whether or not it was taken as such by my daughter Roxanne, the speech ruined her breakfasts, and mine, for several weeks. Roxanne was only sixteen, then, and it seemed to me that her world ought to be beginning rather than ending, and if she was going to sit in tears at the breakfast table every icy morning of that almost spring, it ought to be because of some boy and not because of a Presidential theology adviser and world famous Blues Evangelist.

'Religion is supposed to make you happy,' I told her one morning, 'you are supposed to dance and sing and be joyful in the Lord.' (Actually, it is not my job to be religious. I am suspicious of people

9

who do things like that, but since I am always suspicious in any case, I guessed I could live with it. I would rather have seen her happy than crying into her coffee.)

'The Last Days are beginning,' Roxanne said.

'People always think that. When I was a boy, there was always a man on every street corner carrying a sign that said "Get ready, for the Lord cometh to judge ye". The end of the world is part of the American way of life.'

'You don't understand,' she said, weeping. 'You're not a believer, so you don't understand and you won't be saved.'

'I'll take my chances – you don't really believe that, do you?'

'All of the four horsemen are on their way,' she said. 'There are all the signs. The great plague is AIDS, and the famine is the one in Ethiopia, and the war could be lots of wars, I guess Lazar or something. And then there was that horrible disaster in Wocaluha, I guess that was the death part. Jimmy Ruggins believes it. He really believes it, you can tell.'

'And just because Jimmy Ruggins believes it, you have to believe also?'

'Jimmy Ruggins is a great man.'

I spooned sugar into my coffee, three spoonfuls, which meant it was going to be a bad day. The clock on the wall showed almost 8.30 am; it is the kind that has hands and tick, because although I have gotten used to computers, I cannot understand digital time, not since Ernest Hellbaum explained to me that it is computed in nanoseconds from a random moment in 1856. Ever since then, I have to have a ticking clock to make me believe in time at all. Now it was the third voice in my conversation with Roxanne, reminding me that there was work to do. I watched the minute hand slowly moving ninewards, slicing precious minutes off my travelling time.

So Jimmy Ruggins was a great man. I already knew a thing or two about Ruggins; that he was America's greatest Blues Evangelist, and the Presidential Adviser on theology, that he worked in the White House and gave the President electronic guidance on all matters concerning his spiritual wellbeing.

'He used to be a blues DJ,' Roxanne explained. Her tears were evaporating now, and she had started to drink her coffee, as though the very mention of the great name was a healing influence, 'That was in Portland, Maine, and in those days he couldn't play music or sing.'

Not only do I know about Jimmy Ruggins, I know all about Maine, too. I have had Maine up to the highwater mark. As a boy, I used to go there on strange and depressing fishing trips with my father, which have left me with a permanent phobia about lakes. The insects rose menacingly above the water like hieroglyphics. I couldn't understand the language they talked, or the language my father was talking, if he was, in the insect-filled silences. Clearly, there is a non-communication gene in the Telemann biochemistry. And I never caught a fish.

'When he got the call,' Roxanne said, 'God said to him, "Play guitar," so he picked up the guitar and he found he could play it. Isn't that wonderful?'

I suppose God told him to sing, too. That was not nice of God. Well, I woke up this morning, and God was in my band. So Ruggins stopped being a Blues DJ and playing other people's records in Portland, Maine, and began being a Blues Evangelist and making his own records in Muscle Shoals, Alabama.

'He used to be just an ordinary person. He was really sinful, in fact, I mean even more than most people. Because he used to take drugs and all that kind of thing, you know, and drink and have sex with lots of different women. And then he discovered that religious highs were higher than chemical highs or biological highs. Religious highs are the highest there are.'

I thought of the 10,000 Presidential women in the Sleeping Partner database, and wondered if Warren Pike thought that religious highs were higher than biological ones. Probably he did, when not actually in pursuit of the ultimate orgasm. Intercourse has a way of catching Warren Pike by surprise, perhaps because he never has to arrange it for himself. When I listen, it always sounds as though Pike has just stepped into the bedroom to get a book and is amazed to find a naked woman in the bed. Poor Roxanne, I thought, I guess she's in love with Jimmy Ruggins; she'll grow out of it some day.

Meanwhile, Roxanne continued to cry into her coffee throughout the wintry mornings of that exceptionally protracted dogwood winter, and to refuse scrambled eggs and grape jelly. Her high-school work was suffering; she struggled for two weeks over a book report on *Revelation* which her English teacher described as hysterical and immature. Finally, some kind of hereditary influence took over, and she began, in a tentative high-school sort of way, to follow Jimmy Ruggins. That's my girl, I thought, she can't even be born again without being surreptitious about it. There is an element of sneakiness in her character that must have been left over from her previous birth.

I first heard, or rather saw, the name Ellen Axaxas on my VDU, in an office that looked out, like that of Jimmy Ruggins, on a grey and frozen lawn, smoothly patrolled by men in broad suits and dogs with muscular shoulders. Beyond the lawns was Washington DC, its white facades, its Georgian simplicities, tunafish sandwich shops, Greyhound station, seven universities and 77,000 swimming pools. I saw the name on a monthly report of candidate Sleeping Partners to be considered for admission to the database. There was nothing special about Ellen Axaxas except the absence of sexual partners, and that didn't worry me too much. I don't have a lot of faith in innocence, but I don't have a lot of faith in WHOM either. A system is only as good as its worst data input clerk, Ernest Hellbaum once told me, and I strongly suspected that Ellen had had more input than showed up on her master file. Even a Sleeping Partner has a right to some privacy. I didn't think some obscure sexual encounter in the high-school playing fields that the boy never remembered afterwards, or if he did, thought it had been with someone else, should be an inhibiting factor, just because it wasn't on the file. Maybe she really was a virgin. Even so, what was wrong with that? Pike had had others – at least, he had in principle, and principle is what counts with virgins, so they tell me. Everyone has to start somewhere, and where better than the very top? I want you to remember, though, I was uneasy. Even all those months ago, I was uneasy.

Why? The only possible reason was the two Xs in her name, which gave me a peculiar feeling in my stomach, but it was a feeling I could hardly have explained coherently to the Fred Zolphs of my professional life, and which I can hardly explain to myself today. However, I *did* pass her. If it wasn't for those slightly sinister Xs, it might have been a long time before I took any notice of this particular honey blonde elementary-school teacher: but the peculiar name gave me something to remember her by. Apart from that, there was nothing out of the ordinary. I knew that, if she was lucky enough to be selected by Fred Zolph for an At Home, she would have exactly the same brief and glamorous career as the rest. I knew the routine down to the least detail, from the pass that would be sent to 2054 South Roseberry Avenue, Hillingdon Village DC, a week before, down to the letter of thanks that would be slipped into her purse so that she could find it afterwards:

> Remember that you have had intimacy not merely with a man but with an Administration, and through that, in a sense, with the people of the United States as a whole. Be proud – and be careful.

This message is written in a special ink that fades quickly on exposure to air. The President, naturally, sees neither the pass nor the letter.

But there was something about those Xs which stayed in my mind long after I had forgotten the color of hair, color of eyes, bust measurement (which was unusually slight for a Sleeping Partner), even the absence of previous lovers, long after the pass had been issued and the date arranged. It was as if they were some kind of mystical symbol.

I appear to be examining my recent past for clues to my present state, much as a doctor will ask the patient, 'When did you first notice . . .?' I don't know what my present state actually is, otherwise I would not be trying to diagnose it. There is a mystery, but it is unlike normal detective work in that I don't yet know whether I am part of it. In an illness, the problem is inside; in a crime mystery, it's outside. Here, it appears to be inside and outside alternately, or occasionally at the same time. One clues/symptom is Jimmy Ruggins; another is WHOM; a third is Ellen Axaxas. Putting it like that makes it appear that they, and all the other clues/symptoms, are unrelated, whereas my whole point is that they are, or they may be, related in a way which I don't understand. If the only thing they have in common is me, then I am probably insane. I've contracted something vague and menacing, not an illness, but a Syndrome.

I return to my speculation about Jimmy Ruggins, pausing only to remind myself that it *is* only speculation, that we are dealing here with probabilities and possibilities, with a succession of unavoidable perhaps, as I like to call them. Perhaps are good for the imagination, if you don't have too many of them, in which case they are bad for the health. A moment ago, I imagined Jimmy Ruggins gradually acclimatizing to WHOM, accepting the fact that it was his only route to the President, even (an executive-size perhaps) suspecting the existence of the Sleeping Partner program. Now I imagine him looking out over the same gray lawns I looked out over, and slowly discovering politics. He took to reading the WHOM News Digest every day, in the hope of finding more material for his speeches. Ruggins is a man passionately interested in the end of the world, which he believes will take place in our own lifetime; he studied WHOM to find out as many details as possible about what it was that was going to end. For example, we know from his maiden speech as an aide how he saw the Wocaluha Inquiry. When he read Senator Florian's conclusions, he must have put down his coffee cup and stared at the screen so hard he almost burned the data onto it permanently.

> Senator Florian's Commission of Inquiry into the Wocaluha disaster today published its report. The explosion, which killed 7,000 people, was caused by a leaky oxygen tank, which overheated the electric element underneath the pickle vat, and started a fire. This caused other oxygen tanks to explode. Dangerous chemicals used in the manufacture of dill pickles rapidly worsened the situation, which was not so much an explosion as a chain of explosions. As a result, the poisonous gas potassium divinylchloramine had leaked out over the town, resulting in the regrettable fatalities that occurred. Senator Florian has blamed a junior caretaker for the defective tank, and added that the unfortunate man had since taken his own life. Senior management and government safety inspectors could not be held responsible in any way.

That night, Ruggins returned home at six o'clock to his celibate apartment in downtown Washington, fixed himself a club soda and switched on the TV.

'I say this,' said a crusading chemist interviewed by NBC news, 'Why were they using potassium divinylchloramine in pickles? That's all I want to know. When I know that, I shall sleep a lot easier than I do at the present time. So far, not one member of the Commission of Inquiry, least of all Senator Florian himself, has come forward with an explanation. Until somebody does, this one will run and run, I'm telling you.'

Jimmy Ruggins, watching the crusading chemist on TV, had already come up with an explanation of the Wocaluha disaster, viz., that it was the first in a series of catastrophes heralding the Last Days, and that, to be more specific, it was the Death member of the four horsemen of the apocalypse (the other three were the plague of AIDS, the famine in Ethiopia and the Sudan, and any of several wars which were currently in progress). In that sense, Ruggins too believed that Wocaluha would run and run. When the news was over, he must have turned off the set and reached for the Good News instead. He probably turned up *Revelation* to see whether there was anything in it which looked or smelled like potassium divinylchloramine. Anyway, it wasn't long before he was using what he had read in a speech.

> *And another angel came and stood at the altar, having a golden censer; and there was given unto him much incense, that he should offer it with the prayers of all saints upon the golden altar which was before the throne. And the smoke of the incense, which came with the prayers of the saints, ascended up before God out of the angel's hand. And the angel took the censer and filled it with fire of the altar, and cast it into the earth: and there were voices, and thunderings, and lightnings, and an earthquake.*
>
> Revelation, 8, 3–5

And yet Warren Pike, the President who had to preside over this momentous and terminal era, the Emperor of the Last Days, still had nothing to say on any of it. Why, Ruggins asked himself, why should a man become President if he has no interest in politics? He suspected he knew the answer. He was beginning to understand the true nature of Sleeping Partner.

SUBJECT: Oh God, Karen, I ought not to be doing this, this is wrong, this is wicked, I'm a married man.

PARTNER: You do it all the time, Sir, you like it, don't you? Don't you like it, Sir?

SUBJECT: No, oh God, I hate it, it's terrible, it's wicked. What am I doing to myself?

15

PARTNER:	You don't do it to yourself, Sir, we do it together, that's the beauty of it. And it's not wicked, it's good. It frees up your inner organs and relaxes your muscles, helps the circulation. You like it, Sir, you know you enjoy it or you wouldn't do it so often.
SUBJECT:	How do you know I enjoy it? How do you know how often I do it, you don't know that, you just read it in newspapers and magazines. I am not a bad man, Karen, I know the meaning of the word conscience.
PARTNER:	I know you like it, Sir, just like I like it. You're no better than anyone else is, are you, Sir?
SUBJECT:	That's right, I'm the same as anyone else. There's this guy called Ruggins who keeps sending me memos on the computer about adultery and fornication. I guess it must be getting to me. I don't even remember appointing the guy. Bastard. I told you, didn't I, Karen, about my Baptist upbringing?
PARTNER:	No, I don't think you told me about that, Sir. [PAUSE]
SUBJECT:	Do you know what 1 Thessalonians is?
PARTNER:	No, Sir, I never heard of it. [PAUSE]
SUBJECT:	Bastard. 1 Thessalonians. Oh God, I hate it.

*** DIALOGUE ENDS. SLEEP ASSUMED ***

All right, Ruggins didn't hear any of this. I was the one that heard, and transcribed it. All the same, as Ruggins, under the influence of WHOM and his job title (which no one else seemed to take seriously), became increasingly politicized, he must have suspected that Pike was being depoliticized. Why, for example, had he not made a statement on Lazar, which also featured prominently in the news digest at that time?

Lazar. An island to the east of Malta. To the north: mostly mountains obscured by scrub pine, myrtle, olive and aromatic shrubs.

16

In the center: a valley of orange orchards and farmland. On the south coast, in a narrow strip of sandy beaches: a tourist industry based around the historic capital, Sainte-Fleur, a town founded by the Crusaders. I understand Sainte-Fleur is a beautiful city. It is a city of high cobbled streets, alleys smelling of urine and geraniums, a city of brothels, roof gardens and cafés. The WHOM Geography Subsystem reveals that it has a nineteenth-century Templar Cathedral, round, like the original one, and a first-class Victorian hotel right in the middle of the Esplanade Touristique, overlooking the best beach in Lazar. Also a bakery specializing in hot donuts and cheese danishes, originally opened to serve the US bomber pilots who were stationed there during the war – surviving presumably because the inhabitants have acquired a taste for hot donuts and cheese danishes – lending its own perfume to the Mediterranean air. It has a disreputable dockyard area known as Saint-Sépulcre, an area of oil drums and cranes, where the alleys are narrower and the smells presumably stronger, not just urine and geraniums, but also cumin, basil, seaweed, frangipani, tar. It has its own cuisine: snapper and olives, goat's cheese with red peppers, spiced orange salad.

The island of Lazar attracted Jimmy Ruggins, partly because of its curious religions, but mostly because of its long-running civil war, which consists largely of denials. It is a characteristic of WHOM that somehow it verbalizes politics, making the user more aware of the words in which the event is described than of the event itself. Perhaps because the war is too obscure for the reporters to go to the northern mountains and find out what is happening for themselves, they are content to report President Miraz's denials without further comment, so that the outside world sees the war in silhouette, as it were. President Miraz denied that his Shamanist Defense Minister, General Tuli, had resigned. A few days later, Miraz denied that there was unrest among the Shamanist rural population and riots in Sainte-Fleur. Then he denied that Shamanists in the army were deserting and going to join General Tuli in the mountains. Next he denied in quick succession: 1) that there was a full scale civil war in the island, and 2) that Tuli had won a major battle in the mountains, the first of many defeats which Miraz was to deny in the subsequent twelve months. By the time Ruggins became interested in the war, Miraz was denying things before they had even happened.

Ruggins read in the news digest:

Lazari President Dol Miraz today denied rumours that his health
was failing. His blood pressure was 120 over 85, he claimed, and
his pulse was 65 to 70. He did pushups and pullups every day
and jogged three miles before beginning work each morning. He
said he was full of adrenalin, a fact he demonstrated by pacing
up and down the press room of Republic Palace.

'I am fully confident of the support of my Western allies,'
President Miraz said, 'I hope to have talks with the US Secretary of
State later in the week. I strongly refute rumors that government
forces have lost another major battle in the mountains. There was
not even a first battle.' Asked about the Scorpion, the leader of the
urban guerrilla force in the Saint-Sépulcre area of Sainte-Fleur,
President Miraz denied having heard of him.

'What you mistake for Western-style riots and demonstrations
is the simple traditional carnival atmosphere of our country,' he
claimed, adding that even a family shopping expedition could
become a fiesta in Sainte-Fleur, and that the smallest fiesta looked
like a riot in some of those alleys. What inexperienced journalists
mistook for gunfire was the noise of firecrackers being let off.

President Pike, preoccupied with his sleeping partners, made no
comment on the situation in Lazar, despite the fact that every-
one in the White House who has any wherewithal at all about
Mediterranean affairs, knows that it was the CIA who helped
Miraz to power after Independence, and that he has been supported
by every US administration since. President Miraz is a noted
Americophile, and his eldest son Eric, who once played basketball
for the University of Illinois, became a successful lawyer in Chicago.
Furthermore, they know, as Pike undoubtedly does not, that the
Lazarene Church, to which Miraz belongs, is a Christian one,
probably founded by the Crusaders, although claiming to date
back to the time of St Paul, and that Shamanism is a religion which
has developed under the influence of the Islam brought by Arab
traders. Unlike previous US Presidents, Pike did not complain to
Miraz about the slowness of promised electoral reforms, or accuse
him of detaining political opponents without trial, allowing torture
and abuse of human rights on a scale disproportionate to the size
of the island, or discriminating against the country's Shamanist

majority. Nor did he offer the usual military or economic aid. Jimmy Ruggins, observing Pike's failure to send the Word into battle on its white horse, must have fretted at his terminal and, after 6.00 pm, in front of his TV screen.

As for me, when I look back at myself, I can hardly believe my innocence. I was worse than the President himself: I was less political than he was, less historical, less religious. It must have been my experience as a detective that led me to see everything in personal terms. All I thought about was my job, how much I hated it, and Roxanne. I guess I was jealous of Pike because he had all those women and didn't have to do anything. Transcribing the Pillowtalk tapes is menial work, for one thing, the sort of stuff they normally give to typists. All they need is a typist with the right security clearance, and they could spare me the effort, but of course, there never will be a typist with the security clearance to transcribe Pillowtalk into WHOM. Producing it is a different matter, they are allowed to do that; I'm the one that allows them, so I can hardly complain. Sometimes when I sit back and look round the office, I get so depressed. It's the self-sufficiency of the place that does it – the en suite bathroom, the coffee machine gurgling in a way that has no mechanical function but is apparently meant to be appetizing, the smell of airfreshner which persists throughout the day no matter how many cigarets I smoke. And hours and hours of Pillowtalk.

Partly, I feel guilty about listening to it. I still look round every time I put the headphones on, even though I know nobody will come in. Also, there is something about the tape recording that deadens the passion in the voices, assuming there was any in the first place. The average tape begins with a few minutes of grunting, squeaking and awkward fumbling noises, then a long silence, then the desultory kind of dialogue I have already quoted. On one of Pike's good evenings (ie, one of my bad mornings), there are more grunts, squeaks and fumbles an hour or so later. Private detectives become disillusioned with sex; that disillusionment is my full time occupation. The typical Sleeping Partner is extrovert, bright, bouncy, squeaky, a bit of a bully – a bit like a Swedish aerobics instructress. Warren Pike, on the other hand, is a man in his mid-fifties, dark-haired, handsome, a man who has kept his slim figure at the cost of seeming somehow hollow inside.

Maybe it's the voice, which is too deep for his body, and is even deeper on the tape than it is in his televised press conferences. It has a frail quality along with the depth, a hint of an old man's quaver, which is perhaps merely the result of years of trying to sound deeply moved. Pike naked in bed would not look middle aged; he would look as if he was trembling on the border between being very young and being very old.

So the job was getting to me; Roxanne was getting to me also. Because Roxanne Telemann had inherited her father's surreptitiousness, she had taken to following Ruggins from meeting to meeting, slipping in past the security guards at the door or waiting outside on the sidewalk and walking in when they opened the doors in the interval. It was not merely surreptitiousness, but a kind of spiritual masochism which prevented her from paying and joining the ranks of the elect, as if she somehow did not think she deserved a $10 place in Row K of the hereafter, but must hang around in that New Testament way, watching the goings on from a convenient tree. She would come home late from these meetings, red-eyed and breathless, and sweep upstairs to bed without mentioning where she had been. But I knew; or at least, with my background and experience, it did not take me long to find out. At first, I followed her from a distance, driving slowly after the buses which she took to the various meeting halls, stopping on street corners a block away from the one on which she stopped, watching her as she watched the closed door of the building with longing in her eyes. What was she thinking?

I have spent so many nights like that in the past, warming my hands at the glow of a hot dog, letting my thoughts melt their way through a hundred yards of frozen evening, trying to get inside the mind of a man or woman who did not even know I was there. Now it was my own daughter I was trying to understand, and I had thought I did. I started thinking of her as a case.

The thing about cases is that they are always being driven. There is so much passion out there, it is frightening. It is hard to believe that these people never seem to get a night off from it and do a crossword puzzle instead. In my normal state, I am never driven or urged by anything much after working hours, because I can never find the time for it, or the enthusiasm. But now I, too, was being driven, because I was doing this for a real motive; ie, for her, for that awkward girl on the next corner who had not even bought herself a hot dog, but was waiting for the interval so she could sneak into the hall and find out she was damned. Being urged feels just as cold as getting paid for it, I discovered.

One night, I stopped being so professional about it, and simply paid my money and joined the congregation. There were so many of them, I easily got lost in the ecstasy. The only person who wasn't lost was Roxanne, small with limp hair and large sad eyes, who crept in at the side door in the interval, didn't sing, didn't pray, didn't applaud, stood there close enough to the door to make a quick getaway in case the eyes of the faithful were suddenly drawn towards her martyred form as mine were. Jimmy Ruggins, white-suited, sideburned, and with the twang of Muscle Shoals in his voice rather than the tang of Portland, harangued an ordinary jean-wearing audience on the evil of fornication.

> There is joy in marriage,
> There is joy in solitude,
> But there is hellfire and damnation
> In the bedclothes of the lewd.

'Yes my friends,' Ruggins said, 'as you will read in your Holy Bibles when you get home tonight, Babylon the great is fallen, is fallen, and is become the habitation of devils, and the hold of every foul spirit, and a cage of every unclean and hateful bird.'

Marriage, solitude and the bedclothes of the lewd: Roxanne knew only one of these things, but she seemed to be feeling guilty anyway.

> Well I found myself a woman,
> And I showed her to the Lord.
> He said the dogs will eat your progeny,
> By man and beast abhorred.

Then I saw Ellen for the first time, not knowing, of course, that it was her. I didn't make the connection. She was just a small, slim honey blonde woman, one of a number of witnesses to the healing powers of Jesus Christ who sat in a row behind Ruggins as he sang and preached, and who stood up at fixed intervals to tell their stories. After Ruggins had sung his fornication blues, she stood up and introduced herself merely as Ellen, making no mention of the extraordinary foreign surname, Greek, Maltese, Arabic or whatever it is. She spoke, not about a personal experience of burning bedclothes, but about the sanctity of childhood.

'Children,' Ellen said in a frail voice which was itself childish, 'are closer to God than anyone else. And I *know*, because an angel spoke to me when I was a child. I heard his voice in the garden, and it was just as if it was my own brother standing next to me, and he said, "Ellen, don't be afraid. God wants you." And that is what I want to bear witness to tonight.'

Roxanne's eyes were bigger than ever. It must be part of the sexual development of teenage girls – a part never mentioned in the sex education handbooks – that their eyes grow out of all proportion to the rest of them. Roxanne's eyes seemed to be about to swallow that little blonde woman whole, to draw all the goodness out of her. Oh God, I thought, the reproach she must be feeling towards me, her father, that I let her go through childhood without encountering an angel. Roxanne was now sixteen, and that girl Ellen was the nearest she had ever come to meeting an angel face to face. She did look something like an angel, it was true, whereas Ruggins was plump and middle-aged, had sideburns and wore an expensive white suit which was too broad in the lapel to be fashionable, although undoubtedly fashion does not apply to Evangelists in the same way that it does to the rest of us. At any rate, fashion or no fashion, Jimmy Ruggins as he unstrapped the guitar from round his neck and picked up the Bible from the lectern in front of him was very much of the world. The most you could say of that little honey blonde was that she was in it.

Meanwhile, Ruggins thanked Ellen for her witness, and went back to *Revelation*.

'For all nations have drunk of the wine of the wrath of her fornication,' Ruggins declaimed (he put his halfmoon glasses on when quoting holy scripture, even though he did not appear to be reading it from anywhere). 'And the kings of the earth have committed fornication with her, and the merchants of the earth are waxed rich through the abundance of her delicacies.' Everyone cheered. This, they felt, was something they could relate to.

This is everything I can remember about last year, about the things that seem somehow to be tied together in the Syndrome which I am currently suffering from: Ruggins, WHOM, Ellen, me. Maybe there is another thing I should mention; I don't know. They were beginning to say at that time that Ernest Hellbaum was cracking up. That was the story. They said the strain of finding appropriate metaphors for describing WHOM was getting too much for him, and that once, when he was training a new typist, he went through a map, a forest, a bicycle, a filing cabinet and the White House itself in quick succession, and then couldn't think of anything more to say. He had run out of reality, and he just stood there trembling, large and clumsy as he is.

'It isn't really like that,' he said, when the typist suggested that it was a bit like the Holy Bible, divided into its sixty-six books, each of which had its own kind of truth, and its own meaning for mankind. 'What you have to understand—' Hellbaum wiped his glasses '—is that we are all, every one of us, a collection of ones and zeros. We are just unprocessed data, ready to be chopped up and put into fields, normalized into a database of our relationships, one to one, one to many, many to one . . .'

'Many to many,' the typist said brightly.

'That isn't normal,' Hellbaum said, almost to himself, 'at least it isn't normal enough. When I close my eyes, I see white and green horizontal lines. I have done for years. Do you know what they are? They're standard computer stationery, piano-ruled. I realized just the other day.'

'What does WHOM stand for?'

Hellbaum looked peculiar without his glasses, unfinished, somehow.

'What do you mean "stand for"?' Ernest Hellbaum asked.

Datastream 2; Luke, Saint

I came into the hut, rubbing my hands because of the cold. Paul was sitting on the dirt floor in front of the fire, staring into the heart of the flames as he always did, as if expecting to see a vision in them.

'We might be able to leave tonight, after all,' I said, 'there is a moon. I haven't seen the moon for more than three weeks. I missed it more than I knew.'

'We?' Paul said. 'Who are we?'

He was a small, scholarly man, about fifty, although he seemed older. He gave the impression that he was constantly frowning because his brows met in the middle, and this, together with his querulous voice, made him easily disliked. Most people disliked him when they first met him, and they were right, in a sense. He was arrogant, opinionated, bad-tempered. I was frightened of him; the islanders were frightened of him; even Julius was frightened of him.

'You and I, Paul,' I said, 'just us.'

'And what are you proposing we travel *in*? A hollowed out tree-trunk, perhaps? I assume they have trees on this island. Because, I am, as you know, not a strong man. I have had a lot of practice at swimming recently, but I doubt if I could swim as far as Melita.'

Paul looked at me suddenly, and I flinched slightly before I noticed that Paul was laughing quietly, as if to himself. Paul's smiles were always unexpected.

'They have small sailing craft,' I said, 'quite seaworthy, apparently. I have seen them in the bay.'

'We would sail them ourselves?' Paul was still laughing.

'We could persuade a couple of islanders.' I was beginning to falter. Paul said nothing, and went back to staring at the fire. He had the knack, which I had always admired, of making his point without actually saying anything. Now, for example, he was telling me that it would be impossible to persuade any islanders to come with us. We had no money for a bribe, and besides, the islanders were a devout lot in their barbarous way. They believed in Paul, not in the way he would have wanted, but they believed nevertheless, and would not allow him to leave now that he was there. I was cold, and approached the fire from the other side. We sat there, watching each other through the flames, each of us thinking about the morning, and what would happen. For a long time, neither of us said anything.

'So tomorrow . . .' I began, meaning something along the lines of *tomorrow will take place after all unless you can think of an alternative to it.*

'Oh I never miss a ceremony, as you know,' Paul said gravely. I could not see through the flames whether he was laughing again.

It was pointless to suggest escape in any case. Paul had no intention of leaving the island without Julius and the soldiers. He would not even leave the master and crew of the *Ape*, who would not have scrupled to leave everyone else if they could have got away with it. If Paul had had any sense of the fitness of things, he would have been trying to escape, since he was, after all, a prisoner twice over, a prisoner squared, as it were. He and I were the prisoners of Julius, and Julius and the rest were all prisoners of the islanders. But Paul did not believe in escape. The whole idea was foreign to him. What he did instead was to reverse the situation, or at any rate to make it so obscure that in the end it was impossible to tell which was captive and which captor. Once, when Paul and Silas were prisoners in Philippi, the prison was wrecked by an earthquake. The jailer tried to kill himself and Paul, doubtless without even looking at the man, and in the weary voice he reserved for his most devastating proclamations called out, 'Don't bother! We are all here.' The next day, the magistrates tried to release Paul secretly, but Paul refused, saying that since he had been arrested publicly, the least he could expect was a public release, especially as he had done no wrong, and was, by the way (another weary thunderbolt), a Roman citizen.

The way he coped with being a prisoner was an aspect of his extraordinary practicality. Paul was the most practical man I have ever known. It was another of the deceptive things about him. Looking at him now, as he brooded over the flames, I would have said (if I hadn't known better) that the man was an intellectual, a daydreamer, the kind who look up occasionally from a book, surprised to notice the world is still there. But I knew Paul had been sweeping the hut a few minutes before I came in, with a broom he had made himself from the stalks of some native shrubs. He did this twice a day, to the amazement of the islanders, who had apparently never seen a broom before. Wherever Paul happened to be, he settled into it like a lizard into sand, until you couldn't tell Paul from the background. He did not appear to be exerting himself. He did not even appear to be biding his time until he could get on with the mission. He never made any secret of his plans, and if a diversion came up, he just assumed it was part of the journey, and that he would nevertheless get to where God had intended him to be at the time previously arranged. The islanders were amazed, too, that he refused to have the slave boy they had allotted him to look after the hut. Paul ceremoniously released the boy into the undergrowth to make his way back to his home in the Northern mountains. None of the islanders could think of anything to say after that. They were so shocked, they never mentioned it again.

Paul had warned the master not to set out. It was already October when the ship left The Fair Havens, and he pointed out that we were bound to encounter storms. We would certainly be shipwrecked, he said; there was no doubt in his mind, and of course, the master, who had a lot to gain by finishing the journey before spring, was furious to be told his job by an ugly little Jewish prisoner; nor could he understand why a centurion like Julius took the fellow so seriously. Paul seemed to be saying that it was no skin off his nose, he would arrive in Rome in any case, since his God had promised it, but it would be sensible not to sacrifice the ship and possibly the lives of all the rest of us just for the sake of his mission. He thought he was being very humble about it. When the north-easter sprang up and drove us away from the coast of Crete, Paul didn't exactly crow about it. He just said, very reasonably, that if they had listened to him in the first place we would not have had all this trouble, and that now an angel of the Lord had appeared to him in a dream and told him that we were all going to be shipwrecked on a certain island.

'But don't worry,' Paul said, 'none of you will be hurt. I have God's word for this, and unlike your gods, mine can be trusted. He has decided that I must preach in Rome, and therefore – ' And therefore Paul was going to preach in Rome, though he clearly thought it seemed humbler not to finish the sentence. He spoke like a paying passenger, rather than a prisoner travelling under armed guard.

We struck sail and ran before the wind for fourteen days, eating and drinking nothing, deprived by the storm of the benefits of sun and stars. On the fourteenth night, the sailors took soundings and found that the ship was in twenty fathoms. A little later, it was only fifteen fathoms, and the master knew we were close to land, even though we could see nothing. We stayed there, the ship anchored by the stern to keep her bows into the land, until morning. Paul was the only calm man on the ship. He knew that this was his island.

Next day, he persuaded everyone to eat. 'This will be your last chance before we are shipwrecked,' he said cheerfully. 'I promise you will not lose a single hair from your heads. Eat,' he said, picking encouragingly at a piece of biscuit, 'it's good for you.'

Instead of joining in the meal, the master and crew tried to take the opportunity to escape in the ship's boat. It was Paul who noticed them and who pointed out to Julius that the ship could not possibly be saved without a crew. She still had to be guided close enough to the shore to allow us to swim for it.

She broke up in cross seas later in the morning, as the crew was trying to steer her into the mouth of a river. Those of us who could not swim got ashore clinging to struts and pieces of timber. Paul, weak swimmer though he claimed to be, managed to be the first ashore. And it was Paul whom the islanders assumed to be the leader of the group when they found us later. He had been right, as usual. No one was missing.

I looked up and saw that Paul was asleep on the other side of the diminishing fire. He seldom bothered to lie down to sleep, but closed his eyes and drifted away whenever the mood took him.

I often wondered if this was another symptom of his disease (I was his physician as well as his companion), but perhaps it was just practicality again. It was irritating that he would fall asleep in the middle of a conversation. It seemed, like a lot of his habits, an insult, but it wasn't. At least, as a doctor, I can confirm that it wasn't deliberate, for no one falls asleep deliberately; and therefore it wasn't an insult, for all insults are deliberate – aren't they? But it angered me that Paul could fall asleep at such a time, with this thing hanging over our heads.

In the morning, Paul was going to be crowned King of Lazar.

Datastream 1; Telemann, Alb

Last week, Ellen Axaxas was selected for an At Home. This part of the job is Fred Zolph's responsibility; he handles the subject side of the interface, and I'm just the partner man. Obviously, Fred felt that the Ellen type was what Pike needed at this particular point in history, viz., one of the quietest, dullest winters since the second world war. She's younger than the usual partner – they tend to be around twenty-eight to thirty – so Fred must have thought she would perk him up a little, keep his hormones from freezing. Not my business. My business was listening to the Pillowtalk tape on the following day. Naturally, I remembered the girl in question, since she was the one with two Xs in her name. Just as the name had made me feel strange, so there was something about the noises she made during the main event, some unusual quality in the wow and flutter, that affected me deeply. I've been playing that tape off and on ever since, giving my habitual involuntary guilty look in the direction of the door each time, and I think finally I know what it is. She sounds surprised. She even sounds as if she doesn't quite know what to make of it all. I'm used to the sound of remote female orgasm by now, but there is something poignant about those nervous squeaks which reminds me of my own adolescence. It actually makes me tremble, and sometimes I can't stand it and have to stop the tape for a moment.

WHOM

SUBJECT:	Oh God, Ellen, you're so so beautiful.
PARTNER:	Beautiful?
SUBJECT:	Oh God, you are beautiful. Your skin is like silk . . . no, it's like velvet. I swear Ellen, you're hardly human, you're like an angel in human form, that's what you're like, I really mean it.
PARTNER:	I am human. I am a woman.
SUBJECT:	I have to tell you, Ellen, I've made love to many women before, particularly in my official capacity. It's only fair to tell you that, it seems to come with the job, but never in my life . . . Such radiance, you actually seem to glow. You've never done this before, have you, Ellen?
PARTNER:	I have been saving myself, Sir. I have always known I had to save myself.

Save herself for what? This woman is strangely cryptic. Sleeping Partners, bright, confident, shrill, unemotional, Swedish aerobic types, do not believe in saving themselves, even for the President. It's amazing that the great man can get on so well with someone so unclubbable, since he is even more addicted to talking than he is to fornication. And what about the angel aspect, skin like silk or velvet, angel in human form, radiance, glowing? This, I thought, I have got to see. I went to the filing cabinet where documents are still kept in hard copy form (I don't refer to them much these days), and took out a dossier. The photograph of Ellen Axaxas fell out. The woman I had seen that night at the Jimmy Ruggins meeting.

SUBJECT:	Oh God, Ellen, you're so so beautiful.
PARTNER:	Beautiful?
SUBJECT:	Oh God, you are beautiful.

After all, there is nothing to worry about here, is there? He thinks she's beautiful, and she is surprised and flattered. It may be an unusual reaction in Sleeping Partner terms; a little emotional, maybe, but what the hell? And what does it matter that the girl is or was a Jimmy Ruggins fan and claims to have seen an angel when she was a little girl? My own daughter used to be in the

30

habit of sneaking into Jimmy Ruggins meetings not so long ago, and there is nothing sinister about *her*. There is nothing sinister about Ellen Axaxas, either, she's a pretty, frail, honey blonde who is probably not all there, but basically is a sincere person. No wonder Pike enjoyed it more than usual; she must make a pleasant change after the standard material.

| SUBJECT: | . | Your skin is like silk, no, it's like velvet. I swear Ellen, you're hardly human, you're like an angel in human form, that's what you're like, I really mean it. |
| PARTNER: | | I am human. I am a woman. |

All right, all right, *he* says she's an angel; she denies it. She may be a bit other-worldly, but she is basically in touch with reality. Looking at the picture, the eyes might be far away, but there is something quite stern and confident about that little mouth. She looks like a woman who knows what she is doing. Probably she grew out of Ruggins months ago, just like Roxanne did. Considering her age, she is probably a late developer, and just as Roxanne has given up religion and taken up boys, so Ellen has given up religion and taken up a President.

What exactly do I suspect here? I don't know. Some collusion, some plot, something. Never mind.

I'm unsettled for all sorts of reasons. WHOM is misbehaving. When I log on in the morning, my screen is sometimes full of meaningless garbage, strings of letters and numbers, E011A488 80F1F2E9 etc. Then it clears up again, and I can get on with my job. You may wonder why this is so unsettling, but then you don't have to work in the White House. For eight hours a day, WHOM is the only contact I have with reality – that and the Pillowtalk tapes, which are just as disturbing. Yesterday, I got an electronic memo that wasn't even intended for me.

To:	The President of the United States
From:	J. Ruggins, Theology Adviser
Subject:	The Last Days

Mr President, may I strongly recommend you to consider the spiritual significance of the great tragedy in Wocaluha?

31

The Holy Bible predicted this, along with many other catastrophes, which herald the Last Days and the New World which is to come afterwards. The time may not be long in which to repent of your sins, notably fornication (for more information on this, may I kindly beg you to read 1 Thessalonians, Chapter 4, Verses 3–5). Furthermore, Senator Florian's Inquiry was a travesty, in that it did not explain why potassium divinylchloramine was being used in a pickle factory.

That man again. A harmless idiot, maybe, but I don't like it, him, any of it. Maybe I'm paranoid. When the weather improves, I think I should get out more, take some exercise. Exercise is good for paranoia, and so are fresh fruit and vegetables, wholefoods etc. I am in danger of becoming like Ernest Hellbaum. They say the reason WHOM is going to pieces is that Hellbaum is going to pieces. The latest story is that he had a virtual collapse while lecturing to a group of seventeen highway technicians from Tulsa, Oklahoma.

'Are you feeling all right?' one of the delegates inquired. Hellbaum had stopped in the middle of his online demonstration and was staring dully at the screen, wiping his glasses. He is a large, slow man with a bewildered expression, who looks as if he has just been unexpectedly born.

'What's it like in Tulsa?' Hellbaum asked, 'I always wanted to go there. I guess there is fresh air, sunshine, horses, that sort of thing?'

'Sure, it's great,' a lady said. 'We like it, anyway.'

'If I could just get away from computers. I feel so *virtual* all the time. What was I talking about?'

'File access methods. The importance of file access methods in database maintenance.'

'May I ask a question?' the lady said politely. 'Where does all this fit in with highway design?'

'It's all very simple,' Hellbaum was faltering, 'highways are data, the same as everything else. You don't know what data is? Oh God. Data is what computers eat, that's all. It kind of . . . it tends to be green, and floats, if you understand me. I have the most terrible headache, but don't worry about it . . . I wouldn't want to have you worrying, or you know, losing any sleep in Tulsa, Oklahoma.

Data has a natural tendency to float. If it's numeric, it floats to the right; if not, it floats to the left. Excuse me, I don't feel too good.'

'All right,' a man said. (Probably serious, the kind that has white hair which is standing on end as if eager to get going and do something on its own for once. Independent hair.) 'I understand your point. OK, data. We get that. Why is the computer called number zero?'

'It isn't called number zero.' Hellbaum was sitting in front of the terminal with his head in his hands, not looking at the terminal, or at the delegates. 'The name of the computer is a hash thousand Series. That # symbol is called a hash. IBM have already been through the 1000 Series and the 2000 Series etc, in fact all the good numbers have been taken up as far as 99000, and when the names are bigger than that, they're harder to memorize. We programmers increasingly have to make use of the special characters on the keyboard which we don't use for much else, such as # and @ and §. We use them because there are only a limited number of numbers and sooner or later, people run out. Oh God, what do we do then?

'There is more data in the universe,' Ernest Hellbaum said bleakly, 'than there are numbers to describe it with.'

Datastream 2; Luke, Saint

I opened my eyes and saw that Paul was sweeping the hut again. How long he had been up, I could not have said. Paul's awakenings were as mysterious as his fallings asleep. He always seemed as if he had been awake all along, and moved with particular energy and sprightliness in the early morning, a fact I never failed to find irritating. Now, as he skipped around the dirt floor with his home-made broom, he looked like a small boy instead of the solemn and gloomy scholar he had appeared the evening before. It was all of a piece with his cheery injunction to everyone to eat when we were just about to be shipwrecked, as if he cared in the least what he ate or when! He was always at his most cheerful when there was nothing to be cheerful about.

'You said the weather had cleared,' Paul called. 'I had hoped it would stay fine for my coronation. No such luck, unfortunately. It has been raining all night, in and out of my dreams, so to speak. I could hear it on the roof, quite distinctly.'

'I wouldn't mind,' I said, 'if it was just the noise. This barbarian thatch is not in the least waterproof. I've been lying all night in a puddle.' I was still lying semi-prone in a pool of muddy water which was now warmed by my own body. Even the smallest movement let in cold draughts which froze my skin. I could hear the rain now, crackling as it struck the thatch and making whispering sounds as it wormed its way through.

'Well—' Paul leant the broom against the wall '—it's my coronation, so I must not let the weather put me off. Have you seen the wreaths? They have been arriving all morning while you were still lazing in your puddle.' He indicated some depressing winter blooms, mainly purple and silver grey, in a pile by the door. 'Now, are you going to get up? The morning is half over already.'

I lifted my body gingerly. 'Judging by the light outside, it must be not long after dawn.'

'Ah,' Paul said, 'but how can you believe the light in weather like this?'

I stood up and wrung the water from my woollen tunic. 'I know that whatever you do has a good reason. I know that you have Our Lord's confidence more than anyone except for those who actually met Him.'

Paul sniffed. 'You pay a two-edged compliment, Luke. Do I have to remind you that I *have* met Him? I met Him in person on the road to Damascus, and He has visited me on numerous occasions since, in dreams. That is why I always welcome sleep when it comes, even when it comes unexpectedly.'

'Well,' I said uncomfortably, 'you know what I mean.'

'Of course, I know what you mean, but I trust I still have the right to take issue with it. Physical meetings are not important. Bodies are imperfect things – even His body. You of all people should understand that. However, I had the impression you were about to say something else, so by all means continue.'

'I was going to say that I can't understand why you take this coronation so seriously. That is, I can't understand why you are agreeing to it at all. I know you to be a good man, Paul, and a wise one, wiser than any of us. Even Peter says that some of your arguments are beyond him. So I have every confidence that you are following the Lord's instructions even in this. I just wish you would tell me what they are. Naturally, you are not motivated by vaingloriousness or love of riches.'

'Naturally,' Paul said, with a quick smile that vanished almost immediately, 'Naturally I *am* as you are, as all us poor mortals are. Yes, Luke, I love riches and glory, and even an island such as this one can provide riches of a sort. Oh yes. Oh yes. However,' he continued, raising, with an effort, his enormous eyebrows, 'however, I trust I can combat my nature successfully. I am hoping that the Lord will assist me in this. In fact, I have faith that He will, and that my resolve will hold firm. You see, Luke, these people are simple and savage, and their ceremonies are just the same. They have some kind of pagan religion which they have created in their own image, a religion that mirrors their physical lusts and fears. Yes, it is an evil thing, and they wish to proclaim me king in an evil ceremony for evil motives. But observe the wisdom and mercy of the Lord, Luke, in this as in everything else. Their religion is false, but their desire for it is not. The urge towards God invariably comes from God, even when men misdirect it. They have appointed me a king, hoping and expecting that I will give them the kind of base and corrupt leadership they want, that I will lead them in battle against their enemies, that I will protect them from disease and disaster, that I will bring them gold and silver and whatever else men want. In that, they are wrong. But it was God who told them to look to me for leadership, and to that extent they were right. I will bring them riches that they have never dreamed of, for I will bring them the love of the Lord Jesus Christ, and I will use my kingship to make them part of His kingdom.'

'Then you intend to remain king?'

'What on earth gave you that idea?' Paul said, 'Certainly not. I'm sure I have told you on several occasions that the Lord has commanded me to preach in Rome, and that is where I am going. Now I would advise you not to wear that muddy tunic for my coronation, since it would hardly be dignified and would create a bad impression. Fortunately, I have obtained clean ones from the headman. I am wearing mine already, and I suggest you put yours on before you catch cold.'

The islanders who found us were humble fishermen, speaking neither Latin nor Greek. It must have been a frightening sight for them, some three hundred men, soldiers, sailors and prisoners, mostly naked, lying on the brown mud of the beach in the heavy, freezing rain of mid autumn. Paul was the only one who was making an effort to keep alive, running vigorously up and down the strand, partly to keep warm, partly in the hope that he would discover something to light a fire with, but this task defeated even his practicality. It was a severe problem for the fishermen since there was not enough room in the village for that many men. The passengers and crew of the *Ape* would have filled every hut in the village, leaving no room for the people who actually lived there; and as for clothes, the situation was impossible. Tunics were wealth in this part of the world, and generous as these primitive people were, they owned only enough to clothe a few dozen men.

'The Lord will provide,' Paul said cheerfully to the villagers, who did not understand. Several of them fell instantaneously to their knees and began making gestures of homage, beating their bare breasts and sprinkling dirt on their heads. Perhaps because he was the first person to address them directly, they took him for the leader of this extraordinary invading army, and when they decided to split it up, and send a number of men to each of the nearest villages, Paul, Julius, the master of the *Ape* and myself were among those who went to the capital. Paul instantly understood the nature of the discussions that were going on around us, and the decision the fishermen had come to, and explained it to me.

'It will be a miracle,' I said, 'if most of us don't die of exposure before we arrive.'

'Not one of the Lord's more difficult miracles,' Paul replied.

Our group marched inland for the greater part of the afternoon, through sandy, rocky country, choked with roots and overshadowed by shrubs whose tough and glossy leaves poured trickles of water on to our bare skin. Julius and the Romans, naked as they were, continued to march with swagger, and Paul marched with them – he was a Roman citizen, after all. The islanders trudged in front and behind, heads down, eyes on the path, seemingly depressed by the weather or the terrain, or their own nature. Just as it was getting dark, and I was beginning to wonder how we would avoid tripping over, a sweet, herbal smell reached me. It was the smell of smoke rising through thatch. We had reached our destination.

The village was not much bigger than the one we had seen first, with a big round chief's hut in the centre, a cluster of family huts round the outside, and goat and sheep pens in between. To me, however, it seemed on a completely different scale; an effect of the darkness, and of the cracks of firelight glimpsed through the walls of the huts.

'It is a city, Paul,' I said, awed.

'Yes, I suppose it must be.'

That first night, we were billeted in the huts on the perimeter of the village, one or two men to each hut. Paul and I were accommodated in the house of an elderly man who had three elderly wives, all silver-haired and courteous. Their names were clusters of gutturals which I could not grasp. Seated in the hut in an atmosphere of moist smoke, trying to eat some kind of porridge with pieces of dried meat in it, I felt strangled and blinded. Tears came into my eyes, and I pushed my bowl to one side and lay down. On the ground, filthy as it was, the air was clearer, and I was able to breathe. As I fell asleep, I noticed Paul crouching by the fire with our host, waving his spoon in eloquent but wordless conversation.

In the morning, we were taken to the headman's hut, which seemed to serve as a meeting hall. The headman himself lived in a smaller hut inside it, benefiting from the extra insulation. When we arrived, a couple of dozen male villagers were sitting crosslegged outside the inner hut, waiting for the show to begin. I was surprised not to see any of the others from the *Ape*, not even Julius.

'Do you think they are going to see us all in turn?' I whispered.

'I doubt it,' Paul said.

It seemed like a trial. We were led to the entrance of the inner hut, where we stood with our backs to the villagers, looking into the darkness. I could not see anyone inside.

'There's no one there,' I said, still whispering.

'Look down.'

Two men were lying prostrate on the floor of the hut.

When Paul finally persuaded them to rise, we found that one of them was not a Lazari at all, but a Greek sailor, long ago shipwrecked on the island. He had become half-savage himself; he was dressed in the same clumsy woollen tunic as the natives, and spoke Greek with a peculiar accent and an idiosyncratic grammar which was perhaps borrowed from Lazari. He explained that he acted as interpreter whenever visitors arrived. Yes, there were sometimes visitors. A Roman galley had visited ten years ago, investigating the island, as the Romans occasionally did, to see if it was worth absorbing into the Empire. It had left again a few days later, and they had heard no more about it. The Lazaris were always disappointed to lose a visitor, since they were a race of fishermen who believed that all good, like all evil, came from the sea.

'I therefore also,' the sailor said, 'small god be. Smallest, smallest.'

I opened my mouth to rebuke the man for his blasphemy, but

before I could speak, Paul began asking about the religion of the island. The people believed, the sailor explained, that Lazar was once part of the seabed, and that they themselves were descended from various kinds of fish and crustaceans. No one could eat the particular kind of fish he or she was descended from for fear of offending his or her underwater relatives. They referred to these as their *wet* family, as opposed to the *dry* family of human kin. ('It seems hard to believe that anyone is ever completely dry on this island,' Paul said, 'but let it pass.') The people considered fish far superior to human beings, creatures of perfect wisdom and happiness, a state from which they had been exiled for some sin, which not even Paul could understand.

'Eat why flarg,' the sailor said.

'Eat what?' Paul asked. 'Speak up, man.'

'Why flarg.'

We never found out what it was that the aquatic proto-Lazaris had eaten which caused their exile to dry land. Now, however, they regarded all visitors to the island as emissaries from the fish world, come to reassure them that after death they would return to their former state of tranquillity among the corals. They lived in the constant hope that one day a fish man would come out of the sea to be king over them. The arrival of the fish man would mark the end of human time and the beginning of fish time. He would rule them for one thousand fish years, during which people would gradually develop gills and fins. When the thousand years were up, a huge tidal wave would swallow the island and humanity would be no more.

'There is a paradox in their version of eternity,' Paul said, ignoring for a moment the sailor and the headman who crouched in front of us. 'They believe that people will become fish again when they die, yet they also feel the need to reclaim the whole of humanity for the fish *before* death. And, in fact, they do this in two ways, first by bringing a fish to the land, then by bringing the land back to the sea. It is a most uneconomical view of salvation.'

'We must explain to them, we must tell them what salvation really is,' I said.

'But of course.' Paul smiled quickly. 'That is why the Lord brought me here. To save Lazar from the fish, as it were. Wait a moment – ' he held up his hand to command silence – 'I must marshall my arguments first.'

I looked round the hut, and saw the Lazari audience staring up at us from its seated position. The men were clean-shaven, like Romans, making even the older ones look comparatively young and a little fish-like themselves, especially when they were staring as they were now doing. Nobody moved. They did not even seem to be breathing, and I had the impression that they were all about to explode. Their cheeks bulged and their eyes protruded. I turned back to Paul, and saw to my astonishment that he had assumed the same expression.

'Paul, what's the matter? Are you all right?' Paul did not reply. His small body was locked in a childish posture of attention, the arms thrust straight down and a little behind him and his head thrown back, as if he were playing at soldiers. Suddenly, he took a stiff step backwards and collapsed. The tribesmen let out their breath all at the same time in a brief explosion that might have indicated astonishment or contempt, but was, to me, simply inscrutable. 'Puh!' Paul lay on the ground and waves of invisible liquid seemed to pass through him, beginning at the head, then flexing his shoulders, his chest, stomach, hips, thighs, calves. His eyes turned up, showing only their whites, and foam came out of his mouth. He looked like a fish.

'Well,' Paul said on the morning of his coronation, 'no one has told me exactly what time the ceremony is due to begin. I imagine it will start when I arrive. All the same, I think it would be best for us to attend as soon as possible. The tunic is very becoming. Should I take the wreaths with me, do you think, or leave them? Let us take them. The more ornamentation, the better.' I picked up a great armful of sodden leaves and flowers. Paul took another, and we left the hut together.

Datastream 1; Telemann, Alb

I was hoping if I just left *it* (the Syndrome) alone it would go away, but it seems to be growing, if that is what syndromes do. It's best to record it, so that I can keep track of its development, and perhaps work out eventually what it is. The thing is, I am worried about Ellen Axaxas. It may be my job to be worried, but that doesn't make it any easier. I can't even remember whether this is routine worrying of the kind that I do all the time, or whether I am doing some extra worrying beyond the call of duty. I do less work than I used to, anyway. I sit in my office cultivating my collection of half-full paper coffee cups and cigaret butts smoked down to the filter, watching the snow spiralling onto the lawn. In this weather, the German shepherds wear little woollen coats which made them look like killer poodles. If I was a dog, I would never agree to wear a coat like that, snow or no snow. I drop the butts into the coffee cups, I lean back in my MIT designed tubular steel chair, which creaks warningly – it is so ergonomic that it tries to discourage me from adopting any posture which could eventually damage my spine. Then I get up and pace around the room. Looks good, doesn't it? The private detective wrestling with another difficult case. I'm only kidding myself, though.

The worst days are when I arrive at work to find another tape sitting in my in-tray. Apart from the soap, the band of paper round the toilet seat and the replenished coffee machine, these tapes are the only physical (non-electronic) sign I get that someone knows I'm here: that I'm not in the wrong office altogether, or the wrong job.

Ellen Axaxas has made love to the President three times. I am more or less sure, now, that she is working for Jimmy Ruggins, although I am not sure that *working* is the right word. Maybe she is Ruggins's mistress, but I doubt that. She told Pike that she had been saving herself, and I believe her. After all, I heard her squeals of surprise when she noticed what exactly it was that she was doing. No, Ellen is a disciple of Ruggins, and Ruggins, for obscure motives, is using her to infiltrate the President's bed and win him over to something or for something. What does Ruggins want? If he is cunning enough to plan something like this, is he also cunning enough to be a phony where his religion is concerned? Maybe he has some kind of deep financial fraud worked out. Or maybe he is a spy, working for the Russians. Anything is possible, but somehow I doubt it. Naturally suspicious, I still feel that Ruggins is what he appears to be. My experience tells me that there is no point in complicating things; if a man already has a motive, it is unnecessary to look for another one. Ruggins is a born-again Christian. That's a sufficient motive for just about anything.

SUBJECT:	Oh God, I think I love you, Ellen. I don't always say this to women, not even my wife. It's just that I've never in my life experienced something so . . . Would you understand me if I said it was incandescent?
PARTNER:	Incandescent, Sir?
SUBJECT:	It, the whole experience, making love with you, your body, my body, everything. Do I make myself clear, Ellen? This is a new thing for me.
PARTNER:	I understand, Sir. Of course, it's new for me, too. I'm glad that you love me. I don't think that can ever be wrong, loving someone, do you, Sir?
SUBJECT:	It can never be wrong, Ellen, never. It's just unusual, I guess. It kind of took me by surprise, at my age and in my situation to find myself . . . [inaudible] I don't suppose you would

ever feel in a position, emotionally speaking, to reciprocate . . .? Of course, you have to understand that I'm a married public figure and therefore . . .

PARTNER: Sir.

SUBJECT: Yes, Ellen?

PARTNER: I wish you wouldn't take the Lord's name in vain so much.

SUBJECT: The Lord's name?

PARTNER: Yes, Sir.

SUBJECT: Do I do that, Ellen? I didn't notice I did that.

PARTNER: Yes, Sir, like when you say, 'Oh, God, Ellen', stuff like that. The Lord doesn't like it.

SUBJECT: I see, yes, of course, I shouldn't do that. I understand. I'm a believing man, myself, Ellen. Perhaps I haven't always been as believing as I ought to have been . . .

PARTNER: Sir.

SUBJECT: Yes, Ellen.

PARTNER: Don't you worry about all the unhappiness there is in the world? I think if I was you, Sir, it would almost drive me mad, having all that responsibility for people's suffering, you know, all the ones who were killed, and went blind and got ill . . . when there is so much to do, so many problems to solve. Of course, it's good that you get to rest and enjoy yourself once in a while. People need to do that, too.

SUBJECT: You don't think I'm a very good man, do you, Ellen?

PARTNER: I would never say that, Sir, never. You don't understand me. It's just I think about all those poor people. Sometimes I dream about them, and I just think, was it fair?

SUBJECT: What people, Ellen? Do you mean Wocaluha?

Stop the tape. Son of a bitch, the first time in 279 close encounters that Warren Pike has mentioned politics. Of course, Ellen Axaxas sounds like a wimp, she appears to have no bite, no wherewithal at all. All the same, though, she has wherewithal enough to get three

At Homes when she was only supposed to have one. That is just not supposed to happen, and the fact that she talks like a bunny rabbit does not deceive a private investigator. Bunny rabbits can have sharp teeth, especially in bed. I knew there was something wrong as soon as I saw that name with the two Xs in it, but anyone can have two Xs in her name; and they say this isn't a free country.

To:	Fred Zolph
From:	Alb Telemann
Subject:	Sleeping Partner

According to WHOM, one of the SPs has now had multiple contacts (in excess of two occasions) with subject. Please confirm this, Fred.

To:	Alb Telemann
From:	Fred Zolph
Subject:	Sleeping Partner

This is correct, Alb. It has me kind of worried too. The girl is quite pretty if you like skinny blondes, but she has no kind of conversation whatsoever. To be frank, I don't know what subject sees in this one, and I'm going to try to break the habit. Received your latest Candidates List this am, and it looks good. Maybe a black girl would make a nice change for him, I don't know.

To:	Fred Zolph
From:	Alb Telemann
Subject:	Sleeping Partner

OK, Fred, we agree with respect to this issue. However, it should be borne in mind that subject's encounters are arranged by yourself. In consideration of this, I should be glad to know how you happened to fix up subject with the same woman three times.

To: Alb Telemann
From: Fred Zolph
Subject: Sleeping Partner

Naturally I would not wish to triplicate any of subject's liaisons, Alb; that would defeat the objective of the exercise. I can give you my firm assurance that any subsequent intimacies were not initiated at this end. I guess he just made a date with her. I am not sure how this can be avoided in future circumstances, should any such arise, if subject is going to interest himself in relationships of a steady nature.

What I never said in my electronic memos to Fred Zolph was this: I have a feeling that my job is going to become critical at some time in the future, perhaps very soon. So far I have done what was asked of me, drawn my pay by the invisible, WHOM-controlled process by which my bank account is fattened at monthly intervals, and have never really had to earn it. Maybe soon I will have to start. What is going on in the President's confidential bedroom may soon influence what is going on in the Oval Office.

For example, I took a look at the WHOM news digest this morning and did not like what I saw. In an unprecedented statement, Warren Pike has condemned Senator Florian's Wocaluha Report as 'a tissue of lies'.

'This administration has never wanted a cover-up,' Pike said. 'It is important that we understand the true reason for this calamity, which has brought death to so many. I feel the Florian Inquiry amounts to a betrayal of those dead and suffering people, and of the cause for which they died. I want to see justice done for the people of Wocaluha.'

In a shock move, Pike appointed Jimmy Ruggins, Presidential theology adviser, and a man with no known military or scientific experience, to chair the new Commission. 'The United States has something to prove,' the President said. 'We have to show that we are a truly Christian society before it is too late. I have very close, very intimate reasons for believing that.'

WHOM

Senator Florian hit back, saying, 'My Commission produced its report after a careful sifting of all the available evidence. I was appointed by the President for this task, and I feel I can honestly say I have done the duty he asked of me. I'm sorry if his highly-paid White House advisers, many of them totally un-qualified to discuss chemicals or anything else, see fit to dis-pute our findings, and I'm even more sorry if the President has allowed himself to be swayed by unscrupulous yellow press rumor-mongers.'

If only. If only the press was all I had to worry about.

Datastream 2; Luke, Saint

The children were standing outside the hut in the chill rain of the Lazari winter. Most of them were naked, and, indeed, there seemed hardly any point in wearing clothes in this weather, as Paul and I soon discovered. However, our tunics were ceremonial and could not be discarded. The heavy island wool did not so much let in the water as trap it, so that we were increasingly weighed down as we made our way to the chief's hut. At every step, water flowed out of the saturated wool and ran down our legs. I walked a few paces behind Paul, in keeping with the spirit of the occasion; he looked frailer than usual. As the tunic got bigger, stretched by the weight of water, so Paul became smaller, more bowed under its weight and the beating of the rain: his bare arms and legs were trembling slightly, and I hoped it was only because of the cold. Another fit might confirm the islanders in their belief that Paul really was the Fish Man, if confirmation were needed, but it would certainly be bad for his health.

Looking back, I saw that the children had fallen into step behind us. Surely there were more of them than could possibly be from the village? Some of the smaller ones were imitating Paul's walk, holding out imaginary tunics, bowing their shoulders and staggering slightly. The expressions on their faces were serious, as if the impersonation were a mark of respect. The older girls were singing, in bell-like voices, a song which had the repetitive structure of a nursery rhyme. When they saw me looking at them, they dropped their voices and stared awkwardly down at their muddy feet, but continued walking. 'No doubt they are singing about me,' Paul called.

The Greek sailor was waiting for us at the door of the chief's hut.

'Coming, coming,' he told us, 'is late much.'

Paul apologized gracefully.

'Whose children are these? Do they come into the hut with us?' I asked.

The Greek stepped respectfully round Paul and looked at the children. They laughed mockingly at him, and one or two of the older girls threw their heads back, smiled winningly and pointed their small breasts at him. The Greek waved his arms in a series of semicircles and made spitting noises, 'Thp! Thp! Thp!' The children laughed again, but fell back a few paces.

'Children are fish,' the Greek said to Paul, obviously disgusted. It was one of those occasional remarks he made which I found completely incomprehensible. In what sense were the children regarded as fish? Were they the offspring of shipwrecked sailors and therefore sacred like ourselves? Alternatively, were children considered to be especially fishlike, perhaps because of their recent emergence from the waters of the womb? Why, in any case, should their fishiness be treated as a defect, and cause them to be barred from the ceremony?

'They are probably the children of this village and all its neighbours,' Paul said, seeing these thoughts going through my mind. 'There must be a hundred of them. Remember my coronation is a state occasion, and bound to attract interest throughout the area. Just look inside the hut, and see how well attended it is.'

I stepped towards the doorway. The inner hut, normally the chief's private quarters, had been dismantled specially, but the chief himself sat in the middle of the floor where his hut had been, looking slightly affronted. The floor of the erstwhile inner hut was a dry and dignified circle around him; it had been so effectively shielded from the rain that it was shrivelled and cracked in places. Around the outside, robed men and women of all ages sat with their heads bowed. The women wore flowers in their hair, simple white for the virgins, small purple stars buried in foliage for the married women. The men carried their weapons, spears or bows and arrows. People were packed in so tightly that I wondered how they escaped injury from the points of the spears and arrows. The warmth created by the proximity of so many bodies pulled me towards the building.

'Time to begin. I had better lead, I think.' Paul entered first, with the interpreter at his elbow. I was a couple of paces behind. Immediately, the crowd sent up a chant, more complex musically than that of the children had been, but consisting of only one word (or perhaps two), 'Vaskha-viskh, Vaskha-viskh.'

'Meaning, fish come,' the Greek explained.

'Fish come, fish come!' the chant continued in Lazari. Paul marched through the crowd which, without appearing to change position, left a space a yard wide for his progress. Paul stood before the chief in the circle of dry ground, which grew dark around him as water flowed from his tunic. The chief threw himself on the ground before Paul, but Paul bent down and raised him gently until he was in a crouching position from which he refused to move.

'Vaskha-viskh!' the Chief said in a booming voice.

'Vaskha-viskh!' his people replied.

Paul turned to face the people. 'People of Lazar!' he said. The sailor interpreted. 'You believe that I have come from the sea to save you. You are right. I am here to save you from the consequences of your sins.'

'Sins?' the sailor asked, 'sins be?'

'Wickedness. Crime. Wrongdoing.'

'Ah,' the sailor replied confusingly, 'rainings.' He explained this to the people, who shouted with delight.

'The Lord I serve came from a humble fishing people, like you. He said to his disciples that he would make them fishers of men.'

'Fish men?'

'Fishers of men.'

'Ah?' When the sailor had explained, the crowd made the same confused gasp he had made.

'The Lord I serve is called Jesus of Nazareth. He was a carpenter who walked among the people, preaching and working miracles.' The sailor looked puzzled. 'Well,' Paul said to him, 'what is it?'

'Man was, or fish?' the sailor asked. Paul made a small harumphing noise.

'He was a man, a man like us, but he was also the Son of God.' The sailor was frowning, perhaps feeling it was time Paul skipped the Son of God and got on to the fish. I could sense that it was not going well. Paul had preached to pagans many times before, but they had been educated men and women, versed in the Greek philosophers, sceptical about the vestiges of their own superstitions and, in many cases, familiar with other religions, including that of the Jews. To preach to savages who had never come across the idea of a single omnipotent god was an entirely different problem and required a new approach. I could not help feeling that Paul should have spent the last few days preparing the ground by gradually introducing a few of the basic concepts, instead of following his usual strategy of a big dramatic speech intended to arouse interest and controversy.

The chief now approached the sailor and murmured something to him. Both men shook their heads and tutted a good deal, then the sailor turned to Paul and explained that there would be a time for him to make a speech after the ceremony had been completed. Clearly, Paul's desire to address his potential converts had come as a surprise to them, for they were now talking among themselves in great confusion. The rhythm of the event had been broken, and Paul, by talking too much or too soon, was demystifying it. I was sitting in the front row of the audience, on the edge of the dry circle, a vantage point which allowed me to see two priestlike figures emerge from the crowd at the other side, and step into the circle behind Paul. One of them carried a silver crown, crudely worked, the other a fishing net. Paul, his arms still full of dripping wreaths, turned, saw them, and turned back to face me. Our eyes met for a moment, and, for the first time in my life, I saw Paul at a loss. The crowd began to chant again, 'Vaskha-viskh! Vaskha-viskh!' Paul stared at the cracked ground under his feet.

Paul had intended to use the occasion of his coronation to preach a sermon explaining the Christian faith. He had never planned to accept the kingship of the island, for he felt that, once the people understood his message, they would understand that the kind of king they wanted was unnecessary. Although they were unlikely to be converted all at once, enough of them would be won over to break the hold of this strange fish religion on the thought and customs of the island. No doubt Paul had anticipated some kind of trouble as a result, perhaps even a fight, but he would at least have had his say and been able to refuse the kingship. Now it looked as though they were determined to crown him without allowing him to say anything else. This was what came of preaching to people who didn't speak Greek. Of course, Paul could try to carry on with his speech, but what would be the point if the interpreter refused to interpret, as he quite possibly would? As the priests approached and the crowd chanted, I could see Paul's mind working. Should he accept the kingship, thereby committing himself to rule over the island and its people, at least until he was able to persuade them they no longer wanted him to? Or, on the other hand, should he continue his speech, resisting the attempt to crown him and risking incomprehension and anger from his hearers?

Paul accepted the crown from one priest, and the fishing net from the other. He knelt on the ground when the chief indicated that he should do so, and repeated an oath in Lazari which was interpreted for him in an undertone by the Greek sailor. I knew that Paul would never make a promise that he could not keep, and hoped the translation was adequate to allow him to judge accurately what he was promising to do. After the oath, there was more singing, though the words were different this time, and the chief led Paul around the inner ring presenting him to the people. As each section of the audience was approached, they gave a great cheer, and Paul, following the instructions of the interpreter, waved his fishing net. I caught the eye of Julius, who was sitting with the master of the *Ape* on the other side of the circle. Julius rolled his eyes and gave a little shrug, as if to ask how he was going to get his prisoner to Rome now. Then I prayed passionately that Paul had made the right decision, that God would not allow Paul to fall into sin by reason of the oath he had sworn, that we would be allowed to go to Rome after all. After that, I felt better suddenly. My breathing steadied, and I seemed to see the central arena from a great distance, as if watching it from heaven.

Datastream 1; Telemann, Alb

Spring is approaching, the German shepherds have lost their coats, the Washington blossom is emerging in its dignified way, but Warren Pike's fancy is not turning at all. It keeps straight on in the same direction, Ellen, Ellen, and yet more Ellen. I'm the one that has to listen to the tapes of all this passion, and it makes me nauseous. Not just the fumbles and the squeaks, not just Pike's declarations of undying this and that, but above all the theology seminars afterwards. Ellen is reading him all the Epistles of St Paul (in *bed* – the guy must be turning in his grave). She says that St Paul was the most important man who ever lived, apart from Jesus, who was a special case, and that hardly anyone has ever really understood his message for mankind. Where I come from, Ellen says, we feel we have a uniquely personal relationship with St Paul. Where she comes from: Salt Lake City? Bethlehem, Pennsylvania? I must look up her file again some time. But of course, I know where she gets her brand of religion: it's from her (no doubt) uniquely personal relationship with Jimmy Ruggins, Blues Evangelist, expounder of 1 Thessalonians, stable boy to the Four Horsemen. Most of the time, I try not to think about it. I just lose myself in the problems of getting WHOM to do what I tell it to, which is becoming harder all the time. Hellbaum never answers the phone, or when he does, he puts on a funny voice and pretends that he, Hellbaum, is really in Tulsa, Oklahoma, and that this is somebody else speaking. Meanwhile, the screen is full of crazy data. Today, I got lost in the middle of a confidential State Department report on the Sainte-Fleur hijacking. The plane is still in Sainte-Fleur airport, with some 300 passengers on board, and three Shamanist terrorists. All very important, I'm sure, but not a crisis I can take seriously. Sainte-Fleur is too far from home.

When I first started this job, I thought WHOM was a tool I used to investigate the real world, and to record my observations of it. Now, I sometimes wonder if it is WHOM that I am investigating. There should be a query after the name. Probably there would be, if anyone could think what it would stand for.

There is a whole mythology based around WHOM, which gets passed from user to user in the form of electronic memos. Most of it I never believed until now, but maybe WHOM has just become so big that anything is possible. Perhaps I myself am the subject of a myth, the 'myth' that they actually employ a man to keep tabs on the women the President sleeps with . . . You see my point?

Myth 1

This is concerned with what the acronym WHOM actually stands for. They say that, in the days before memos were electronic, one of them landed on the desk of a VIP on the top floor that ran roughly as follows:

To:	Senior Executive, Admin. Strategies
From:	Agnes Johnson
Subject:	WHOM

From today's date, WHOM will stand for White House Organizational Module, and not White House Organizational Methodology, as previously.

Now here is the point of the story: *there was no WHOM in those days*! It hadn't even been invented. The guy asked everyone he knew if they could tell him what WHOM was, and nobody knew. So he tried to trace this Agnes Johnson, with the same result. Either there was no Agnes Johnson working in the White House, or she was someone he wasn't allowed to know about – he was big, but not huge. Anyway, years passed, and the people who were writing the computer system to run the White House called him in on the human factors side. They wanted to know what they should call it. So the man assumed that this was the system he'd read about in the memo all that time ago, and he said that as far as he understood, it already had a name. None of the people who were working on the system knew any different – they just assumed in the usual way that he knew something they didn't – and the result was that the system became known as WHOM.

If all this is true, what happened to the original WHOM? Does it still exist? What does it do?

Ernest Hellbaum has always denied that WHOM stands for either of the meanings given in this story. Agnes Johnson is a well-known White House catchphrase, often abbreviated to AJ, and meaning a sort of human glitch, as in 'we have investigated the problem, and believe it may have been caused by an AJ'.

Myth 2

There is a man in the White House whose sole duty is to keep track of world events and relate them, Jimmy Ruggins fashion, to the *Book of Revelation*. He uses WHOM to keep track of things like plagues of locusts, stars falling into the sea and so on, and he has a hotline to the President, so that he can get through to him day or night, as soon as Armageddon comes. (God alone knows what Pike would do about it if he got the call.) Some versions say that this Armageddon operative has already worked out exactly when the big day will happen, and that no more WHOM subsystems are planned after that date. They say that if all the programming staff involved in subsystem development got together and compared deadlines, they would be able to figure it out for themselves. An alternative myth is that there is a WHOM module known as Armageddon Corner which collects all the evidence relating to the possible destruction of the world, including Biblical prophecies, Nostradamus, pollution, environmental balances, probability of nuclear war, extraterrestrial invasion, etc etc, with the aim of maintaining the status quo. They say the Armageddon operative has power to intervene in any way in any political situation if WHOM thinks it's necessary. He (or she) is the most powerful man (or woman) in the world.

Myth 3

This myth concerns the contagious bug. Every user knows what a bug is; it's an oversight in the programming that makes mincemeat of your data. The thing about bugs is that they are small and notoriously difficult to spot, also they have disproportionately large appetites. One of them got into the Sleeping Partner database once, and changed every name on it to Kirsten May Barcowitz. It had to be eradicated by Ernest Hellbaum, and the original names recovered from the archives under the lawn. Normal users can never understand bugs, which just seem to them like the computer screwing up again. In fact, they are conceived at programming time and brought forth when some unforeseen set of circumstances arises, such as a leap year or a new tax rule. They say that on New Year's Day in the year 2000, all the systems in the world will collapse, because the programmers will have forgotten to tell the computers about the new century. This seems unlikely to me, but then I have never been able to figure out the bit about nanoseconds and 1856.

The contagious bug is a bug that works like a virus. To understand it, you have to know that data is not kept in a big heap, but tends to be isolated in different partitions. The contagious bug is said to destroy text, though not everyone agrees on how it does this. Some say it will take a page like this one and gradually eat away all the vowels, till it looks like a Confederate flag after Gettysburg. Other descriptions suggest that it fills the page with periods, or that it changes the letters randomly to the IBM alternate character set, featuring such useful symbols as $\underline{a}$ and f. The aspect on which everyone agrees is contagion. They say that if you receive an electronic memo in which one of the characters has been changed by the bug, it will rip through all your data in no time, and it will be impossible to stop it. Users whose data is affected by the bug have to be barred from the system to prevent it being transmitted to other people. Remembering Kirsten May Barcowitz, I find the contagious bug easy to believe in, but Ernest Hellbaum says it couldn't happen.

Fred Zolph gave me another contagious bug story just a couple of weeks ago. He says the bug is passed in numerical data, and converts plus signs to minus signs, with unsettling results. The consequences of this in accounting systems do not bear thinking about, especially as the bug is said to develop very slowly over a period of months.

They make thrilling reading, these WHOM legends. They seem to imply that there is more to work than any of us knows, that we may all, Fred, Hellbaum, me, Ruggins, even Pike, be caught up in a huge informational network that runs us for its own purposes. Like all fairy stories, they make it easier to believe in God. Still, the fun kind of goes out of fairy stories when they become true, doesn't it? I mean, if people really did get abducted (or hijacked) by elves, no one would tell their kids about it any more. It's the same with the digital myths – if I started to think there was anything in them, I would feel . . . you know how I would feel. Data Lock, they call it, that feeling of sudden horror that can come over the most hardened computer user and prevent him from ever touching a keyboard again. It can strike in the middle of a piece of data – one minute you're typing away happily, and the next: Screen Scare, File Freeze, Silicon Psychosis. There are lots of expressions for it. Fred Zolph says he heard it was induced by the radioactive emissions from the VDU, but probably it's just the experience of staring into the heart of the machine and seeing all those ones and zeros, the binary nature of reality. I never heard of an actual case of Data Lock, unless that's what Ernest Hellbaum has. Or unless I'm getting it.

Datastream 2; Luke, Saint

When I raised my head again after my prayer, something strange and terrible was happening. The fishing net priest had retired from the circle and was standing in the crowd quite close to Julius. He had someone with him, and they were approaching the circle again. It was a woman.

It was a woman: tall, dark-skinned and beautiful. She was dressed only in winter wreaths of flowers which did not succeed in hiding her breasts or the crown of hair on her pudenda, let alone the wide, flat expanses between. Paul was facing her, so that I could not see the expression on his face, but his body was so straight and still that I was afraid he would have another fit.

The woman and the priest arrived at the edge of the circle and knelt before Paul. The interpreter whispered something in Paul's ear.

'What did you say?' Paul said loudly, in a way which suggested he had heard the first time.

'Fish woman, belong king.'

Paul gave a great howl of horror. He, too, fell to his knees. When he was able to speak, he began saying, 'No, no, no,' in an intimate voice, raising his eyes to the thatch, perhaps speaking to God. The priests, the interpreter and the chief looked at Paul in astonishment, stepped back and seemed about to argue or to apologize, but none of them spoke. They waited for Paul who rose slowly to his feet.

'It is not lawful,' Paul said at last, in a sick and weary voice. 'You would defile me with wreaths and crowns and with a maiden, but it is not lawful. Don't you understand me? I CANNOT DO THIS!'

He turned, wild-eyed. Face to face with him, suddenly guessing at the answer to my prayer, I rushed into the centre, seized Paul's hand and led him into the crowd. Shocked cries sprang up around us, there were thrashing limbs, shouts and snarling teeth, but we clawed our way through. When we reached the door of the hut, the children had gone. Only one remained – I recognized him at once as the slave boy Paul had released into the undergrowth. Paul half-smiled, panting.

'I have allowed, even for this. Where is – '

His question was answered even before he had finished asking it by the appearance of Julius and the master of the *Ape* at the door of the hut. The boy seemed to have been expecting us, and led us quickly through the village. On reaching the outskirts, he ducked into the undergrowth and we followed. I did not dare look back to see if the Lazaris were in pursuit, but I felt that God had given us a way out and would not let us down now. For hours we struggled through the undergrowth, pelted with bitter rain. The boy led us to the small but seaworthy boat he had been keeping for us. We were free at last.

Datastream 1; Telemann, Alb

I lost my car. It's really embarrassing to write this down, especially as I don't know who will eventually have access to the data, but I guess I must record everything, as originally planned. You see the point is, I may be a WHOM user, but I am essentially a man of action and I couldn't resist any more. One evening after work, I drove to Hillingdon Village, DC.

Hillingdon Village, spring evening, quiet, pretty, secretive. Its suburban streets at night that smell of matured daylight. Its dogwoods whose cream/orange/pink flowers float in front of them like water lilies, seemingly unconnected, its redbuds, its black youths gyrating outside liquor stores, its wheezing, rattling nightbirds. This is the background, all that's known of it, to Ellen Axaxas. I see Hillingdon Village as the unconscious side of the White House, the yin to its yang. Perhaps this is because I went there at night and I am only at the White House in the day time. Presumably it is just another suburb, no more mysterious than any other. For me, though, that trip was a journey into the darker side of my work. By coming to Hillingdon Village outside working hours, I finally allowed the worries and obsessions of the office to spill over into my spare time.

Explain this to me. I went to Hillingdon Village to keep an eye on Ellen, even though I knew she wouldn't be there. Her visits to subject are always made around the cocktail hour, although neither of them drinks. Perhaps I was planning to break into her house and look for evidence (of what?). Those perhaps again. I ought to cut down.

So I was sitting in my car absorbing the atmosphere, checking out the exterior of 2054 South Roseberry Avenue, a modest wood house, wondering what to do next, and I got picked up. I, Alb Telemann, White House aide and Washington family man, allowed myself to be picked up by a prostitute called Rose. I was kind of offguard, I imagine, because I knew I was doing those things which I ought not to be doing, and I just didn't think.

'Do you always sit around like this in your car at night? I can show you somewhere much nicer you can sit.'

'What is this,' I said, surprised. 'This is supposed to be a respectable neighborhood.' She didn't look much more than seventeen. She might have been my daughter. In fact, she looked a lot like Roxanne, only not the same color.

A nightbird woke up suddenly in one of the dogwoods, and began chirping. The noise it made was like this: rattle rattle rattle pfuieee. The girl rested her pink fingers warmly on my right arm.

'What's your name, honey?' I said.

'Rose. It says on the button, look.'

She was wearing a button on her T-shirt with the name Rose on it in pink letters. White flowers twined among the letters on luminous green stalks. They were supposed to be roses, but they looked more like balls of cotton wool. Cute, in a pathetic sort of way (and the wrong color again). The button rose and fell nicely as she breathed, and, as I watched it, I began to wonder whether I had had some ulterior but unconscious motive in coming to Hillingdon Village. Had I really intended to sit in the car for an hour or so, watching an ordinary (and empty) house? What would I have done when Ellen showed up? I'm used to following people, but normally I do it to find out where they're going. I don't usually know where they're going and go there first. My own motives were a mystery to me, unless I was really here to look for a piece of the action I keep listening to in stereo. I guess I needed the yin.

Rose took me to a wooden house, just like Ellen's, in the next street. She seemed to have it all to herself, and there wasn't much furniture in the room we used, only a bed on bare boards, a naked light bulb and floral wallpaper with a design like bugs creeping through foliage. At first, there was a certain amount of nervous negotiation about the price, and I kept changing my mind and thinking I ought to go back to the car after all, until eventually Rose dropped her price as low as it was going to go, then locked the door and sat on me until I decided I was enjoying it. We cavorted on an unmade bed, a suburban breeze tickling our skin through a broken windowpane, the nightbird rattling and wheezing in the background.

Later, I emerged into the shadows, with my yin satisfied, if not my professional curiosity. I had almost forgotten about Ellen, but I made a mental note that Rose was a black woman, such as Fred Zolph had suggested for subject. She might be a suitable candidate, provided she fitted the requirements. The requirements, I thought, and heard the wingbeat of a suburban bad angel. There is a whole computer system to make sure that Warren Pike does not share a bed with anyone inappropriate, and I, Alb Telemann, had just leapt into action with the first woman to put her head inside my car. I thought of all the terrible diseases I might contract from an evening like this one: AIDS, syphilis, herpes, compromising photographs, babies. God, I thought, I must never do anything like this again, never.

When I got back to South Roseberry Avenue, there was something wrong with it. I knew right away, the moment I entered it, though I couldn't tell what it was. It had been deserted when I parked the car; it was deserted now. It looked almost as if the streetlamps had been moved, a different pattern of shadows on the sidewalk. Of course, it had been twilight when I parked, and night had arrived since, but that was not the problem. The problem was that some son of a bitch had stolen my car.

It was not actually my car, fortunately. It was a Tenessee-built Datsun stationwagon, as supplied to Grade S60.B White House employees and its loss was more a cause of embarrassment than of panic. First I had to report it to the police, who kept me waiting for two hours in a dingy room where the dirty fluorescent lighting made me feel like a criminal, and the boy next to me offered to murder anyone I named for $15,000 dollars. This was carrying private enterprise a bit too far – surely no one would take him up on an offer like that in a place like this. Probably the boy was a police spy. Having refused the offer, I hope politely, I spent the next ten minutes peering sideways at him. He had straight black hair, parted in the center, and a solemn bony face. Could he be

someone from the White House? The person who stole my car?
No, I was becoming paranoid, an effect of guilt about Rose. I
filled in the multiple choice which a sulky receptionist (brown
cascades of hair, pouting lipstick, flicker of sardonic humor
beneath eyelashes) offered me, marvelling half-heartedly at the
crimes I could have been the victim of:

Offense: Rape / Mugging / Indecent Assault / Burglary /
Physical Injury / Theft / Verbal Abuse / Dangerous Driving

Items Stolen: Wallet / Purse / Jewelry / Money (State Sum)
/ Credit Cards / Car / Bicycle / Motor Bicycle

Injuries: Head / Neck / Hands / Arms / Upper body / Groin
/ Legs / Feet / Other

(Please delete where not applicable)

State Severity Level on Scale of 1 to 10

(1 = Superficial scratches or bruises, 10 = Severe disable-
ment or danger to life)

Will any of this information end up in WHOM some day? If so, will
it mean anything to the person who has to monitor it? I hope anyone
who monitors me is a woman, preferably one with cascading hair
and sardonic eyes. I wouldn't want my intimate data monitored
by a man. No wonder Ernest Hellbaum flipped. There is just too
much data in the world, and there doesn't seem to be any way of
getting rid of it.

Next morning, I went through a similar process explaining the
loss to Roly Entwhistle, with the difference that the forms I filled in
this time were electronic ones. Naturally, I did not mention either
Ellen Axaxas or Rose; my memo told Roly that I had stopped off
to buy flowers for my wife, an excuse which, no doubt, externalized
the guilt I was feeling about the cavorting. For a couple of days, I
had to take cabs in to work, until the replacement arrived.

Why I went to Hillingdon Village. By Alb Telemann. Actually, I
have already explained why I went to Hillingdon Village, but I
am not concerned now with yin and yang and the dark night of
the suburban unconscious. What I mean is the ostensible reason
for my going, the rational reason, if you will forgive the tautology.

A week ago, Ellen Axaxas, who is now seeing the President on a day to day basis, began to talk about the Lazar hijacking.

PARTNER: Those poor people, kidnapped by heathens like that. I expect they must be undergoing the most terrible tortures and suffering. I can't help it, I think of them night and day, trying to imagine the fear and the heat and everything.

SUBJECT: I heard some of them were Americans.

PARTNER: They're Christians, anyway. It's a Christian plane, and those heathens are going to martyr it, just like in the days of Nero. We must try to forgive, Sir.

Pike took the hint, as I guessed he would. The very next day, I read in the WHOM news digest:

> President Warren Pike today made his first statement on the hijacking of the British 747 in Lazar. 'We in the West can no longer tolerate terrorist violence,' he said. 'The hijacking in Lazar is just one more example of the lengths to which unscrupulous and heathen men will go in pursuit of their perverted ideals. I have pledged my full support to President Miraz, and to the British Ambassador in Sainte-Fleur, in their attempts to end the hijacking. A battalion of the 87th airborne division is standing by in Malta, in case they are called upon to intervene. In fact,' President Pike continued, 'all of us Americans are standing by at all times in case of all or any eventualities. We are all, of course, praying for a peaceful end to the crisis, but we are prepared for whatever end God may have in store.' He called on the nations of the West to support him in a stand against terror.
>
> A US spokesman later denied that the US was planning military intervention to end the hijacking. 'I guess that isn't what the President meant,' he said.

Lazar is dominating the news digest at the moment, and it is beginning to dominate me, too. While I'm on the subject, I'll quote from the digest of the following day:

> The semi-legendary Shamanist streetfighter known as the Scorpion gave a rare interview today to a British newspaper, in which he

condemned US President Warren Pike as an 'international pirate and the incarnation of evil upon earth'. The Scorpion already controls much of the dockyard area of Sainte-Fleur, and is believed by many observers to be the key to recent Shamanist successes in the civil war.

'My men are ready to fight day and night,' he said, 'We are fighting in the name of God, and of destroying US militarist oppression. We do not fear death. I call upon the whole world to rise up and overthrow the heathen government of the tyrant and fornicator Pike.'

It is getting confrontational. Does Ellen really mean to get us involved in a war? Another one? Maybe now you'll understand why I just had to go and sit in a car outside her home. I wanted to know if she was the sort of woman who starts wars. (I haven't reached a conclusion on this one, yet.)

Meanwhile, I have been trying to find out why they consider they have a unique personal relationship with St Paul in Ellen's home town of Colophon, Minnesota, which, according to WHOM, is where she comes from. I even borrowed a book on St Paul from the White House library, but it hasn't been much help. It's a popular theology book published by BBC Publications, England, and illustrated throughout by pictures of a man in shorts standing on various Mediterranean beaches. The man in shorts is not St Paul, but Hugh Stephenson, a sort of British Jimmy Ruggins, except that being British, he has more style. Anyway, he is an Episcopalian talking head; the head in question is long, grey, sharp-edged and would never last five minutes on US television in competition with all those game shows. The book is based on a whole film series about the missionary journeys of St Paul which was shown on British television, and Stephenson got to stand on all the right beaches. I learned from this book that no one really knows what happened to Paul in the end. He was arrested, and taken to Rome, where he arrived after various adventures. There he was kept under house arrest and did a lot of preaching, and eventually, according to legend, he was beheaded with a sword during the persecution of the Christians by Nero, but there is another story that he 'reached the Western limits of the world', whatever that means. Colophon, Minnesota?

Datastream 3; Prunewood, Kate

I watched him continuously from the time he boarded the plane at Rome, and sat with his long legs stretched in front of him and an expression of boredom and anxiety on his face, like somebody in a dentist's waiting room. In the film, which I couldn't help glancing at occasionally, even though I was without the benefit of earphones, Jeff Bridges also was waiting, shuffling his feet in the dust, as a bus slowly approached him across miles of prairie. It was a modern type of film, and I had to watch the whole wait, every twitch and shuffle, and all the time I was half-watching the man across the aisle, the blankness in his eyes, his straight, motionless legs.

I decided that he was a German, and that his wife had just left him. And then later, when I leant over to the window, and looked at the blue and olive carpet rolling by, trying to pick out the islands by their shape, I found that I was still dreaming about the blond man. Presumably, he was going to Greece as well. And I had always thought when I finally went there it would be with Hugh, and we would stagger about the ruins talking guiltily about Judy and repentance. This German was getting over his wife, I decided, and I was getting over Hugh, and we could do it together. Me in a pastel dress, the German in shorts, stumbling over a landscape of white rocks and broken columns. Long guiltless nights in a tent, the squeaking of cicadas, pineneedles and desire. Now I had the German to fantasize about, I could really enjoy my memories of Hugh, which were really only fantasies in reverse, only more satisfying because the experiences were already in the bank.

And the son of a bitch hijacked us. You can't trust any of them, can you? First Hugh, now Jalal. There are three hijackers, actually, two of whom have the regulation appearance, thickset, suntanned and sinister, but Jalal? You would never have picked him for a Lazari terrorist. Of course, I don't think he's actually a bad man, just a misguided idealist. There's something almost gentle about the way he talks to the passengers, compared with Faroun, who shouts, and Haq, who stands to attention as if on parade, and says nothing at all.

The first thing the hijackers did after taking over the plane was to smash all the bottles of alcohol in a fit of zeal. I spent the first day being sick, staggering out of the bulkhead afterwards, clambering dizzily and wretchedly over the seats, and joining the back of the line so that I could crunch my way over the broken glass to the bulkhead and be sick again. Even now, on the second day, the air still reeks of the hijackers' impromptu Shamanist cocktail of beer, whisky, gin, vodka, red wine, white wine, sherry, tequila, Southern Comfort, Bacardi, brandy, advocaat, cherry brandy, Cointreau, more beer. The Lazari spring has arrived, and even with the door open, the air is so foul and stifling that people have been passing out in the line for the toilet, and have been unable, because of the crush, to fall down. Faroun has decided that it is time to reassert his authority. All right, so he made a mistake, and will no doubt atone for it later, but in the meantime he has decreed that the passengers will eat. There is no shortage of food, because Government troops have brought large metal pails full of cold tinned fish and cold rice to the plane this morning. Nobody wants the seige to finish in anticlimactic starvation. Jalal is moving about the cabin with a pail of fish rice in each hand, smiling nervously, urging, 'Eat, eat,' with impartial solicitude. I think he is beautiful.

All the same, it is a shock to find myself in Lazar. Hugh never mentioned it when we walked on the beach in Clacton or Climping discussing Lesbos, Delphi and Rhodes; it is not one of *his* islands, the ones where he explored the early history of the Church in shorts, prising shellfish away from rocks, Greek girls away from grim chaperones and, in his televised disquisitions, homoousian bishops away from homoiousian ones. Lazar is current affairs, not art or history; it is not the sort of place we would ever have wanted to go to, because of its very low tranquillity quotient. Hugh is very keen on tranquillity, and always made me take into account the tranquillity quotient of a town before he would consider investigating a miracle there for his programme (it was for that reason that he tended to avoid little boys saved from bullets in Londonderry and the recoveries of riot victims in Brixton).

Foreign travel is not good for Hugh, for moral reasons. Whenever he is away from his wife for long periods, he has an affair, and this causes him terrible guilt. That was why he decided, after many years of making religious documentaries set either in the Holy Land or, for preference, in the footsteps of Saint Paul, to make a series in England. The series was *Modern Miracles*, but the idea proved counter-productive, because that series provided me with my first job as a researcher, and so Hugh had an affair anyway, but longer and hence even guiltier than the ones he had had in Italy, Greece and Israel. I contrived to find many of the modern miracles in seaside towns, and so Hugh was able to walk with me on the beach in shorts and yearn for the Mediterranean, musing about St Paul.

'When I was a child, I thought as a child, but when I became a man, I put away childish things. How very hard that is. Now you and I, we worship a Mediterranean God, I think. That's very important to both of us.' Hugh has an American wife; she, of course, worships an Atlantic God, and this is a major obstacle in their love. He wrote a lot about the sea in his St Paul book. 'When one thinks of this sea, and how central it was to the people who lived around its shores, how they went out on it every day, how it brought them life in the form of the fish they ate at nearly every meal, how it brought them death in its sudden storms and squalls, how it was their lifeline in terms of communication with the rest of the civilized world, how it was in fact the very centre, in a literal sense, of that world . . .' Hugh envied them that world with its literal centre. He would have liked a simple world like that. He once said to me, 'I am fundamentally monogamous. I have just lost my way in the wilderness of modern morality.' Of course, I was so bitter about it then.

'I think I could stand it better if I knew I was being used,' I told him. 'The trouble with you is you're so horribly responsible.'

'NOTHING TO FEAR' says the leaflet I am reading as I eat the fish. I was too afraid to read it when they were first handed round, and too ill to read it thereafter, but now some of the journalist's instinct for getting inside people's skin is reawakening in me. I need to know who these people are, and what they want. In particular, I want to know about the blond hijacker Jalal, about the source of that gentleness and sweetness I feel in him. Where does it come from, his own nature, or the nature of his beliefs? I am almost in a mood to get converted – almost, but not quite, for there is a wayward element in my personality which always spoils my conversions, and makes me turn instead to people, not creeds.

'NOTHING TO FEAR', it says in ferocious red letters, and underneath, in smaller black print:

> You are seized by non-violent members of Shamanist Revolutionary Party of Lazar, purpose to humiliate socalled President of Lazar Dol Miraz and imperialist US allies. This is acceptable process, and no harm will come at you unless unexpected. Dol Miraz is evil man in pay of US military barons. He is become President in 1958 in legacy of British French imperialist rule. Shamanist role in government is technically assured, with General Tuli appointed Defence Minister and head of all armies. However, life of everyday Shamanist peasant in North of island remains for hundreds of years pursuit of difficult crops, such olives, oranges, suffering tax of severity imposed by neoimperialist rule of Miraz. Supposed representation of Shamanist in Parliament remains charade, represent only rich Sainte-Fleur merchant class not devote to Shamanist cause and religious, even not keeping fast. Finally, in 1969, war arise, and is punished of brutality, farms set fire after crops seized by Christian. Ravishes of Second Crusade is repeat for modern time. From this date, beginning of revolution philosophy of Scorpion.

Jalal has appeared beside me, repeating the slogans. 'Nothing to fear. We are non-violent terrorist. No harm will come at you. You are temporarily seized.'

'What is going to happen to us?'

'No one is hurt,' Jalal says, 'no one hurt unless Miraz not resigns. Then we are blown up.'

'Blown up?'

'Miraz will resign,' Jalal says. 'Forces of Scorpion are overwhelming. Even Lazar official army is now with General Tuli on hills. However, if you are dead, you will die democratically, for Shamanist cause at world politics. We are negotiate now with government.'

The blitz spirit is now returning to the other passengers, who enjoy this kind of thing. Every now and then, a brave little murmur and rustling starts up somewhere, and two or three quavering voices begin to sing 'The White Cliffs of Dover', or even, if they are old enough 'It's a Long Way to Tipperary'. I hope I don't die when they're singing that, it would be as if the last seventy years had never happened. The hijackers allow it, perhaps feeling that Christian passengers should be allowed the comfort of their hymns during their temporary seizure.

'Is no need for alarm. You will not die,' Jalal lies. Actually, I know I am going to die very soon. I am going to be blown up in this plane, and my body covered with undignified soot, like a cartoon.

Hugh on death. 'What you have to remember,' he said, throwing stones into the sea, 'is that there is no time in the world of death. Not only [stone] no day and night [stone], no this year and next year [stone], no dental appointments and mortgage payments [stone], but no sense of self, because the sense of self is entirely dependent [stone] on watching oneself change through time, and no sensations even, in the way we understand the term, because we only recognize sensations by their boundaries, like picking up a coin [stone] by its edges. Now that is almost impossible for us in our present unenlightened and fallen state really and truly to [stone] understand. And that is why St Paul says *then* face to face, because the world of death is as different from life as the sea from the dry land. I must get some more stones. Did I split an infinitive just now?'

'I don't think so,' I said.

'Yes,' Hugh continued, 'and that is also why tranquillity is so important in my life, because it is only through tranquillity that we can approximate, even through a glass, darkly, to the state of timelessness which is death.' [Stone. Stone. Stone. Stone. Stone.]

I know I am going to die. That is why, talking to a blond Teutonic-looking hijacker whose English is poor and whose grasp of Western sexuality is minimal, I tell him, speaking as a liberated, sexually experienced woman, that I love him.

Datastream 1; Telemann, Alb

I have a confession to make. You may not have realized this yet, because I'm ashamed, and don't really know how to talk about it, but I'm scared. It dates from the time Roxanne used to weep over the grape jelly, and I used to assure her that the end of the world is part of the American way of life. We have all lived with the apocalypse so long we hardly notice it any more. We have all seen the bumper stickers which announce to the world:

> In case of RAPTURE
> this car will be DRIVERLESS!!!

The basic idea here is that God intends to seize all the believers and take them to heaven, before the world goes up in smoke, fire, brimstone, fallout etc. This gives believers a certain amount of confidence in contemplating Armageddon. What excuse have the rest of us got for complacency? I have been to Jimmy Ruggins's meetings, and they have converted me, brothers and sisters. Not to Christianity, but to fear. For I have seen Jimmy Ruggins put on his half-moon glasses and expound the text:

> Then shall two be in the field; the one shall be taken and
> the other left. Two women shall be grinding at the mill;
> the one shall be taken and the other left.
> Matthew 24, 40–41

WHOM

I have heard him say that when the great day comes, believers will be snatched from their houses, their beds, their cars, just like that, leaving the rest of us behind to suffer the plagues of the apocalypse, hundred pound hailstones, stinging locusts, seas turning to blood.

And I was not comforted when he pointed out, 'Of course, we don't have to take the Holy Bible literally when it speaks of these things. I tell you, brothers and sisters, that when John speaks of hundred pound hailstones, he is referring to falling masonry, the debris of a multi-megaton nuclear explosion. And when John speaks of stinging locusts, he is referring not to locusts but to Cobra helicopters spraying forth nerve gas from their tails. And when he speaks of seas of blood he is referring to the aftermath of a major sea-battle between the NATO and Warsaw pact fleets. It is horrors like these, brothers and sisters, that you will have to endure if the Lord does not take you. You just better make sure, brothers, when you're working in those fields, that you are the one who is taken, not the one who remains. And sisters, unless you know you are the chosen of the Lord Jesus Christ, you had better look over your shoulder when you're grinding away in that mill. I think you know what I mean now, don't you? I mean rapture.'

I have heard him quote 1 Thessalonians. (Yes, St Paul. Yes the same book he used to quote in electronic memos to his President – subject: chastity.)

> *Then we which are alive and remain shall be caught up together with them in the clouds, to meet the Lord in the air.*
>
> 1 Thessalonians, 4, 17

I have seen him take up his guitar and sing his own composition 'Rapture Blues':

> I was driving on the freeway,
> When I disappeared from view,
> Yes I was driving on the freeway,
> When I disappeared from view,
> For the Lord had taken over,
> I just spread my wings and flew.

There's a big wind coming
That will blow away the just
Yes, there's a hurricane coming
That will blow away the just
It will sweep us clean to Heaven
When the earth is full of dust.

When the locusts come from Syria
I won't be here to see,
When the midnight comes from Moscow
I will not be here to see,
I gave everything to Jesus,
And he's looking after me.

Sometimes, when driving home, I stare hard at the driver of the next car and imagine him suddenly vanishing, seized instantaneously by the Lord, while the car proceeds blindly on without him. I am not a Christian; I can't help it, I made half-hearted attempts to become one when everyone else seemed to be doing it, but I couldn't work up enough interest. I just worry that they might turn out to be right after all. There are times when I quite like the idea of all the Christians disappearing, despite the road accidents it would cause. But that isn't logical, because if that happens, it proves they are right, and there is no time left for me to get saved. I hate the idea of a nuclear holocaust *followed* by hell. It doesn't seem fair. One or the other I could probably put up with.

Warren Pike is scared of the rapture also. Ellen keeps trying to explain it to him, and Pike, despite his Baptist upbringing all those years ago, just can't take it in.

SUBJECT: You mean, I'll lose you, Ellen? You'll go to
              heaven and you won't even be dead?
PARTNER: You don't have to lose me, Sir. You can come
              with me, but you have to be saved, first.

Pike doesn't know whether he is saved or not. Probably he will be. Ellen will save him. I guess I ought to be pleased about this, as I am in a sense quite close to the President, but actually it upsets me. For one thing, I don't like being left out. I always hated this when I was a boy, you know, when everyone got to go and pick blueberries and I had to stay behind and do the chores. With all the sins Warren Pike has committed, it will just make me sick if he goes to heaven and I get stung by the Cobra helicopters. Besides, is it good for the country to have a President who feels confident in his physical salvation? It's bad enough letting him have a fallout shelter. In the inner recesses of my brain, I have been doing a great deal of what Ernest Hellbaum calls *What-If* modelling recently, and the results are not encouraging.

I went to Hillingdon Village again, on account of the rapture. My new car is not as large or as impressive as my Tennessee-built Datsun stationwagon, and it is, significantly, of a type usually supplied to White House employees of a security rating well below S60.B. However, now that I have a car again, I can continue with my unorthodox policy of keeping an eye on Ellen Axaxas in her absence. While Ellen was in bed with Warren Pike, alternately squealing nervously and talking born-again Pillowtalk, I was once more parked in the leafshadows of South Roseberry Avenue, where, once again, I was picked up by Rose and ended up cavorting on her unmade bed with the draught from the broken windowpane cooling my buttocks.

'Why am I doing this?' I asked her afterwards. 'I don't even enjoy it all that much.'

'Why did they take away your car, Alb?' Rose said. 'Was it because of me?'

'I lost it.'

'I thought it might have been because of me,' Rose said rather wistfully, as if she thought it would have made her more of a *femme fatale* to have been responsible for the loss of the Datsun.

Long, selfconscious pause. I was aware of my toes protruding from the far end of a dirty sheet, of the bulge in the middle of the bed where my stomach was, of my clothes neatly folded on the bare floorboards under the broken windowpane, of Rose breathing discreetly beside me.

'Shit, what's the time?'

'It's only six-thirty,' Rose said. 'Don't worry, I don't have another customer for an hour.'

'I don't understand, why do you work in an area like this? It isn't a red-light district, is it? I would have thought it was all quiet respectable families round here.'

'The quiet respectable ones are the worst.'

'I guess so. But even they have got to know you're there, haven't they, Rose? I mean you can't find many men just hanging around the sidewalks waiting for you to come along.'

'Well what were you doing, Alb?'

'Yeah,' I said, 'what *was* I doing? I swear to God, Rose, I find my own motives completely mystifying. I must be crazy to spend my time screwing a woman like you in the present circumstances. I hope you don't take this personally, of course.'

'Not at all, Alb. After all, I don't do it personally.'

As I made my way back to my car, I felt better. Rose, I realized, was just an ordinary working girl, and I was just an ordinary customer. There was no reason why I shouldn't sleep with a prostitute; people were doing it all over the world, and had been for thousands of years with very little in the way of ill-effects. What was Warren Pike himself, but a customer much like me? And what was Ellen Axaxas but a slightly more complex Rose, an elementary-school teacher doubling as a prostitute and being paid not in money but in the coin of power politics? There was nothing, ultimately to be frightened of. The White House was full of people whose only duty was to watch the President and make sure he didn't do anything political. It wasn't just me and Fred Zolph and Roly Entwhistle – there were probably hundreds of others. This being the case, I reasoned, there wasn't the slightest chance of Pike getting the US into something he couldn't get it out of. Anyway, Pike doesn't want the end of the world, I thought. He likes the world, and considers he is just getting good at it.

I was thinking these comforting thoughts while unlocking the door of my car and getting into the driver's seat. That was when the bicycle wheel appeared. It was just a regular bicycle wheel, except that it had no bicycle attached to it. I watched it rolling towards me, expecting that at any moment someone would come running after it, perhaps half-wheeling, half-carrying a maimed bicycle, but no one came. The bicycle wheel was an event without an obvious cause and, perhaps, without a sequel. There is something sinister about wheels. If they could get away from us, they would.

Ten minutes later, I was still thinking about it; I drew up at the side of the road so that I could think about it better. I rested my hand on the steering wheel and thought about rapture. Naturally, it

WHOM

could not be happening. Bicycle wheels escape every day. I thought
of a multiplicity of plausible explanations for the appearance of
a solitary bicycle wheel, and found none of them to be plausible
after all. On the other hand, was God seizing bicycles as well as
believers? Even if He were, He would undoubtedly seize the front
wheel as well. Maybe He had intended to, and the front wheel had
fallen off. I could not believe I was thinking these things. I must
be ill, I thought, it must be the stress of the job and the Syndrome
catching up with me at last. I am losing touch with reality.

I drove back to Hillingdon Village. If I could just see Ellen
Axaxas, I would know that she at any rate had not been seized.
If the rapture had already taken place, Ellen had presumably not
made it back from the Presidential bed. She was undoubtedly
one of the elect, having been intimate with an angel from early
childhood. In any case, I had come here in the first place, not to
go to bed with prostitutes and see ghostly bicycle wheels, but to try
to understand Ellen, to put her into her natural context, dogwoods,
redbuds, nightbirds and all. It was time to talk to her. I had been
wasting time for so long. I needed to confront her at last.

As I drove back through the post rush hour streets, I found that
another Jimmy Ruggins blues anthem was going round and round
in my head:

> That big wheel keeps on rolling
> Keeps on rolling down the road
> That big wheel keeps on rolling
> Keeps on rolling down the road
> I heard a voice call in the darkness
> Let me help you with your load.

Datastream 3; Prunewood, Kate

I feel a little guilty to be the cause of Jalal's dilemma, but he is, after all, the cause of mine. The emergency conference of the three hijackers has lasted hours, with a lot of shoulder-shrugging, and now Jalal is back. He isn't able to look me in the face.

'Negotiations are not good,' he explains.

'No?' This is something, he confides in me.

'Yes. Possibly we explode plane.' He half turns towards me, catches my eye and winces, like someone forgetfully using an injured muscle. Not looking at me, he continues, 'Faroun will kill passengers on daily basis. This is however murder.'

'Isn't it murder to blow the plane up?'

'Is only collective murder, therefore not relevant. I am not murdering individuals if possible.' He chews his lip and stares at the pocket in the back of the seat in front, where I have stowed the first page of the hijacking diary I am keeping. I follow his eyes, hoping he doesn't read any of it. My handwriting is so naked, the cross that always just misses the 't', the 'g' with the huge loop, so naive. I have had the idea of writing an article about my experiences, possibly expanding it into a television documentary later. But Jalal ignores the diary and carries on talking.

There are three reasons why Jalal is embarrassed by my feelings for him. Firstly, he is currently busy with negotiations by radio with the government spokesperson at the airport terminal. Secondly, he is a warrior of the Shamanist Socialist cause, hence not at liberty to indulge affections like a small boy. Finally, he says, I am a woman, and therefore have neither the right nor the ability to fall in love. Women marry, Jalal explains, because of a threefold gratitude: to their father for having them, to their husband for proposing to them and to God for giving them an opportunity to produce children for the armed struggle.

'What about sex?' I ask quickly, and hold my breath. The reply will not only be important in itself, but central to the article when I get round to writing it. As a matter of fact, despite being a liberated Western woman, I didn't give very much thought to the central issue when propositioning Jalal. I have never really pictured the two of us doing it, because, of course, the plane is full of hostages. Besides, neither of us has washed since the hijacking began, because of the state of the toilets after everyone has been sick. Even my remaining pack of small cologne-soaked tissues is unlikely to make any impression on my skin after this time. My hair is like damp string; Jalal, too, is beginning to fade slightly, as if what little colour he has is draining out of him. In the circumstances, sex is something of a theoretical crux.

It would have been better, this being the case, if I hadn't mentioned it, because then Faroun would not have wanted to have me shot. Faroun has told Jalal that, if they allow me to live, the other female passengers will also be infected with unwomanlike lust. He has seen women on Western television, removing the clothes of musicians. One woman screams, and then many women scream. By being shot, on the other hand, I will be a hero and a martyr of the Shamanist cause, as well as prevented from committing sin. Jalal was nice about telling me; he said he was reluctant to do it because of his scruples about individual murder. All the same, I hate them, all three of them. They think they know it all, don't they? Well, I know a hell of a lot more about sin than they do. I work in religious television. I have a professional insight into it. Also, I cannot see that there is anything unwomanlike about lust. And my death is not in the popular interest; it isn't popular with me, anyway.

'No, no,' Jalal says. They have rejected the murdering. They have reached a compromise, and are going to throw me off the plane.

I don't want to go.

'You must go for good of Shamanist cause,' Jalal says. It's very late by now, and the passengers in Economy are trying to sleep, some lying in the aisles on the dark stains of gin, whisky, Southern Comfort and beer, others, (the more respectable ones) in the seats, hooking their legs over armrests or pressing them against the seat in front. 'Already disease is spreading to other females,' Jalal says. 'Stewardess red hair in love Haq.'

'She's only pretending,' I tell him. 'She probably heard you were planning to let me go and decided to try the same herself. How could anyone be in love with Haq, it's ridiculous.'

'Haq very sad also frightened.'

'Why should he be frightened? She's so skinny, and anyway, he's the one with the gun.'

'No, Faroun is with gun. Haq has moustache,' Jalal says quickly.

'You mean you only have one gun?'

'Certainly, Faroun bring in camera case Rome. Haq bring ammunition. Guns are difficult past machines unless wood.'

'So it's a real gun?' I ask. I cannot help thinking of the article.

'Of course is real gun, otherwise how possible shoot passengers?'

'And you have real explosive in the hold?'

'Yes, if necessary to blow up aeroplane. However you are not here.'

'But I want to be here, Jalal. I want to be in at the kill.'

'Do you mind,' a man says. He is short and bald, lying curled up a few feet away from us. There are several short bald men, almost indistinguishable from each other, all troublemakers. From time to time, they form a little knot outside one of the toilets and start muttering about 'having a go'. Strangely, they only do this when one of the hijackers is around, perhaps because they want to be stopped, or perhaps because the 'have a go' talk is intended as a gesture of defiance. I look hard at the man. The bald contingent have me marked down as a traitor because I have been fraternizing with Jalal. Perhaps they think I am a terrorist myself.

'Yes, I do mind as a matter of fact,' I say sharply. 'I'm having a very important conversation on which all our lives may depend, and you are interrupting me. Go back to sleep.'

'I'm sorry, Jalal,' I say, 'but I can't go. It would be running away.'
'If not running away,' Jalal says, 'you are shot.'

3.45 am. The spring night is scarcely cooler than the inside of
the plane, but uncontaminated by beer, gin or Southern Comfort.
There are no stars in the sky, and Faroun has put off all the lights
in the plane. Only the runway lights, crisscrossing, illuminate a few
weedgrown strips of tarmac. The airport building, two hundred
yards away, is unlit. I brace myself to jump. It is probably equivalent
to jumping out of a second floor window, but I have no choice. I
want to live to finish my article. There is a crackling noise in the
distance.

It is remote, as if heard over a public address system. Having
made up my mind to jump, I want to go ahead, but Faroun and
Jalal are over-reacting. They shush me, as if I was making the noise,
and then pull me away from the door and swing it shut. 'Gun,' Jalal
says. Gun? Really? It didn't sound like anything much. It seems to
be slowing now; yes, it has stopped.

'What did they do that for,' I ask stupidly, sitting on the floor.
'Don't they know I'm on their side?' Jalal puts his hands under
my arms and pulls me to my feet.

Datastream 1; Telemann, Alb

I was sheltering under a dogwood tree in which the same nightbird I have heard everywhere since my nocturnal visits to Hillingdon Village was rattling and wheezing. A slim blonde young woman with a grim face was getting out of her white Volkswagen a few feet away, unaware of my presence. A wheel was rolling somewhere, a big wheel, like the wheel of fortune. I didn't know yet where it was rolling to, but it was rolling somewhere.

'Good evening, Miss Axaxas,' I said, as she closed the garage door, and passed my dogwood tree on the way to let herself in to the house.

I at least expected her to be surprised. Ideally, I thought she would gasp with surprise and horror, scream or faint. However, she did none of these things. Instead, she stopped, gave a rueful little smile and walked across to kiss me.

'Hi,' she said, 'I've been expecting you.'

'You must think I'm someone else,' I stammered stupidly.

'No, I think you're you.' She looked very hard at me as she said it, with eyes that may have been gray or blue in the suburban darkness, and I had a terrible feeling: this woman had seen through me.

Ellen unlocked the door and led me into the house. We stood together in a dark, shapeless room, and I felt her breathing calmly beside me. Then she switched on the light and I looked around.

The room was surprisingly large, apparently too large for the house that contained it, but this was a delusion caused by the lack of furniture – Ellen had no chairs, no table, no sofa. This appeared to be policy rather than poverty, since there was at least a carpet, with a few big cushions scattered on it. Apart from these, there were no *things*, no evidence that this woman ever watched TV, read a book or listened to a record. Ellen saw my expression and looked at me with amusement. 'I'm just passing through,' she said.

I sat on one of the cushions with my knees protruding awkwardly into space. Suits were not designed for this kind of decor. I wished I was wearing something more appropriate to the occasion, whatever that was. Ellen Axaxas sat about four feet away in a more practised manner, her weight on her left hip, her bare legs drawn up beside her. She was wearing a light summer dress, an efficient minimum of clothing, the kind of garment you wear for just passing through.

'I know they sent you,' Ellen said.

'Who? Nobody sent me.'

'You're here to kill me, aren't you?'

'What? No, of course I'm not here to kill you.'

'It's funny. I thought you would be different. I was expecting a thin, silent type who would just get on with it. You look kind of flustered to me, as if you were lost. Do you feel lost? I'm sorry, I don't know your name.'

'Alb.'

'Do you feel lost, Alb?'

'I guess I do. All the same, I want you to know, I'm not here to kill you.'

'You don't have to hide it from me, Alb. I've been waiting for this moment ever since I was a little girl aged six, picking flowers in the backyard. I spoke to an angel. No, I guess it was the angel that spoke to me. I was just a kid, of course. I don't remember it too clearly.'

She spoke in a flat, matter-of-fact voice, but I saw the scene clearly: the tiny grim-faced blonde child, a posy clutched in her hand, the terrible angel, a car passing ignorantly in the road.

'It was just a voice really,' Ellen said. 'I thought it was my mother at first. It said, "God wants you." That's all. It's not so much the words that are important, it's the meaning. And it means you're going to kill me.'

'Ellen, I don't want to kill you.'

82

'You mean it?' She looked at me suddenly in confusion, a startled look. It reminded me of how it felt being a kid, when you grabbed a stranger's hand in the street because he looked like your father.

'Sure I mean it. I don't want to kill you. I won't kill you, I promise.'

'Why not?'

'What do you mean, "Why not"? You don't actually want to get killed, do you?'

'Try to understand, Alb. It's not a question of wanting to or not wanting to. It's just what God has in store for me.'

'Yes, maybe. I can understand if that's what you think the angel meant. But what about me? What has God got in store for me?'

'I guess if you kill me, you'll go to hell. Unless you repent, of course.'

'Wouldn't it be better not to kill you at all?' I found this conversation hard to cope with.

She looked at me again. This time, in the naked bulblight, I could tell definitively that her eyes had no color at all. Color of eyes: not applicable.

'Maybe you're right,' she said at last. 'I don't think the one that's going to kill me will spend so much time arguing about it. It's curious, though. I was so sure this would be the night.'

She wanted to die, that was the difference between us. The difference between her and most people. Ellen Axaxas was actually looking forward to it.

We talked for half an hour. I was not frightened of her any more; I felt so natural with her that I had an urge to confess everything, even the little things I had hardly confessed to myself. I told her about Rose. I told her about my job listening to tapes of her sexual activities in the White House. I told her that I was worried about her influence over the President, and even about the fishing trips I used to take with my father. Ellen hugged her bare knees with her bare arms, elfin and innocent. When not looking grim, she had a pretty, childish laugh.

'But that's wonderful! Do you mean I'm famous?'

'Everyone who sleeps with the President is famous,' I said, and bit my lip.

'Don't worry, Alb, I don't care. I see, so you had recordings. I never guessed. But it doesn't matter. You see, sometimes, Alb, people have to do things that are against their principles, just because God wants them to. You know about Abraham and Isaac, don't you? Well this was like that. Sometimes, it's necessary to sin in order to overcome sin. Sometimes it is only through the flesh that the flesh can be conquered. As a matter of fact, I think that's always true. We are as God made us, men and women, sex organs and all, and we become something greater and purer than that, angels, who are beyond sex organs, but the flesh is, if you understand me, a sort of ladder. You have to climb up it if you want to get to the top.'

'I see.' I felt ashamed.

'You've got your job to do, I understand how important it is. You did the right thing to come to me, Alb.'

I felt more peaceful than I have done at any time since my Syndrome began.

'Ellen,' I said as I was leaving, 'I wanted to ask you. About the world.' I couldn't say what I wanted to. It sounded stupid, and a little selfish. She was both the most beautiful and the most innocent woman I had ever met. It was sacrilegious to associate her with my own neurotic fears.

'What about the world, Alb?' Ellen asked, smiling. 'The world isn't important.'

Half an hour later, I stood in South Roseberry Avenue, cursing, 'Shit, shit, shit, Jesus Christ.' It was kind of incongruous, seeing that I had just that moment come from a conversation with a woman so pure and virtuous I felt changed for life. Not that she wasn't dangerous – maybe she was. I just felt that she really was what she seemed to be, viz. a Saint, even if a dangerous one. She was incapable of harming people deliberately. When I left Ellen, my soul was at peace, and I had decided to be a better person. I promised myself that I would not go back to Hillingdon Village, that I would abjure fornication with Rose (or anyone), that I would look for another, less obsessive job. Ellen was right; there was no point in worrying about the world, which usually manages to take care of itself. My life was transformed. When I finally emerged from her passing-through place, however, it was untransformed again by the disappearance of a second car. 'Fuck. Goddamn it.' My life never stays on a transcendental plane for very long. I have no idea why.

What really hurt was the fact that, as a private investigator, I have always supposed myself tough, cool, and above all, streetwise.

Things like this are not supposed to happen to people like me. First of all, private investigators do not go to bed with prostitutes – they are above such things, and if they go to bed with somebody, it should be a beautiful suspect or, better still, a beautiful client. Second, private investigators do not tell all to anyone, let alone the chief suspect in the case, Saint or no Saint. Finally, they are supposed to be immune to car thefts of this random and insulting kind. I shoved my hands deeper into my pockets (the night was suddenly cold) and stared at the place where the car ought to have been. This is what comes of thinking you know the street, just because you spend a lot of your time walking along it. 'But Goddamn it, this isn't a street. This is an Avenue!'

The same girl in the police station. Pretty and knew it. When I came in, she recognized me at once and fluttered her eyelashes.

'Hi,' she said, 'so soon?'

I looked sulkily at her, and she looked sulkily back. The difference was that, for her, sulkiness was part of the image. It went with thick lipstick, cascades of brown hair, a blouse made of some glossy cream-colored material.

'I lost my car.'

'I know it,' she said. 'I never forget a crime victim. You're a little premature, aren't you, Mr . . . Er?'

'Telemann.'

'That's right, Mr Telemann. We would have phoned you if we'd found it so soon. Forty-seven percent of crimes in this town go unsolved, did you know that?'

'In Hillingdon Village?'

'You'd be surprised, there isn't such a thing as a respectable neighborhood these days. You do get a better class of crime in Hillingdon Village, I guess. More burglaries, fewer rapes. You want to see the statistics?'

The girl leant forward across the desk, covering most of her in-tray from view.

'No thanks, I want to report a car missing.'

'Another one?'

'Another one.'

'Is this some kind of tax dodge?'

'No,' I said, 'I guess I'm unlucky.'

'I guess so,' she said. 'Did you know there's a man in Idaho who was struck by lightning four separate times?'

'No, I didn't know that. You're very hot on statistics tonight.'

'It's my hobby. A girl needs a hobby.' She gave a little wriggle of the shoulders. Thank God there is still someone who treats me like a real detective. But probably she treats everyone that way.

'You want to fill out another form?' she asked.

'Why don't you just photocopy the last one?' I said, 'and I'll write the new date and the model of car on it.'

'Sorry, we don't work that way. Rules are rules.' She opened the desk drawer and got out another thick form, full of slashes and asterisks. Two pages of it were footnotes.

'You know,' she said, 'some people are kind of magnetic, they draw trouble. Actually they enjoy it, it's a masochistic thrill for them. Are you that kind of guy?'

'No,' I said, 'I don't think so.'

Back at my desk in the White House, enjoying the sunshine that dazzles my computer screen and the prospect through the office window, I am beginning to feel better. The moral surely is to stay away from Hillingdon Village, and as long as I do that I will be safe. I haven't been drawing trouble, I've actually been going out to look for it. In a way, the theft of the two cars was providential. It has taught me a lesson, and I have escaped from the dark night of the suburban unconscious without losing a penny, only a bit of pride and credibility. Roly Entwhistle says it is impossible to get me a car through the normal channels until there has been a thorough investigation into the loss of the other two, but when I pleaded that I had to have transport, Entwhistle finally agreed to get me one. 'I shouldn't be doing this,' he wrote, 'you apparently are the kiss of death to automobiles. Do you have any condition of a psychological nature that I haven't been told of? I was thinking maybe something related to kleptomania, only in this case a compulsion to have things stolen rather than to steal them. I'm not an expert on these things, but you ought to see a good psychiatrist and check it out. Hellbaum is doing really well with his, by the way, and expects to be back at work soon. The car is a convertible, smaller than you asked for and better than you deserve. It was all I could get at this kind of notice. Try not to park it too often. And don't take it to Hillingdon Village. It isn't insured for going there. I don't know what you see in that place anyway.'

Datastream 3; Prunewood, Kate

I am in the first class cabin, alone for the first time in three days, stretching my legs in the unfamiliar space. It has begun to rain with a fierce, tropical sounding hiss. Now the lightning begins. I listen to the silence inside, amplified by the rattle of rain outside. Free at last (almost). I don't even have to think, make plans, nothing. Thunder brings back memories from the pre-Hugh era; it makes me feel a small girl again. It all seems remote from my new cocoon, and the remoteness makes the very vehemence of the storm seem comforting, as it always did when I was a child . . .

I must have fallen asleep. Suddenly, Jalal is standing in the aisle unbuttoning his shirt.

'What are you doing?'

'Taking clothes.'

'Why are you taking your clothes off?'

'We are consummating.'

'What are we doing?'

'Consummating.'

Consummating?

'Well, wait just a moment. What, now? Why?' I have to get him out of here, for God's sake, no, anything but that. Did I really want to do this? With him? I must have been crazy.

'You are want, I are want, very nice,' Jalal says.

'But we can't!' I say. 'I haven't even had breakfast yet.' Jalal folds his shirt and places it on the seat in front of me. His chest is flat and narrow, with a small tuft of unexpectedly dark hair on the sternum. He looks younger without the shirt. I take several sniffs, sampling his smell, wondering if I like it, whether I could become passionately carried away, or whether I would only feel queasy. He smells strong, but clean, like a stables.

'Is no breakfast,' Jalal says, 'rice is finish, imperialist forces suspend negotiations, therefore eat impossible. Apologize for inconvenience.' He bends down and begins to unlace his military boots.

'So you want me for breakfast, is that it? Perhaps you would like me to wash that shirt for you afterwards.'

'You think I using you. Yes?' Jalal says.

'I do, somewhat.'

'Not so. You are not whore now, respectable married woman.' I get up, as if to edge out of my seat and move further away from him. Pointless. I sit down again.

'Married woman.'

'Married, yes. Faroun is Shaman of Shamanist church. We are married at dawn in simple dignified ceremony. You are remarkable privileged wife as Christian woman.'

'We are married,' I say.

'Yes, married, certainly.'

'I wasn't there.'

'Not necessary in Shamanist marriage.'

'Not necessary.'

'No.'

I am crying. It was the only response I could think of on the spur of the moment, and it works quite well on Jalal, who is stopped in the act of removing a boot. He remains with his boot clutched in his right hand, while I try through my tears to explain that sex is one thing and marriage another, and that while I may have wanted to make love, at least in theory, I never wanted to make vows. Then Jalal puts the boot down carefully and slaps my face. I cry again, watching him between my fingers, my face stinging with indignation. This is typical male violence, he has no chance now, he has totally forfeited all rights to love or sex or being respected as a human being. Jalal is walking up and down wringing his hands, like a character in a play. Sometimes he stops and looks at me with an expression that is part embarrassment, part confusion, part – perhaps, but I can hardly see this part through the tears and the fingers – tenderness. He walks right up to me and stretches out a hand as if to touch my shoulder, but draws it away at the last moment.

Am I being fair to him? I'm not sure myself – after all, I am a liberal, and have grown up believing that other people's views should be respected. Also, I find him attractive. Now that the first shock of pain and indignation is fading, I suspect that I am showing a deplorable insensitivity to the ideals and beliefs of Jalal's culture, a culture in which violence is important and women aren't. I have been failing to see that he could only have developed as a man and a human being in a limited number of ways, and considering his background, he hasn't done badly. He is my husband after all – at least, from his point of view he is. Naturally, the marriage will have no legal standing in Britain, since I didn't consent to it and wasn't even there at the time, and it has no ecclesiastical value either (assuming that, as an ex-Christian, I still care about such things). As Hugh always said, we live in a relativistic age. He would regard me as only relatively married. (Hugh regards his own marriage in a similar way with far less excuse, but perhaps that is because his wife is American.)

We are consummating on the floor of the first class cabin, when a row of bullets rips through one side of the plane and out the other, missing Jalal's shoulder by about a foot.

'My God,' I murmur, 'We're going to die.' We are a modern play suddenly interrupted by a newsflash. I pull his body down on top of me, remembering great action broadcasts from the BBC archives, swivelling snatches of jungle and flames, foreign voices swearing just out of sight of the camera.

Faroun is here, waving the pistol. He shouts at Jalal in Lazari, and Jalal says something in reply. On the verge of death, I am seeing the whole history of the BBC flash before my eyes. The plane is perforated with ragged daylight. Passengers are screaming and moaning in the other cabin, perhaps being wounded or killed, but I stay clinging on to Jalal, holding him close for protection. Faroun, still waving the gun in one hand, tries to pull Jalal off with the other.

'Put that gun down,' I say, 'It will go off.' And then something happens.

Datastream 1; Telemann, Alb

Several days after my visit to Ellen. Nothing is happening. No Pillowtalk. Ruggins is full time on the Wocaluha Inquiry and doesn't have time to make speeches. He gets in the occasional word about Armageddon. Little Alb is bored. I have been monitoring the news digest carefully for want of anything else to monitor. Even so, the main news item is now over, since the hijacking of the British 747 was terminated by the blowing up of the plane. According to the news digest:

> One consequence of the government's carefully planned move has been a wave of anti-British feeling among Lazari Shamanists. Shortly after the destruction of the hijacked plane, Shamanist terrorists acting on the orders of the Scorpion attacked the British Embassy in Sainte-Fleur using rockets. The Ambassador was among those killed. British subjects have been advised to use the US Embassy from now on, and to leave the country as soon as possible.
>
> President Dol Miraz has denied, not only that his army has lost another battle in the mountains, but also that there are any mountains in the country at all. 'The highest mountains in Lazar are only 270 metres above sea level, so this shows the extent of unscrupulous foreign press exaggeration,' he said. 'I have my rifle loaded and ready at all times in case it is necessary to protect my

grandson.' Even President Miraz could not deny that his carefully planned assault on the hijacked plane had led to the deaths of all the passengers.

President Pike issued the following statement about the destruction of the hijacked plane in Sainte-Fleur airport: 'The mass murder of the passengers in the hijacked British 747 by Communist heathens is evidence of the brutal savagery to which man can stoop in the name of his ideals. Politics will not save you, and machine guns and bombs and hand grenades will not save you, there is no power on earth that will save you, if you have not the Lord Jesus Christ in your heart. But the time is coming shortly, my friends, when the Lord will be revenged on all them that do not have the Lord Jesus Christ in their hearts, because the levee is going to break, and when the levee breaks all those heathens and Communists and unbelievers, and that means you, too, are going to have no place to stay. I tell you, this massacre in Lazar is a sign, as the disaster in Wocaluha was a sign, that the levee can't hold out much longer.'

Observers were surprised at the uncharacteristic tone of the statement, which alluded to a well-known traditional blues song:

If it keeps on raining,
The levee's going to break,
When the levee breaks,
Have no place to stay

President Pike's theology adviser Jimmy Ruggins is an expert on the blues, and often uses this particular song in his sermons and speeches.

Meanwhile, in another part of the White House, Jimmy Ruggins has been listening to witnesses and yet more witnesses. Scientific evidence has been brought to show that potassium divinylchloramine is not used in the making of dill pickles as the defense claims. An expert witness maintains it has a smell very similar to that of a Macdonald's hamburger, making the pretense of a dill pickle factory the perfect cover for a factory whose sole function was that of creating nerve gas.

'You are telling us that this factory was used for the manufacture of nerve gas,' a Senator asked.

'Yes, that is the only reason for the presence of potassium divinylchloramine.'

'Yet Mr Rice alleges that the factory was used to make dill pickles.'

'Potassium divinylchloramine is not used in dill pickles.'

'Is it used in the manufacture of catchup?'

'No.'

'How about mayonnaise or thousand island dressing?'

'Absolutely not.'

'Let me get this straight,' Ruggins intervened, 'you are telling us that potassium divinylchloramine is not used in relishes or pickles of any kind?'

'The stuff is poison, for Christ's sake! Why should you want to put it on a hamburger?'

'Please do not take the name of the Lord your God in vain,' Ruggins said.

'I'm sorry.'

'You should understand, Mr Rogers, that a great and terrible day is coming in the not too distant future.'

'It seems to me,' Mr Rogers replied, 'that a great and terrible day has already come. Maybe you missed it.'

'What is your name?'

'Michael J. Fudokowski.'

'How old are you, Mr Fudokowski?'

'I was thirty-three last birthday.'

'Michael,' Ruggins said, 'let me ask you a question. Do you consider your life so far has been worthwhile?'

'What?'

'Has your life so far been worthwhile? Do you go to bed at night thinking I really got something out of today? I mean, if the Lord came to take you tomorrow, would you be ready to go, or would you want to say "Hold it a minute, Lord, I didn't get everything done"? Are you the kind of guy that would want to wash his socks first, you know, and mail that letter to your cousin that you wrote last week? And what about that envelope for a well-known charity that's been sitting over your fireplace for a month now? That's what I'm asking you, Michael. Are you packed and ready?'

'Yeah, sure. I think so.'

'You think so? Or do you know so?'

'I think so. I mean, I know so. Hey, do I get to talk about my eye now?'

'You're thirty-three years old now, Michael, I think that's what you said, isn't it?'

'Sure.'

'That's the age of our Lord when he suffered on the Cross for us, Michael, you've heard about that, haven't you?'

'Sure. Of course, I go to Church. I've been born again.'

'Yes, Michael, but have you really been born again? I mean really. Because you know when you're really born again, it's when you can face the end of your hopes and dreams, the whole of your life. It's when you're ready to go, Michael. A true Christian travels light.'

'I have trouble with my left eye. I don't see too good out of my eye. Not since the pickle factory exploded.'

'Are you Col. Lawrence F. Feenbaker of the US Army?'

'Yes.'

'Were you posted to the Snakattak dill pickle works as part of your military duties?'

'I refuse to answer that question on the grounds that it may tend to incriminate me.'

'Were you aware that potassium divinylchloramine was being produced at the factory?'

'I refuse to answer that question on the grounds that it may tend to incriminate me.'

'Do you know what potassium divinylchloramine is, and what it is used for?'

'I refuse to answer that question on the grounds that it may tend to incriminate me.'

'Now just a moment, Colonel,' Commission Chief Ruggins said, 'this isn't getting us anywhere. You may think we're just a normal Commission of Inquiry into just another technological disaster, and in a sense I'd have to agree with you, that's exactly what we are. But there is another sense, Colonel, in which things are not normal. Do you understand what I mean by that? Well, don't answer yet, just you think about it. When I say that things are not normal, what I mean is that the hour is getting late, and it may be later than you think. Now what I'd like to ask you, Colonel – and I don't want you to answer me just yet, please – is do you intend to take the Fifth Amendment at the Day of Judgment? Because let me assure you, Col. Feenbaker, there are no amendments to the constitution of the universe, and the reason for that is that the Lord got it right first time. Now it's in our interest to tell the truth here today, because the Lord is listening, and I may say He is listening even harder than He usually does, because He knows that the hour is not going to be long. So I want you to think about that before you answer this question. Did you know that the Snakattak factory was being used for chemical weapons, and not for pickled preserves?'

'I refuse to answer that question on the grounds that it may tend to incriminate me.'

Outside the Wocaluha Inquiry, there was a shock revelation today when President Pike admitted that the factory was being used to make nerve gas. 'A healthy supply of chemical weapons is essential for the defense of world freedom,' he said. 'It is important that we understand the true reason for this calamity, which, I still believe, was an Act of God. On the other hand, we are talking about a very precious and strategically important chemical here, and there is just a chance that the explosion may have been caused by deliberate terrorist type action by the enemies of our democracy. If this is so, we want to see justice done, which is why I appointed my dear friend Jimmy Ruggins to this post.'

To: Alb Telemann
From: Fred Zolph
Subject: Wocaluha

Yes, OK, Wocaluha was being used as a nerve gas factory. I knew this as soon as I read the mention of dill pickles. All our nerve gases smell of characteristically American things such as pot roast and hot fudge sundaes, so that it's easy to tell our guys what smell to avoid on the battle field. If you give them a whiff for identification purposes, they tend to keel over, so it's useful to have something you can just describe. Psychologically, I'm told it's a dubious idea, because in the stress of battle, a guy might easily be overcome by nostalgia and just follow his nose. But there you are, at least he would die happy.

The thing is, no one can work out how the President knew about it. I cannot get anyone, either in the WH or the Pentagon to admit to telling him. Of course, maybe he didn't know it at all, and is just pretending he did. If so, it just confirms what I've said all along, that the guy is a screwball – Presidents are not supposed to pretend they *did* know about things, for Christ's sake. All the same, I think we can assume he was aware of something of an incriminating nature, or he would not have re-opened the inquiry. Why Jimmy Ruggins, though? The guy doesn't know shit about chemistry. All gossip here suggests the P and Ruggins are now good buddies, and practically on fishing trip terms. If you know any more about this relationship, I should be glad to hear it.

EA continues to be highly reciprocal. Why no Pillowtalk recently? Burn this.

I obediently deleted this message from my electronic mailbox, wondering as I did so, whether a backup copy would be filed away under the lawn, and if so, whether a new, revitalized Ernest Hellbaum, relieved of his complexes, would have enough wherewithal to make capital out of it in the unlikely event of a WHOMgate. Alb is nervous again. Pike quotes blues numbers and defends chemical weapons. EA continues to be highly reciprocal, does she? Then, as FZ says, why no Pillowtalk?

Datastream 4; Paul, Saint

It was Jesus. I recognized him at once, not from his appearance, which was hard to make out, but from the egg-shaped aura of brilliant light that surrounded him. The light was hard and bluish at the edges, and soft and yellow in the middle; but it was the middle of the egg I found hardest to look at. In between the edge and the middle were shifting prismatic shades which never stayed long enough for me to make any of them out. They were not substantial like the bluish shell or the yellow yolk. I thought of them as splinters of colour cast off by the central glow, by-products. Jesus himself was – no – the entire egg was Jesus. The human form of Jesus was a tiny straggling figure in the very centre. Sometimes, the figure seemed like a spider without enough legs, sometimes a snake with too many, but at all times, it was a miniature man, a homunculus. Looking at it, in so far as I could see it at all in the yellow dazzle of the nucleus, I found myself thinking, is this what a man looks like? It was curious to think that I, too, was one of those strange, insectlike creatures. But, of course, this was a dream, and, for the time being, I was not a man at all, but an ear, an eye, a receptive brain, waiting for a sign from my master.

The voice rang like a bell, shaking the aura, but it was, otherwise, not an unearthly voice. It was deep and had a quaint, peasant tone to it.

'Paul,' the voice said, 'Paul.'

'Yes, Lord.'

'Say to the folk which are in Lazar, I have chosen them. They shall be first in the battle. They shall be first in the air. The woman shall be first and the others after. They shall be the best and the worst. And the best shall be saved. And the worst shall be destroyed. Utterly.'

'But, Lord,' I said, 'there are no saints in that country. They are heathen people.'.

'I have chosen them. The seed of the saints is planted. And the seed of the Enemy will be planted also.' Suddenly, I remembered the slave boy I had released into the bushes, the boy who had reappeared in time to rescue us and lead us to the hidden boat. We had left the boy in Melita – had he sailed back to the island to convert his friends? But surely the boy knew nothing of the faith? He had had no time to find out.

'Lord,' I said, 'the seed of the saints? Is it the boy?'

'When?' the voice continued, 'In Time. How? By woman opened and by woman closed. Why? Because.' The voice and the light were getting fainter, the voice asking and answering vague questions. 'What . . . that which . . . Where . . . in that place . . . Whom . . .'

'Lord.'

'Time,' the voice said, 'going now.'

It was late when I opened my eyes. As always after a dream like this, I had a slight headache. For a long time, I lay in bed, listening to cries from the street: fish, jewellery, olives, copper, leather, silver, pots. Pots, as always. The Romans are obsessed with earthenware. Surely they cannot need so many pots. The smell of bread reached me from the kitchen, awakening my stomach. I was hungry after my dream. Soon Gaius, the soldier appointed to guard me, would enter with breakfast. And after that, visits from Jews, visits from pagans, visits from Christians wanting to keep my spirits up, as if my spirits could be down in such a place, with so much preaching to do. But the voice had been right; time was going now, and there was never enough to do the Lord's work. I must start writing immediately. Then later, I would have to find one of the saints who was willing to go to Lazar, to take the letter and to look after the seed which was even now growing there.

I got out of bed and moved at once to the writing desk by the window. Sunlight fell across the parchment like the Holy Ghost, and the voices of Rome came through the window, crying pots. I took up my pen and began to write.

> *Paul, an apostle of Jesus Christ by the will of God, and the prisoner of the Lord to the saints which are in Lazar, if there be any. Also to the chosen of the Lord who continue to walk in ignorance of their predestination: grace be to you and peace, and may the light of understanding fall across you.*

Datastream 1; Telemann, Alb

Today I learned of the Epistle of St Paul to the Lazarenes, an apocryphal book which is the most sacred text of the Lazarene Church. I sit at my desk as an oblique stroke of sunlight crosses the table and falls on the terminal, which was the medium for this most terrible of revelations. I was reading an article in the WHOM news digest on the religious dimension of the Lazari war, and suddenly it all made sense. I learned of the Epistle to the Lazarenes, and I learned of *Acts* 27.5.

Acts 27 is the chapter of the Bible which tells how St Paul was shipwrecked on his way to Rome. *Acts* 28 begins with the words, 'Now when they were escaped, they knew that the island was called Melita.' Melita was the old name for Malta, and every self-respecting theologian concludes from this that Paul was shipwrecked there. The Maltese will even show you the place where it happened. The Lazarene Christians, on the other hand, possess a document which they claim to be a missing chapter, belonging between *Acts* 27 and 28. Students of Lazarenism (yes, there are such people) refer to this as *Acts* 27.5 and dismiss it as an obvious medieval forgery. It tells how St Paul was really shipwrecked on Lazar at a time when the Lazaris were primitive fish-worshippers. Paul was declared king against his will and escaped with the help of a slave boy he had previously released. That's how the Lazarenes make sense of the first sentence of *Acts* 28. Ingenious, huh? Paul then went on to Rome, as described in *Acts*. There, he had a vision, in which the Lord told him that the seed of the saints had been planted in Lazar. The slave boy had returned to the island and begun the process of converting the people to Christianity. The Lord told Paul that Lazar had a special place in his scheme, for the best (Lazarene Christians) and the worst (Shamanists?) of men were to live there. Lazar's saints (ie, Christians) would be first in the air (ie, taken up in the rapture), and first of these saints would be a woman. The phrase 'by woman opened and by woman closed' in the second sacred Lazarene text (the Epistle) is usually taken to mean that humanity, and human sin, began with Eve, and will end with this mysterious second woman. Needless to say, the students dismiss the Epistle also. The Lazarenes don't, is the point. Ellen Axaxas doesn't.

The reason all this theology is such bad news is explained in the memo I received yesterday from Fred Zolph.

To:	Alb Telemann
From:	Fred Zolph
Subject:	Ellen Axaxas

Hold your horses, cancel your dental appointments and pour yourself a stiff bourbon, Alb, the woman is *interesting*. My inquiries have revealed some disturbing discrepancies in our data. First of all, she does not work at Mimosa Park Elementary School. They have never had a teacher there called Ellen Axaxas, or one who answers to her description. She certainly does live at number 2054 South Roseberry Avenue, because I had her followed there, but the house does not belong to her. It belongs to a company called Sunny Smile Real Estate Holdings, which is a subsidiary of Alabama Blues Evangelism Inc, owned by J Ruggins. Axaxas is her real name. She is the only daughter of one Thadde Axaxas, a Lazari olive oil merchant who arrived in this country in 1971. Dad is now dead, and Ellen does not appear to have held any job before meeting Ruggins at a Crusade in Minnesota a couple of years back. Story goes that he told her, 'God wants you, Ellen', which is what he says to everyone, and she broke down because she claimed an angel had said the exact same thing to her when she was a little girl in Sainte-Fleur. It would appear that EA is using her position to foster the cause of JR and probably of Dol Miraz as well. Guess you could call it a missionary position. Will let you know any further news when I have it, Alb. Keep monitoring the Pillowtalk.

I truly believe I have to do this. Listen. The missiles are ticking in their silos. The nerve gas (potassium divinylchloramine) is loaded in the tails of the Cobra helicopters. The fleet is pacing up and down the Mediterranean, and the Atlantic and the Pacific. The seed of the saints is planted in the Presidential bed. He used to be a Baptist, remember. Revelation is nearly upon us, and I, Alb Telemann, have found out before it's too late. Maybe in another day or two, the sky outside that window will explode like an egg in a microwave and fill the land with fire. There is some kind of providence that put this information into my hands. I have the qualifications: I'm a man of action, I have in my pocket the Government issue WH (for White House) 38 automatic with silencer, and I know how to use it. It isn't murder. She wants to die, she told me, and besides, if I don't kill her, she'll die anyway. And me, Roxanne, Warren Pike, Ernest Hellbaum, everyone, fried, poisoned, irradiated to death, all because of some screwball legend about St Paul. If only they had stuck to worshipping the fish. Never mind, it's too late now. Don't argue with me, I've been arguing with myself for three hours, I smoked so many cigarets I lost all feeling in my throat, and there is only one answer. It isn't just for me, it's for everybody. It's the only real justification for my job, it's what my job is really for, only nobody dared tell me. I'm going to use my initiative now. This evening, when she comes back from her non-cocktail hour, I'm going to kill her.

I drive slowly around the suburban streets, watching the black kids breakdancing outside liquor stores in the twilight. A big, lazy owl is offended by my approaching car and flaps away slowly from its telephone wire. As a boy, I knew evenings like this, when I used to go on fishing trips to the Maine woods with my father, and the darkness would close unexpectedly around him, much as it is doing now.

Something has bitten me on the neck, not a mosquito, something bigger and hairier. I have the feeling it is still there, although I can't see it in the rear view mirror. Maybe it's inside my shirt. Even the goddam insects remind me of those fishing trips. I don't think it's a mosquito. It is something with a lot of legs, some kind of poisonous earwig. It's still running around in there, and the bite itches like hell.

I draw up the car in the leaf shadows and begin to unbutton my vest. I drape the vest over the back seat, wrench off my tie and unbutton my shirt. There is a girl walking on the other side of the street, but she doesn't seem to notice. Probably used to half naked men in parked cars, and in any case she is plump and dark, only about sixteen, not at all like . . . I feel around inside the shirt. Nothing. My skin is cold and sticky. I hadn't realized I was sweating so much. This sweat is really unprofessional. No earwig. Or maybe I touched it with my fingernail. I think something fell.

A tall black man in a red armless T-shirt and satin finish shorts swerves up on rollerskates.

'Too late to catch the sun, man.'

'I've got some kind of a bug here,' I tell him nervously.

'You're damn right you have. Looks like the measles to me.' He floats off, laughing a squealing extraterrestrial laugh. And he is right about the bug, it does seem to be spreading. The earwig got away without my noticing, but it had already bitten me in five or six places. The lumps show up red and sore in the light from a streetlamp which has just come on. I feel sick and dizzy, with the bites or with fear, it is hard to tell which. And Ellen will not be here for an hour.

'You have a very nice chest, Alb,' Rose says.

'Thanks,' I say automatically. I look up, exasperated. 'Rose, where did you come from? I can't see you tonight, honey, I'm busy.'

'I thought you couldn't wait, Alb, I thought you started undressing already because you couldn't wait to see me.'

'Listen, Rose, I unbuttoned the shirt because I was bitten. By an insect.'

'Really? Let me see. I used to be a nurse, you know.'

'Like hell,' I say.

Once again, Rose's pink fingers play warmly over my skin. The nightbird wakes up on cue.

'I got some calamine lotion in my room,' Rose says.

'Calamine lotion. Jesus,' I say under my breath. 'No, thanks all the same. I'm very busy tonight.'

'Yeah, sure, you look real busy, in a car with your shirt unbuttoned. Another car, Alb? Is this a convertible?'

'Yes, it isn't really my image, but it was all they had. I don't seem to be too lucky with cars. Look, Rose, I have to meet someone. I just unbuttoned the shirt because of the insect.'

'You ought to take the top down. It's a lovely evening. When are you meeting the someone you have to meet?'

'In about an hour.'

'You like to be early for dates, don't you. Is she pretty?'

'Very.'

'Prettier than me?'

'Much prettier. No, actually, I guess not.'

'You're nice, Alb, I always thought so. Why don't you come and spend the time with me?'

I look at the flower-entwined name on her badge, the comforting way it moves up and down when she breathes, and think what the hell, an hour is an hour. If you're planning on murder, a little fornication doesn't make much difference.

Once again we cavort on an unmade bed, a suburban breeze tickling our skin, the nightbird rattling and wheezing in the background. I have almost forgotten about Ellen when suddenly a foot creaks on a floorboard close by and I know, without having to look, that the bedroom door is open. Suddenly I am moving and not getting anywhere, as if this is a dream and the air has turned to treacle on me. Rose is giggling with embarrassment and waving her hand to make someone go away, go away.

SUBJECT:	What is it? What's the matter?
PARTNER:	You came sooner than I expected.
SUBJECT:	I didn't come at all.
PARTNER:	Not you. Him.
SUBJECT:	Him? Him? Who is it, your next customer?

I have the absurd idea for a moment that it might be President Pike, who certainly has other plans for the evening. The eyes of the INTRUDER *behind me are summing me up, dwelling disdainfully on my insect bites.*

INTRUDER: You through, or not?

I roll over. The INTRUDER *is revealed as the young man who passed me earlier, minus the rollerskates, but still wearing the red armless T-shirt and satin finish shorts.*

INTRUDER: *confidently,* *like one who* *knows he is* *the only* *person in* *the room* *with clothes* *on.*	Hi. Stay open, OK?
SUBJECT:	Open?
INTRUDER:	Open. And flexible. This is what we wish to see. You haven't given those measles to Rose, have you?
SUBJECT:	No.
INTRUDER:	Good. You keep those measles to yourself. We do not want no white measles here, those are non-requisite in this environment, capeesh?
PARTNER: *sulkily.*	You came early, man. Anyway, those are earwig bites?
INTRUDER:	What kind of thing might that be, earwig bites?
PARTNER: *calmly, but* *her limbs* *are rigid* *under the* *sheets.*	He was bit by some earwig. Some earwig bit him. Totality. Period. End transaction. You came early, man. You know you don't come early when I'm with a fish. I like to think of myself as in some sense a professional. I give value for money when I give.
INTRUDER:	Well you can carry on if you want to. Do you want to? So you had value for money, right? He isn't complaining. You aren't complaining, are you?
SUBJECT:	No.
INTRUDER:	Listen, you guys, let's be flexible. We're mature individuals, aren't we? Are we mature individuals? I know we are, and I know we do not need intercourse in order to communicate. Do we need intercourse? Do you need it? No, man, we are beyond crap like that, and you know why, because we have something better, and that is mutual respect. Hi, I think we met before. My name's Warburg.

'Hi, Warburg,' I say, shaking hands (still in bed, still partially wound round Rose's indignant limbs), 'Alb Telemann.' Alb Telemann, what is this, some kind of conditioned reflex? Didn't my mother teach me to tell lies when necessary? I swear to God, I must be crazy. Here I am in bed with a black prostitute when I should be preparing my soul to murder a white elementary-school teacher. Here I am shaking hands with a black pimp when I should be grabbing my clothes and running for the car. Here I am introducing myself by my real name when the world is full of imaginary ones.

'Listen, Alb,' Warburg says, 'are you in a hurry or anything? Because it would be nice if we could just sit here and absorb toxins for a while. I just want to be friendly, you understand. I believe in flexibility.'

'I'd like to, Warburg, but I really have to go. I'm very busy tonight.'

'Sure,' Rose says jealously. 'He has a date in an hour, that's how busy he is.'

I wish I hadn't told her that. I just wish.

Warburg rolls about on the carpet, kicking his training shoes in the air and squealing with extraterrestrial laughter. 'I just love that Jimmy Ruggins, Alb, he kills me. I listen to him on the radio whenever feasible. He's about as feasible as they come.' He begins to sing:

> There's a brown dog barking,
> And his voice will soon be heard
> Yes, there's a brown dog barking, baby,
> And his voice will soon be heard . . .

'I used to be a detective,' I say, waving the joint antisocially in the air. 'I was a good detective, too. I used to enjoy it.'

'I think that's very important,' Rose says. 'I get job satisfaction, too, in my own small way.'

> You know they call him the hound of heaven,
> Oh yes they do, baby,
> And he's barking out the word.

'I used to follow people,' I continue. 'They would walk down the road and I would walk down the road after them. Or else they would drive down the road and I would drive down the road after them. Or if they just stayed where they were, I would stay where I was, about fifty yards behind them, and then they would move off again and I would move off again too. If they caught a bus, I would catch the same bus, and when they got off I would get off, too. You learn a lot about people that way.'

'Alb,' Rose says, 'are you stoned?'

'No, what do you mean, stoned? I am a government employee, I am not stoned.'

'You know,' Warburg says, 'that Jimmy Ruggins, he knows a thing or two about blues. He says the trouble with blues is why do they always have to be so sad all the time? You know, your house falls down, your baby leaves with your best friend, the levee breaks and you have no place to stay and all that crap. Jimmy Ruggins says, sure, the world is full of natural disasters and they're getting more disastrous and less natural all the time, but you know what? If you really are a believer, Alb, God will save you from disaster.'

'Sometimes they caught a cab,' I say reflectively, 'and then I would go after them in a car. It was always a problem if they got into an elevator, because then I wouldn't know whether to follow them or not. It depended on the context, I guess. If they knew me, I wouldn't get into the elevator with them, I would just wait for them to come down again. People who go up in elevators usually do come down. If they don't, it could mean someone has shot them on the 25th floor, which shows I was right to be following them in the first place.'

'You see, Alb,' Warburg says, 'this is no longer the age that the original blues came out of. This is not the age of slaving in the Mississippi cottonfields or starving in the ghettoes of Chicago. This is the age of the affluent black pimp in Hillingdon Village, Alb.'

'This is the age of Love,' Rose says, weeping.

'I want you to know,' I tell them, waving the joint, 'I want you to know that I believe in this evening as a kind of existential fact of existence, the quintessential whatever it is that makes me Alb and Rose Rose and Warburg Warburg. Rose, sitting on the bed in that faded housecoat with artificial silk round the real silk of

106

her neck, is Rose is Rose. Warburg, snatching that joint out of my hand, is Warburg snatching that joint out of my hand. That rattling nightbird I can hear outside is both a nightbird and rattling. The air coils and uncoils itself. What, after all,' I say, 'is time?'

'You know what I am?' Warburg asks.

'You're Warburg. You are my friend Warburg.'

'I said what I am, not who. I'm a black pimp. That is my role in the order of things, and this young lady of whom you have so recently and so virtually partaken, she is my employee, and also the woman I love.'

'That's beautiful, Warburg,' Rose says, crying.

'You know what I am?'

'What are you, Alb?'

'I am a random collection of images, for example, the mist rising over a lake where I used to go on fishing trips with my father. I am an owl. I am a nightbird in a dogwood. I am true spirit of America.' I say sententiously, drawing the smoke into my lungs, 'I am Walt Whitman, I am Abraham Lincoln, Horatio Alger, Warren Pike.'

'Yeah,' Warburg adds. 'Also Booker T. Washington and Martin Luther King and Jimi Hendrix and the Four Tops.'

'I am Diana Ross,' Rose says.

'I could partake of that,' Warburg says out of smoke-filled lungs.

'You know what I am?' I ask. 'I am the custodian of American sexuality. I am the man who determines who the President screws.' Long pause. It seems longer than it really is. Either that or it is longer than it really seems. I'm not sure whether I . . . What the hell.

End of pause. 'You are a man worth knowing, Alb,' Warburg says, 'you are a personage. Do you think you could get Rose in there?'

'Certainly, Warburg, I don't see why not. The President has no prejudice about race, creed or color.'

'He's a good man,' Rose says.

> I was driving on the freeway,
> When I disappeared from view.

He sits back on the floor and tries to blow smoke rings using smoke that is no longer in his mouth. The effort exhausts him.

'The Day of Judgment is coming,' Rose claims. 'I just hope my faith is strong enough. I just hope so. I don't believe I'm a really bad person, but I just hope my faith is strong enough.'

'My faith is really strong,' Warburg says, laughing deep inside himself. 'I mean *really*. I have no problems in the faith department, man. When that rapture comes, I'm going to be right in there. I mean, when it comes, I'm going to be right out of everywhere. I am planning to disappear, Alb, even in the twinkling of an eye. How about you, Alb, will you be saved? Better think about it, you may not have much time.'

'I think about it a lot. It scares me.'

'Your faith is not strong,' Warburg says. 'America needs faith, Alb, especially at the helm and in the wheels of government. And the corridors of power, those too.'

'I'm not a bad man, either.' I move away from Rose in the bed, an action which she seems completely indifferent to. 'I'm not a bad man at all. I'm a government servant and a good detective, and I just don't feel I'm ready yet for some Goddamn Almighty cock-up.'

'That's a hell of a way to speak about God, Alb,' Rose says, 'you ought to be ashamed of yourself. Don't you want to go to heaven?'

'I am in heaven at this very moment, people.' Warburg is trying to suck back the smoke he has exhaled. 'It may be,' he continues, 'that I am already raptured. Can you still see me? Am I present? Am I in a state of hereness?'

'You don't really believe that, do you, Warburg? About the Day of Judgment?'

'Sure, Alb, everyone believes in the Day of Judgment. That is not mere theological speculation, that is scientific fact. The great war will begin between the ungodly lands of the East and the Holy Lands of the West, and the true believers will disappear from the face of the earth. The chaos will be really something to see, Alb, only I have no intention of being here to see it. Just imagine, Alb, you're sitting in the back of some guy's car and he's driving along the freeway at ninety miles an hour, when suddenly he vanishes and your car goes ploughing across the road and under a truck. He's a true believer, Alb, and you're not. That's what rapture will mean in your life.'

'It seems, it seems, it seems kind of antisocial.'

'Sure, Alb, you mean believers should not drive at ninety on account of people will get killed at the Day of Judgment. But people will be getting killed anyway, and if they don't believe, that's their problem.'

'It's illegal,' Rose says, sadly.

'What is, honey?'

'Ninety, it's illegal. Speed kills you know, Warburg. You ought not to do it.'

'I do not believe what I am hearing, man. What is this illegal shit? You're illegal, I'm illegal, just about everything is illegal. What counts is that your faith is strong. If your faith is strong enough, man, there is no speed limit.'

I have an appointment. I mustn't forget the appointment.

'Jimmy Ruggins has given me a whole new outlook on life,' Warburg explains, sitting on the carpet, trying to catch smoke rings with his teeth, 'Jimmy Ruggins understands the genuine essence of our epoch more than any other authority. I tell you, Alb, if I owned an aircraft company, there is no way I would ever employ believers as pilots. When the big day comes, man, those planes are going to be dropping out of the sky.'

'Jimmy Ruggins is an asshole,' I say.

'Don't say that, Alb,' Rose says, crying more than ever, 'Jimmy Ruggins loves Jesus, and Jesus loves Jimmy Ruggins, and God loves Jesus, and Warburg loves Jesus, and Jesus loves me, and I love Warburg, and Warburg loves God. Life is so beautiful, when you think about it.'

I have to go see Jimmy Ruggins. I have to see St Paul. Any minute now, I shall kill someone. You think I don't mean it but I do. I am a murderer. The arrangements have all been made.

'I don't believe you, Alb,' Rose says, 'you wouldn't do anything like that. You're a good man. I can always tell with a customer.'

Did I say anything?

'I told you, man,' Warburg says, 'I told you you were not saved. When the rapture comes, man, you are going to be right here with your bootlaces rooted, because there are no murderers in the Kingdom of Heaven. That is really unhinged, man, it doesn't even have a handle. What got into you, Alb, to want to do a thing like that anyway? Who are you going to kill?'

I seem to be weeping.

'Now don't cry, Alb,' Rose says kindly. 'It isn't as bad as that. You don't really want to do it, do you?'

I do want to, I really do. I don't really want to want to, but I have to want to. She's so beautiful, too.

'Who, man?' Warburg says jealously. 'Whom are you planning to kill? We are not taking this on unsupported testimony you understand. Whom will you kill, and why, and how? I am not going to sit here and listen to you boasting about some felony you claim to be perpetrating under false pretences.'

I am out of the bed, rummaging through the pile of clothes. I had some undershorts.

'What murder? I had some undershorts, I know I did. Can I go home to my wife without undershorts?'

'Jesus, what a fish!' Warburg shouts, 'Undershorts! What kind of fish are you anyway, Alb? You are no barracuda, man; a barracuda doesn't even have undershorts, man, it just eats people. And you are telling me you're a murderer.'

I am snivelling. The room is full of blue smoke and laughter. There are clothes all over this bed. I reach for the undershorts, which fall off the bed, apparently on purpose. I climb carefully off the bed after them.

'Did he say he killed somebody just now,' Warburg asks Rose, 'or was that someone else?'

'No, I think it was Alb. Did you kill someone, Alb?'

'Don't keep asking me that,' I say, losing my balance and falling heavily to the floor. 'Don't keep asking, I don't want to talk about it.'

'Hey man, are these your undershorts?' Warburg picks them up and begins examining them critically. 'They say you should always wear clean ones in case you get hit by a truck. When the Day of Judgment comes, Alb, how clean will yours be?'

'Give them back, Warburg,' Rose says, 'leave him alone.'

'Don't talk to me. Just give me those undershorts.'

Rose begins crying again. 'That's so like a man. Men are always saying don't talk to me, just give me my undershorts. That's all you ever say, any of you. You too, Warburg.'

I am sitting naked on the floor among my own clothes, trying to remember what I was looking for.

Warburg holds the undershorts up to the light and turns them over as if looking for evidence of the presumed crime.

'All I want is my undershorts.'

'Are these them?' Warburg throws them over. 'I wondered what they were.'

I am a good man. I work in the White House. My mission, should I choose to accept it, is to prevent Jimmy Ruggins.

'To prevent Jimmy Ruggins what, Alb?'

'What do you mean, Jimmy Ruggins what?'

'He means, Alb,' Rose says, 'you can't just prevent people period. You have to prevent them from something.'

'I'm going to prevent him because of something,' I say, picking up my jacket. 'I intend to prevent him because of Ellen Axaxas.' I am not wearing trousers or a shirt. I turn the jacket upside down, and the WH38 falls out of the pocket.

Centuries pass, and I pass with them. I am walking through a street at night, I don't know how long I have been doing it. It feels like the ocean. When I take my eyes from them, I think the cars parked along the curb are wrecks, slowly settling into the road. Apart from that, I feel great. Apart from that and the birds watching me from the trees, fidgeting scratchily. I know walls have ears, but nobody tells you trees have eyes. The trees are watching me with their thousand eyes; I don't know what they see. Alb Telemann walking in slow motion down the streets of Hillingdon Village, probably. A thousand Alb Telemanns.

I can bear anything except losing another car. This must be the place. I remember that house over there, with the wishing well in the backyard. This was where I was bitten by the insect, whatever it was. (The bites have swelled up like balloons. What with one thing and another, I never did get any of Rose's calamine lotion.) Question: where is the car? Thank God. I was looking for the wrong one, of course, because I had forgotten it is now two sizes smaller than it used to be. A tall black man is leaning on it.

'Warburg! you bastard! Are you stealing my car?'

'What car, Alb?'

'You know damn well what car. This car that you're leaning on. You know it's mine, Warburg. You went past on rollerskates when I was sitting in it about six o'clock.'

'Alb, I am definitely not about to steal your car.'

'Then what are you doing hanging around in the shadows? You don't look like a man about his legitimate business, Warburg. It's the middle of the night for Christ's sake. Your suntan is already as good as it's going to be.'

'My business is not legitimate, Alb, you know that. But be reasonable. If I was going to steal your car, I would have done it earlier when you were busy with the inflight refuelling. I would not wait for you to show up so I could steal it before your very eyes and have the satisfaction of seeing your little face fall, man.'

'I'm sorry, Warburg, it's just that I've lost a lot of cars recently, so I'm kind of sensitive.' Too much has happened already. This evening, I have done the following:

1. planned a murder
2. been fished by a prostitute
3. smoked narcotics

I am no longer thinking straight, and the insect bites, marijuana fumes etc, have exhausted me. I sit down suddenly on the sidewalk, and rest my head comfortably in my hands. I am weeping (again). Warburg is sitting beside me. His arm is unexpectedly round my shoulders.

'You didn't do it, did you, man?' Warburg is asking gently.

This is confusing. I don't know how to answer. 'I lost two cars already, Warburg. I need to go home. It's late.'

'Yes, Alb, yes. You didn't do it, did you?'

'I'm worried, Warburg, and I wish you'd stop humoring me, Warburg, and let me go home and worry some more . . . I just want to go home, you see.' Instead, I am shaken by a hurricane of sobs from somewhere outside myself. Warburg shelters patiently beside me until Hurricane Alb has passed on, and then steps cautiously into the open again.

'I hear you, Alb, I hear you. First, though, we have to answer a very important question between us. You know what that question is, Alb?'

'What question?'

'What did you do with the girl? You know, the girl with the weird name, Miss Axes or something. Is she still alive?'

Goddamn him. I am indignant, between sobs. 'You really think

112

I'd do that? Kill that sweet, beautiful saintly woman? Let me tell you something about Ellen Axaxas, Warburg. She heard an angel calling her in the backyard when she was six years old. It told her God wanted her.'

'OK, maybe she did. The question I'm asking is, did God get her yet?'

'I'm telling you, God has had her ever since then. She's a good woman. I wouldn't dream of killing her.'

'You did more than dream about it, Alb. You planned it. You didn't come to Hillingdon Village for the ultraviolet any more than I did. You told me, and you told Rose, that you intended to murder this Axes woman for the good of the world or something like that, and then when you realized you'd gone too far, you suddenly told us you'd changed your mind and vanished into the night. Well what were we supposed to think, man?'

'Is that what you're doing here? You thought I was going to do it? You wanted to stop me?'

'I've been worrying about what you said ever since you left us, Alb. That was more than an hour ago. Now, suppose you tell me what you did to her.'

'I didn't do anything to her. I told you, I changed my mind. All I did is talk to her.'

'You talked to her? That's all?'

'Yes, that's all. I talked to her.'

'And she's still alive? You mean you talked to her like just talking? It wasn't any special CIA type talking? She's still alive?'

'I have nothing to do with the CIA, Warburg. And certainly, she's still alive.'

'So what was so interesting, Alb, that made you want to talk to her for an hour at this time of night?'

So I tell him. I tell Warburg:

1. that I saw Ellen
2. that I told her about my plan to kill her
3. that I handed over the WH38

And Ellen was so pleased, she really was. She had always thought I was going to kill her – maybe that was what put the idea

113

into my head in the first place, a sort of self-fulfilling prophecy.
Then:

4. she forgave me

Because there is more joy in heaven over one White House aide
that repents. (More joy than what?)

'Well, if you're so sure, Alb, maybe we better check it out,'
Warburg says. 'Maybe we go and talk to Miss Axes and make
sure she didn't mind you talking to her.'

If I wasn't so confused, I never would have agreed to do this.
Warburg says that he and Rose talked it over and got scared, and
then Warburg went out to look for me. When he couldn't find
me, he stood by my car until I showed up again. All this argues
that Warburg has a considerable social conscience. I suppose I
should appreciate that as it is a rare quality in a pimp. On the
other hand, it does mean that I am here for the second time this
evening, standing outside this door which I had earlier resolved
never to stand outside again. Ellen and I have already talked
once this evening. What do I say to her this time? Oh, hi Ellen,
sorry to wake you up, but the thing is . . . Meet my friend
Warburg. He's a pimp, and he just wanted to know if you were
still alive or not. You *are* alive, aren't you? Actually, it is none of
Warburg's business whether she is alive or not, anyway. This is a
free country.

I press the doorbell for the second time, and hear it buzz somewhere deep in the house. Warburg is shuffling beside me, perhaps
having the grace to feel ashamed of himself. The house inside is
bare, saintly and silent, a passing through place which we are rudely
attempting to pass into. In her bedroom (does she have a mattress
on the floor, like Rose?) Ellen Axaxas must be waking up, shaking
herself, rubbing her eyes, questioning the sound, discovering that
it's really there, that it's not a dream, that it is in fact a doorbell
etc. She must be wondering if it could be burglars, remembering
that burglars don't ring doorbells, trying to decide whether or not
to answer it, weighing up the possibilities of passing drunks, news
of a sick relative, psychopathic axe murderers, messages from the
President. Maybe she is thinking if anyone wants to get in touch

with her there is always the telephone. She may be unworldly, but is she unworldly enough to answer a doorbell at one o'clock in the morning?

'She's not going to answer, Warburg.'

'How do you know that, man? You know that because you made sure she wouldn't answer before you came away, right?'

'She's not going to answer because it's the middle of the night, that's all. Would you answer a doorbell at this hour?'

'Sure I would, Alb. It might be a customer. We work late, in my profession. Besides, all time is relative, you know. It might be some quite different time to her, not so? Didn't you say she was the sort of girl who screws presidents?'

'I don't see what that's got to do with it.'

'Screwing takes place at night, right? Copulation is a naturally nocturnal activity. If that weren't so, Rose would be a nine-to-five guy like any other guy; like you, for instance. Why don't we break in?'

'You're crazy.'

'You told me she won't answer the doorbell because she's afraid. That may be true. It's also true that she undoubtedly won't answer it in the event that she has already passed over and left her brains behind. This being the case, I don't see how else we can make sure, do you?'

'Sure, I can break in if I have to. I used to break into places when I was a detective. But I'd just like to point out, Warburg, that there's a law against breaking into people's houses. It constitutes a felony. I am not going to commit a felony just to satisfy your morbid curiosity, is that understood? This has gone far enough, Warburg. We rang the doorbell and no one answered. Now I'm going home.'

Warburg has produced an automatic from his pocket and is pointing it at my head, as if to blow it off. I am shocked rather than frightened; it seems to me that pimps should stick to pimping and not wave hand-guns around. Besides I, Alb, ought to be the one with the gun in this situation. But I gave it to Ellen Axaxas.

'I'm sorry this has become necessary, Alb,' Warburg says. 'However, between us we have got to get that door open. If you don't open it, I'm just going to have to use this hole-punch, and you are going to be the one with the hole.'

What is it with this man? If he really thinks I have committed a murder, why doesn't he just phone the police? I don't like this sudden access of muscular morality. Warburg is hardly a representative of the American Way himself, is he?

'Warburg,' I tell him between clenched teeth. 'You are annoying me. You are attempting to impose your will on me by force. You're violating my integrity as a human being.' I make this sound as tough as I can. I think I do a pretty good job.

'Alb, fuck your human integrity. Just open the goddamn door.'

So, under pressure from Warburg, I finally agree to open the door. Having no wish to be mistaken for a burglar, especially as Ellen has my gun, I call out loudly as I unpocket my skeleton key, 'Ellen, it's me, Alb Telemann. I'm just coming in for a while to make sure you're all right.' This sounds ridiculously inadequate, so as I throw open the door, I call out again, 'We're not going to hurt you! Whatever you do, don't use the gun!'

'You're crazy, Alb,' Warburg says in a demented whisper. 'You know what kind of a neighborhood this is? This is a quiet suburban respectable neighborhood, and you come along and sing about guns at one in the morning. What are the neighbors going to think, Alb? They are going to think police, that is what they're going to think.'

'So? If you haven't done anything wrong, you have nothing to fear from the police.' I am whispering, too, now.

'Alb, I have always had something to fear from the police, but this is not the time or the place. For God's sake, let's get inside and close that door. First you won't open it, then you won't close it.'

I am the victim of an intermittent paralysis, which freezes all my muscles after every action. Now, for example, after closing the door, I am completely incapable of putting out a hand and switching on the light. Instead, I stand on the doormat in the darkness and silence, not thinking.

'Alb,' the voice beside me says, 'do you know what the first law of opthalmology is?'

'What is it, Warburg?'

'I can't see when the light isn't on, I think we should return to basics, shouldn't we, man? Put the light on, Alb, then we can see. Remember Newton.'

'Yes, yes, of course.' Where is it? I paw the smooth wall help-lessly.

'Come on, man, you must know where the light switch is for Christ's sake. What a fish, man, a real fish. And I actually thought you might have murdered someone. Here it is, here.'

It was not so bright as this before, surely? The naked bulb prints little purple horseshoes on my retinas.

This was the room where we talked, her passing through room, the place where she lives while still in the world. It still retains that atmosphere of mystical emptiness that it had on those previous occasions, only now it has no Ellen in it to give it point and purpose. Rooms look lonely without people in them. But then Warburg and I are in it. I guess it has to be the right people.

'Isn't anything here, man,' Warburg remarks, 'and I thought *I* was underprivileged. Or did you steal the furniture as well?'

'Now come on, Warburg, you didn't notice a credenza under my arm did you? I was not carrying a grand piano when you stopped me.'

'She wouldn't have things like credenzas and grand pianos. All the same, I would expect a few chairs at least. This room gives me the creeps.'

We walk into the hall. No lampshade here either, no carpet on the unpolished floor, an uncared for room, an inbetween room. We try the kitchen, and it is not what I would have imagined. It contains: 1 cooker (covered with grease and bits of food), 1 refrigerator (choked with ice), pots and pans (insides heavily scratched and stained white from boiling eggs), several cupboards, 1 pedal operated trash can (broken). The refrigerator contains: 3 eggs (1 broken), 1 quart Sonoma Valley mango ripple ice cream, 1 packet frozen chicken cutlets (best before February 7), 1 tin tomatoes (open, half-used, rusty), 1 hardy potato (successfully putting forth a long green shoot in the arctic conditions of a cracked vegetable tray). The cupboards contain: crumbs, 1 tin baked beans with pork fat, 1 bottle tomato catchup, 1 empty packet long grain rice, rice from aforementioned packet. The trash can contains: – no, that's OK. There isn't much point in going through everything in the kitchen. For some reason, it makes me think of a bus station. Another passing through place, I guess.

'Let's go upstairs,' Warburg says.

One of the bedrooms is being used as a storeroom, and is full of trunks and suitcases. The other is clearly Ellen's own room; the bed unmade, and the pillows all over the floor, as if she had a rough night. The carpet is scattered with half-eaten TV dinners, used coffee cups, tracts and pamphlets by Oral Roberts and Billy Graham, cigaret ends, contraceptive packets. This is where Ellen does her real passing through. This is the terminus. Where exactly has she passed through *to*?

The bathroom, obviously. We try the door, but it is locked.

After I force the bathroom door, I reel out of it again, closing the door, and sit at the top of the stairs. Warburg sits beside me. Both of us are panting with our heads in our hands.

'Oh man, what have you done?'

'Yes, what? Done. What have *I* done?'

'What have you done?'

'Nothing, Warburg, I haven't done anything. She's dead, isn't she? I think she must be dead.'

'Try to understand, Alb. You killed a girl. You could be in trouble, Alb. Do you understand?'

'I don't understand, Warburg. I just don't. You said I killed her, but I can't have done. I don't remember it. I don't remember anything.'

Warburg raises his head and looks around, as if he has the feeling we are being watched. I have that feeling, also.

'Now let's try to stay calm,' he says. 'First of all, I want you to know how very sorry I am. I mean that. If there's anything I can do.'

'Is she dead?' I ask again.

'She may not be dead. We have to check that out, but I wouldn't be too hopeful. It looked bad.'

'Check out? You mean go in there? No, I don't think so, really. I mean, she's dead.' I am not going to switch that bathroom light on again. I would rather let her be dead. As far as I am concerned, she *is* dead.

Warburg stands up. 'Alb, you have had a terrible shock. I know that, I appreciate it, believe me. But you must remember that you caused it. If you kill someone, you have got to expect them to be dead, that is all there is to it. Learn to take responsibility for your actions, Alb. Deal with it, rise above it. Grow through it.'

'Wait, wait,' I tell him. He speaks too fast. Every time he says *dead*, my mind slows a notch, and I end up not hearing what he's said. I am still struggling with the idea that he wants me to switch on the light again, and now he's saying something about responsibility.

'Wait, you don't know I did this, Warburg. I didn't do it. I wanted to do it, but I never actually did it.'

'You intended to kill her tonight, Alb, you told me that before a witness. And then you admit that when you left us, you went to see her. You've shown me tonight how easily you can force a door, and I know you had a gun. It adds up, Alb. Face it, there is no use crying over spilt fluids. Now let's open the door.'

Ellen. She is lying comfortably on the floor, face downwards, in the position recommended for asthmatics and other bad sleepers. She is naked, and her body from behind seems plumper than I would have figured. Her buttocks have a matronly fullness, and there are dimples over her kidneys. The blood is congealing on her hair, so that one side of it is dark, the other blonde. There is a pool of blood around her head and upper body, covering her mouth and most of her nose, so that she looks in danger of drowning. The blood is not so red as my previous impression of it. If anything, she reminds me of a high-school biology experiment. The bullet has passed through her brain, like so, destroying nerve centers here and here, smashing the artery here and causing the expulsion of blood from the opening here. The gun is held lightly in her right hand, here. Ellen Axaxas, elementary-school teacher, Presidential mistress, visionary.

'Is that your gun, Alb? You can't tell unless you look at it, man. Is it your gun?'

I look at it quickly. It is a WH38. I nod.

'She's holding the gun in her right hand,' I say. 'That means she killed herself. I told you it wasn't me.'

Warburg looks thoughtfully at the gun, and then shakes his head with an expression of wistfulness and regret. 'Nice try, Alb.'

'Try? What do you mean, try? This is proof.'

'Alb, you said yourself that this woman was a Bible-believing Christian. Such persons do not knock themselves off, Alb, they call it a sin. You're a smart enough guy to think of pressing the

119

gun into the hand after the fatal. You read detective stories, don't you? It happens all the time.'

'All right, it's possible, I admit it. But why shouldn't she have done it? What makes you so sure it wasn't suicide? Warburg, in this country, a man is considered innocent until proved guilty, that is the law.'

'But what about Ellen, Alb? What about this poor innocent female? You want me to assume she's guilty just so I can assume you aren't? She didn't even have a motive. Would you shoot yourself in the head the very same night you had been to bed with a President?'

'Supposing I did plan it, *this* couldn't be what I planned, surely? This isn't an example of a nice orderly efficient White House deletion job. If I had killed her, I would surely have done it in a professional manner. I did have a plan, I did intend to commit a murder, but this is not the murder I intended to commit.'

It is Warburg who insists we have to hide the body, Warburg who knows the perfect place, Warburg who volunteers to use his own car for the task so that my newly acquired convertible will not be compromised by bloodstains. 'I'll take care of this potato like you won't even know you dug it up,' Warburg says. 'What are friends for?' As he hurtles round the streets of Hillingdon Village in the dark, skidding and squealing, occasionally bumping against the curb, some sense of proportion is beginning to return to me. I can remember what it feels like to be afraid for one's life.

'Warburg, you bastard, one person's been killed already tonight. What are you trying to do, start a business?'

'Sorry, man.' Warburg grins in a way that suggests the old Warburg is returning. 'This is my new car. I haven't gotten used to the power-steering yet, that's all.'

'Well, do you have to drive so fast? You're only making us look suspicious. It isn't a matter of life or death, is it? I mean, not any more.'

'I thought you were in a hurry to get back to the ancestral, man. I just do what I can. If it wasn't for me, you'd be in a hell of a mess. Call yourself a professional! First you announce your intentions in advance to two witnesses, then you shoot her with your own gun. I think it's about time we had a little sang-froid and savoir-faire in this murder. You just leave it to Warburg, Alb.' As he says this, he misses an unexpected turn in the road and drives with two wheels on the sidewalk for several yards, thereby distracting me temporarily from the uncomfortable thought of Ellen rolling about in the trunk.

'For God's sake, Warburg! Where are you taking us, anyway?'

'I know a real good lake near here, just a few miles out into Virginia.'

'You sound as if you've done this before.' Is it another felony to take a dead body across a state line? Do I care?

'I'm going to a lot of trouble for you, Alb, just remember that. I didn't have to do any of this. OK, so you maybe didn't have a real value for money encounter with Rose earlier in the evening, on account of me screwing up my timing. I made that up to you, didn't I? You smoked my substances, we had a nice talk, it was sociable.' He takes a corner too fast and goes into a spin, from which he extricates us without pausing in his conversation. 'It was sociable, Alb, I like to consider we're friends, notwithstanding the gulfs between us. So that's why I'm helping you, man, because what are friends for? We'll just consider you owe me a favor from now on, OK?'

'OK.' The road is dark now. We have left the suburbs and are driving through some of that suspicious-looking countryside that hovers on the edge of big cities waiting to get its own back. Tall trees hang over the road, talking to each other. Between their trunks I can see dark tangled shadows which look ideal for hiding bodies. Perhaps the trees and shadows stretch back for miles – alternatively, perhaps they stop a hundred yards from the road, at the limit of visibility. Perhaps there is nothing beyond what I can see, no trees or scrub or animals. Certainly, there are no people out there, because if there were, I would sense it. We are driving through an uninhabited part of the United States, close to Washington DC.

The invisible lake makes its presence felt suddenly as we go round a corner. There are no stars in the sky and no lights to reflect in it, but I didn't go through all those adolescent fishing trips with my father without knowing what the presence of a lake feels like. The car window is open, and I can smell the coolness and hear the peculiar light breeze which water generates even when there is none blowing elsewhere. And suddenly, there is a blank in the darkness ahead of us, huge and oval and undulating gently. Warburg half buries the car in a spiky bush and brakes violently. We get out.

'You think you can go through with it, man?'

'Is there a choice?'

'No.'

'I don't like this place much.'

'This is a secret lake, Alb. No one but me knows it's here.'

'How can a lake be secret, Warburg? This isn't the Amazon jungle, this is Virginia.'

'I never seen anyone here but me, Alb. There's a lot of lakes in this country, anyway. It isn't surprising one gets overlooked every now and then. You throw that poor girl in here and the turtles will eat her before anyone knows she's missing.'

That poor girl. We pull her out of the trunk as if she were a heavy suitcase. Warburg has covered the body with a blanket, and as we are swinging her, it slides suddenly to the ground. When we pitch her in, there is hardly a splash, and I am reminded for a moment about King Arthur and that hand that came up out of the water and caught the sword. But only the turtles will catch Ellen Axaxas.

'Come on, man,' Warburg says finally, 'I'll drive you home.'

Datastream 5; Fane, Robert

I don't know exactly why I came here. Lazar is east of and more primitive than Malta, and I am aiming eventually for the primitive east. I haven't got any money at this stage to go further, and my friends at the Valletta Youth Hostel told me that it is easy to find work in Sainte-Fleur, and that all this talk about a civil war is typical Lazari exaggeration, and simply means there are a few bandits in the mountains. I am living in the Sacred Heart Youth Hostel, Sainte-Fleur. My long term objective is to find my identity. My short term objective is a job. On my first evening here, I had a conversation with a hook-nosed, melancholy barman which was not encouraging.

'Your excellent wife is well?'

'I haven't got an excellent wife.'

'I am desolation. And your children?'

'No.'

'Your father is well?'

'Yes, very. Cambridge University, very intelligent. Want job.'

'You are not been at the Department of Strangers?'

'No. Want job.'

'This is a photograph of our glorious President, Miraz. There is war in Sainte-Fleur presently.'

'Yes. Very good barman. Experience. Very intelligent. Job.'

'You are not been at Department of Strangers?'
'No.'
'Also your brothers and sisters, well?'

The Department of Strangers. A small boy with one eye is sitting at the desk.

'English,' I tell him, 'want papers.' The boy nods, thoughtfully. 'Do you speak English?' I ask. The boy nods again, and points to two paraffin stoves sitting on the desk beside the in-tray. On one of them is a small copper urn from which sweet tea vapours are rising. On the other is an iron frying-pan containing peanuts in hot oil. The boy produces two small tin cups from a desk drawer, empties half the peanuts into each, then pours tea on top of them and hands one to me. The tea is highly sugared and has some kind of herb in it, basil or perhaps oregano. Small salty flakes of peanut-skin float to the surface as I drink.

'Cambridge University,' I remark, 'very intelligent.' I hand my passport to the boy, who has drunk his tea and is now crunching the peanuts. The boy looks at the passport with great interest, studying the photograph for a long time, and then reading the Lazari visa, incomprehensible to me, which is four pages long and handwritten. Then he puts the passport in the desk drawer and locks it.

'Enchanted,' he says suddenly. He holds out his hand to me. My mouth is full of peanuts, and I am stunned at hearing him speak so suddenly. I shake the hand.

'Can I speak to your father?' I ask him.

'Enchanted,' the boy says again, and stands up without letting go of my hand. He is about ten, dressed officially in short-sleeved white shirt, blue tie and long white trousers. Still holding my hand, he leads me to the door.

'Passport! Passport!' I shout, doing an impromptu mime of panic, but the boy either ignores it or doesn't understand, and I am left outside the locked door before I really know what is happening. I knock for about ten minutes, but there is no reply. The door acquires a 'Not at Home' look as I watch it.

Left alone outside the Department of Strangers, rejected in a war-torn island, I walk away through crowds of young boys who are pointing at the sky, doing aeroplane impersonations and chanting in Lazari. (They associate English people with the plane which was recently blown up in Sainte-Fleur airport.) A policeman in a brilliant white uniform shoos them away; a Lazarene priest in black, a negative image of the white policeman, walks carelessly across my path, apparently not seeing me. The priest's bag is being carried by a Christian woman with a moustache. A mule loaded with oranges runs past, scattering chickens.

I cannot help thinking about the one word the boy spoke during the whole exchange, 'Enchanted'. I have this neurotic fear that some kind of spell has been placed on me. I have always been superstitious and I am beginning to suspect that Lazar is unlucky for me. I would go back to the Sacred Heart Youth Hostel, pack my bags and leave on the next ferry if I had enough money for the ticket, and if my passport were not in a locked drawer at the Department of Strangers. I am also beginning to feel hungry. Four hours have passed since my coffee and doughnut at the American Bomber Pilots' Bakery, and I am wondering how to afford lunch. I counted my money in the doughnut shop – only seventeen riba left, enough for one good meal or three bread and cheese ones.

I suppose it's funny, in a miserable sort of way. I am travelling in search of my identity and I have lost the only specimen of one I have ever owned. The hook-nosed barman who asked in such detail after my family won't give me a job without papers. Nobody will give me a job unless I have a passport. I have allowed myself to be humiliated, robbed of my identity by a one-eyed ten-year-old. I will just have to go back and demand both passport and papers, or I may find I have been enchanted out of existence. But not now. It is now lunchtime in Sainte-Fleur, and the Department will certainly be closed until after the siesta.

I have to go to the Café Européen for lunch. I am meeting my room mate, Ravidan, a nomadic Lazari who spends his life wandering the islands of the Eastern Mediterranean, washing dishes or waiting at table, a job he currently performs in his occasional spasms of conscientiousness at the Hotel Folio. When I walk into the Café Européen, I see Ravidan sitting with a friend I don't know, eating goat's cheese with red peppers in it. The friend is eating bread and grapes and drinking black coffee;

he has a two day growth of beard, and occasionally picks out chords on a guitar.

'This is Carlos,' Ravidan says. 'Only he isn't Spanish.'

'Fuck the system, man,' Carlos says.

I order red snapper with olives and a quarter litre of white wine.

'I don't tell anyone where I come from,' Carlos says, 'I live on the road, man.'

'He is ashamed,' Ravidan explains, 'of not being American. He has good taste in rock music, nevertheless. You like music?'

'No,' I say. I am not going to attempt to explain the Robert Fane rag to Lazaris. This is a musical genre of my own invention, which many people, even those with more advanced tastes than Carlos and Ravidan, have called discordant and alarming. I have a sudden flashback to my Cambridge days, in which I see myself sitting on a chair in an intense posture playing RF Rag VII to Susan Gray, who is lying naked on the bed reading *Brideshead Revisited*. It was, I suppose, an early phase in the search for an identity, but it was wrong somehow. Those numbers made it too abstract, too mathematical.

'You English, you are very cold, you know. The English are not very emotional people.'

'I'm not English any more,' I tell Carlos between mouthfuls of snapper. 'I've lost my passport.' Having swallowed the snapper, I laugh carelessly. Carlos and Ravidan hold out their glasses for me to fill.

'Great, man, now you can be anything you like, just like me. I get you a passport. What do you want, French, German?' Carlos says.

'I want my own passport back. It was stolen by a one-eyed boy at the Department of Strangers.'

'No problem,' Ravidan says, 'I fix it for you. You come with me and I fix it. After the siesta. First we find some girls.'

This is unnerving. I have never *found* girls before, and was brought up to believe they just develop. I don't feel ready for a girl, not until I have my identity back. 'You're supposed to sleep during the siesta,' I say.

'Sleep is for old people. Ravidan never sleeps.'

'And before that,' Carlos says with an unexpected flash of generosity, 'more wine.'

A whole bottle arrives with a plate of green almonds and little slices of watermelon. It is Lazari Loup de Mer wine from the outskirts of Sainte-Fleur. It is pale green, and tastes, as its name implies, of sea water. I don't like it, but perhaps it is growing on me. If I stay in Lazar long enough, I may find it is part of the enchantment.

We arrive at a small plum-coloured door. Ravidan knocks. The door is opened by a shrivelled widow; without saying anything, Ravidan holds up three fingers as in a restaurant, and the widow leads us up a roofless staircase resembling a fire escape, and through another door at the top. It is a roof garden which apparently serves as a waiting room for the brothel. Wine and watermelon are already waiting for us, on a table surrounded by white chairs. (Has Ravidan arranged this in advance?) We sit down on the white chairs and drink Loup de Mer. I am tense because I have never been to a brothel before, and the others must feel the same for the conversation quickly dies away, and we drink the wine seriously, as if this were the main business of the afternoon.

We are sitting among nervous green leaves, the leaves of potplants I do not recognize, oval and spear-shaped, dark, pale, striped and spotted, under a sky now so blue that it seems purple. The sea wolf is gnawing my brain. I am no longer worrying even about how to get my identity back. I am not content, merely apathetic – and I cannot keep track of time. It does not surprise me when I find that Ravidan and I are alone with a new bottle. 'Where's Carlos?' I ask, as a gesture in the direction of conversation, and Ravidan makes a gesture of his own, not one I have seen before, but its meaning is obvious. Oh yes, I had forgotten we were here for that. A while later, it is dark suddenly and I am alone. A thin rain has begun to fall on the roof garden. A light, like that of a paraffin lamp rather than an electric bulb, shines under the door which leads to the brothel. I wonder dazedly if I have missed my turn, and if it is time to go home yet. When I am able to turn my head, I notice the shrivelled widow. She is standing beside me.

'Please,' she says, 'pay now.'

Datastream 3; Prunewood, Kate

I am still naked and still horizontal. Everything is white. No, this is untrue – I am seeing the world through a kind of coarse white veil. I am in a small room with a table, a chair and a window. There is a man sitting in the chair, and a vase of spiky flowers on the table which stands beside my head. Obviously, I am in a bed. My body feels cool for the first time in days, almost too cool, but it is such an alien sensation at the moment that I can't tell whether I like it or not. There is another alien sensation that I like very much; I feel clean. The white thing over my face is a sheet, and it is in contact with my whole body. There is no layer of sweat and grime interposing itself between Kate Prunewood and the universe. It feels as if I have just been invented. Nothing has happened to me yet. It is probably a long time since I have been so free of wear and tear – not since the pre-Hugh era.

I move my head, and the sheet which is moulded to it moves too.

'Please not remove sheet,' the man says nervously. I had forgotten about him.

'Where am I?' I ask, not that I care.

'Women's ward, Sainte-Fleur Hospital. Please not remove sheet. It is believed you are naked. Also you are wife of Lazari citizen.'

'Can't I at least take it off my face. I can't see you.'

'Is not necessary you see me. You are Lazari citizen wife, there-fore not right to look man. Your face is naked also that your body.'

'Are you a Shamanist?' I am vaguely disappointed. I had been led to believe, after all, that Lazar was a Christian country, and somehow, after Jalal, Faroun and Haq, I feel a lot less hostile to Christianity than I used to be.

'Lazar land of equal to all,' he replies, 'Shamanist, Christian, all alike. Your husband understandably very bad man, wishing overthrow of legally constituted popular state government of Lazar by men of violence. But you are married by official Shamanist Shaman, therefore marriage acceptable. I hope you understand this my respect.'

'I am very flattered,' I say through the sheet, 'but we can't have been legally married. I wasn't even present at the time. I want to see the British Ambassador.'

'British Ambassador is unfortunately dead at the moment, I regret. Also your marriage is still legal in Lazar, which is where you have the honour to be. Your husband will attend trial shortly for crime of treason against lawful constitute state. And also you.'

'Me? What have I done?'

'Doing not necessary for wives. Being is adequate.'

In my bed remote from the troubles, I am kept completely ignorant of everything that is going on, apart from the facts that my husband (if this is what he is) is charged with treason, and the British Ambassador is dead.

In the morning, I sit in a chair in a heavy black nightdress loaned to me by the matron and look out of the window at a view of rocks and olive trees. The hospital is several kilometres outside the town; I can see the main Sainte-Fleur road a couple of hundred yards away, but nothing passes along it except lorries full of dejected looking soldiers being ferried in from their rural outposts for the final confrontation. The talk in the hospital is that Sainte-Fleur is in danger. The matron has told me it is doomed, and that not St Paul himself can help President Miraz now. However, I am getting used to the melancholy national temperament by this time, and don't take her too seriously. Not that a Christian defeat would do me any harm. My situation is about as bad as it could possibly be anyway, and perhaps as the wife of a Shamanist freedom-fighter I might at least be safe. But in the meantime, I watch the lorries passing and listen to the boom of the jets overhead and pretend that the war and my trial are subject to some infinite postponement owing, perhaps, to the fine weather. The weather is usually fine in Lazar in the late spring, of course, but that would explain why procrastination, too, is a part of the national temperament. I could happily live for ever in this sunny room: an unmarried wife, a healthy patient, a peaceful war victim.

Unfortunately, the little Shamanist from the government turns up every day before lunch. He tells me to get back in bed and pull the sheet over my face again, because he considers the black nightdress almost as shocking as complete nakedness. Then he asks the questions, some connected with his investigation, some not. The unconnected ones are the same every day:

Why did you not marry earlier?
Why were you sent abroad without your father?
Why does your family allow you to have a job?
Why did you marry a Lazari and not an Englishman?

I have decided that he is incapable of understanding or accepting my answers, so I now invent new ones each time, in the hope of finding one he likes. I console myself with Hugh's words, 'The majority of people never really think after a certain age – they merely go on repeating the reactions they have learned earlier, when they were thinking, regardless of whether those reactions are still appropriate or not.'

The man's more official, investigative questions are usually about Jalal:

Did he really intend to overthrow the popularly constituted democratic government of Lazar?
Was he in pay of the Soviet Union?
Did he torture you or other passengers?

I prefer to reply that he will have to ask Jalal, since it is all nothing to do with me. The man replies that it is much to do with me since I am the wife of a terrorist murderer, and besides, he is asking Jalal but receiving only terrorist lies in reply. I ask why he expects anything more from me, since I am supposed to be a terrorist, too. He weeps. He tells me that his job is a very difficult one, and that no wise man would ever do it because there is no truth or honour left in the world. This conversation follows much the same pattern day after day, the monotony being broken by my improvised answers to the questions about my private life. This pattern has a catechistic quality which I find especially comforting. After all, I was brought up in the Church of England.

Datastream 5; Fane, Robert

I am standing among the shadowy potplants, oval and spear-shaped, dark, pale, striped and spotted. I am trying to explain to the widow that I can't pay. Rain is tapping impatiently on the leaves. As darkness has arrived, the plants appear to have grown taller, so that I now find myself in a rain forest.

'Please,' the widow says, 'pay now. Three and wine.'

'But my friends are going to pay, they said so.' Actually, they didn't say so, but I assumed they intended to because it was their idea.

'Friends gone. Three and wine.'

'Anyway all I had was the wine. No sex, you understand? Just wine.'

'Yes, you are screwed.'

'No, not me. My friends, Carlos and Ravidan. They screwed, I no screwed. Only wine. How much wine, please?'

'No more wine. Pay now.'

'No want more wine. Pay wine. No pay screw. Understand?' As if I would actually want to pay for it, when I never even wanted it in the first place.

'NO PAY SCREW,' I say clearly and simply.

'Ah,' the woman says, 'SCREW NO PAY NO EXIST.'

This makes me think. I look into her eyes, expecting to find there a kind of hard sympathy, a deep sexual wisdom. I cannot make out an expression at all in the darkness, and perhaps her remark was just a Mediterranean brothel owner's platitude. Speaking slowly and forcefully, distilling each syllable into an essence of reasonableness, I tell her, 'SCREW NO EXIST NO PAY.'

I am rather proud of this, but the widow is unimpressed. 'Ah, screw exist!' she replies indignantly. She waves her arms in the air and calls in a high voice, 'Fall-e-la, Fall-e-la!'

The door opens. A small, meek figure emerges from the brothel. She is wearing heavy robes, which makes her look ghostly in the darkness and drizzle. The widow squawks a few syllables in Lazari, and the girl studies my face carefully from the shelter of the yashmak. Rain is running down the face in question; the eyes studying it are dark and religious.

A stream of harsh consonants and infuriated vowels comes out of the muffled body, like words coming out of a loudspeaker rather than someone speaking. A hand emerges from the bundle of clothes and strikes me across the face. The widow seizes Fallela's hand and begins to shake it, muttering something soothing and urgent through her teeth. Then she tells me, 'She saying you are beaten her.'

'I never touched her. It must have been Ravidan or Carlos. I drank too much wine and fell asleep.'

'You are beaten her. Pay, please.'

3 SCREWS	30 RIBA
WINE	5 RIBA
BEATEN	10 RIBA
WATERMELON	1 RIBA
TOTAL	46 RIBA

'The watermelon is free,' I say. 'Anyway, I didn't beat her. I didn't screw her either. You can have five riba for the wine.'

'Watermelon dangerous, war in fields.'

WATERMELON	1 RIBA
3 SCREWS	30 RIBA
WINE	5 RIBA
BEATEN	5 RIBA
TOTAL	41 RIBA

'I have no money. Five riba is all I have, look!'

I know this is true because I have been counting and recounting the money in my pocket for the last five minutes.

'OK.'

    NO MONEY FOR WATERMELON

    BEATEN IS ON THE HOUSE

    WINE   5 RIBA

    3 SCREWS   33 RIBA BECAUSE VERY GOOD WITH
                       BEATEN

    TOTAL   38 RIBA

Eight riba off the price already. If I did not have such an unsound financial base for haggling from, I might have negotiated a bargain. However, my best offer is:

    NO MONEY FOR WATERMELON BECAUSE FREE

    NO MONEY FOR BEATEN BECAUSE ON THE HOUSE

    NO MONEY FOR SCREW BECAUSE NO EXIST

    WINE   5 RIBA

    TOTAL   5 RIBA

The widow has now realized that I meant it when I said I had no money. She goes into a shocked conference with Fallela. After this, she turns to me very politely, as if afraid she might be about to make an unforgivable mistake, 'No money?'

'No money.'

'Five riba?'

'Yes, yes. Five riba for wine.'

'We are beaten you,' she says matter-of-factly. I nod to show her I understand.

Chances of escape: I could run down the stairs, but if the plum-coloured door at the bottom happens to be locked, I will be trapped. I could stay and fight, but if they intend to produce a professional beater, I don't fancy my chances. I am not even an amateur. My morale is low following the incidents of the day and my head is still ringing from the Loup de Mer.

Meanwhile, the widow speaks again to Fallela, who turns self-righteously and walks with sharp and angry steps back into the brothel. I could jump over a low wall on one side of the roof garden. There are flat-roofed buildings everywhere round here; possibly one of them is underneath the wall. I look over the edge, but the light from the door does not carry far enough to let me see. However, a spotlight now shines on the roof garden, touching the oval and spear-shaped leaves with white and turning the rain into hard streaks in front of my eyes. It looks like a roof down there. On the other hand, maybe it isn't. I think I can hear the rain beating on some hard surface. Two brittle young men in white suits run out of the brothel, and I decide to find out. I climb over the wall, lower my body down the other side, and drop.

Datastream 3; Prunewood, Kate

This morning, the man who normally interviews me in my hospital bed has not shown up. His place has been taken by a plump, unshaven-looking man in an expensive suit, who allows me to leave my face outside the sheet, tells me he is my humble servant, and that he is sorry from the deep bottom of his heart for much inconvenience I have suffered at hands of misguided Shamanists both before and after my liberation from terrorist incarceration. He does not regard Jalal as my husband. 'Naturally not. Shamanist ceremony has no legality in Lazar, especially in aeroplane.'

My previous interrogator is under arrest for treason.

'He didn't seem very treasonable to me,' I say.

'Nowadays, Shamanist may not hold government position. That is itself treason.'

'What, just having the job?'

'Yes, treason. Since 12.00 pm this morning. Same time as Shamanist marriage ceremony illegal.'

'So now he is charged with treason, just like me.' I begin to see why the Lazaris are all such fatalists.

'No, you are not charged now, because not married to traitor. However, it is believed you have consorted with one, so please answer questions.'

Then he asks:

> Why did you not marry earlier?
> Why were you sent abroad without your father?
> Why does your family allow you to have a job?
> Why did you marry a Lazari and not an Englishman?

I demand to see the British Ambassador, who is, however, still dead.

Datastream 1; Telemann, Alb

I have been involved in a death. That is the culmination of the Syndrome I have been trying to describe. The Syndrome has turned out to be fatal, though not, admittedly, to me. Whether it will kill me also remains to be seen. In that case, the death of Ellen might be regarded merely as a side effect or perhaps the result of contagion. It is, however, the only objectively verifiable symptom I have to go on, and I have to try to understand it. I don't know yet how deeply I am implicated, or what the consequences may be. I have never been involved in a death before, only that of my father, and I was never actually suspected of *killing* him.

I know she died within an hour after I left Rose's house – at least, I guess the house actually belongs to Warburg, since pimps are the ones with the money. On leaving that house, I went straight to Ellen's and she let me in. It probably took me five minutes to walk round there, and the time must have been around midnight, although, of course, I was under the influence of a narcotic which meant I had no sense of time and no interest in it, either. Ellen was up and dressed; she let me in without any hesitation. Now this is an important fact in view of the subsequent chronology of the evening. Because I had lost interest in time, I never looked at my watch all evening, but Warburg told me when I met him at the car that it was 1.00 am and that it was an hour since I left his house. I have no reason to doubt any of that. The chronology is therefore as follows:

5-00 pm approx	Ellen arrives for rendezvous with Pike
5-30	Alb leaves office
6-00	Alb arrives HV, sees Warburg
6-15?	Alb picked up by Rose
6-45?	Coitus interruptus by Warburg. Marijuana session
7-30 approx	Ellen leaves White House
8-00	Ellen arrives South Roseberry Avenue
12.00	Alb leaves Warburg's house
12.05	Alb arrives Ellen's house
1.00 am	Alb and Warburg discover Ellen's body

This chronology raises several questions. The first thing to say is that I don't know for certain that Ellen was with Pike between 5.00 pm and 7.30 pm, because of the absence of Pillowtalk over the last few days. But I assume that the normal pattern of the relationship is continuing (as Fred Zolph's recent memo suggests), and that they have found some means of escaping the bugging, following my admission to Ellen the first time we met. Anyway, it doesn't seem to me to make a lot of difference what she was doing at that time. The second gap in my knowledge is caused by my unfortunately mislaying my sense of time after leaving Warburg's house. It means that I don't know how long I talked with Ellen, and how long I was walking around the streets afterwards in slow motion. I don't think I talked with her very long – say about fifteen minutes. That means she died between 12.20 am and 1.00 am.

I said the fact that Ellen was dressed and ready to open the door at 12.05 am was significant. Assuming she did get home around 8.00 pm, give her till 9.00 pm to prepare and eat one of those postcoital TV dinners (I could have checked her carpet to see which of the leftovers was the freshest, but it's too late now), what was she doing for the next three hours, praying? Bear in mind that the woman had no TV or radio or record player. I would have figured her for Benjamin Franklin sleeping habits, but I have abandoned most of my preconceived ideas by now. The fact that she was up and dressed at midnight and opened the door right away suggests to me that she was expecting someone, though it *is* only a suggestion. And bear in mind that she was naked when she died. If someone murdered her, did she undress first, or did he undress her afterwards? (Why should anyone want to do that?) All right, she undressed first, either voluntarily or under compulsion. Either way, the undressing and the shooting have to be fitted into forty minutes. Pretty fast work.

Thesis 1

After I left, Ellen took the WH38, took her clothes off (why?), went to the bathroom, locked the door (why?) and blew her brains out. This fits all the facts, though it doesn't explain why my visit should provoke her to such an act, or, alternatively, why she waited three hours to do something she could have done as soon as she got home, or, at least, after eating a hearty TV dinner.

Thesis 2

Ellen was naked because she was being visited by Warren Pike. This presupposes some development in their relationship which has taken place since I lost auditory touch with it. Say, Ellen has tried to persuade Pike to leave his wife, Pike has agreed in principle, he visits her at her home, she takes off her clothes to make love and (bang) he changes his mind. Problem: she locked the gun in the drawer. How did he know it was there? The fact that the bathroom door was locked on the inside is not the bar to murder it at first seems to be. I took a good look at that lock after I picked it. It was the kind that's set into the doorknob. Flick it, close the door, and it locks. It doesn't matter if you go out or stay in, that door stays locked.

Thesis 3

Jimmy Ruggins shows up. Ellen takes her clothes off (are they lovers?) and he shoots her. Same problems as with the Pike theory. As with that theory, she could be expecting him. Additional problem: Ellen is Ruggins's trump card, she is the key to his control of the White House. Why should he want her dead?

Thesis 4

Warburg is the murderer. He is certainly a shady character, and the more I think about it, the more certain I am that he stole my cars. He got organized suspiciously quickly to find me and then take me to the body, and he was suspiciously ready to help me dispose of it. It was almost as if he expected to find it. This explains one problem which applies to all other theories except Thesis 1. Why did the murderer do nothing to dispose of the body? Apart, that is, from making it look like suicide by pressing the gun into the hand after the fatal. Wouldn't it have been better to make her disappear altogether? Certainly, a dead naked woman in a bathroom covered with blood is a newsworthy event, and one would expect our hypothetical murderers to want to avoid scandal. New problems: motive again. Could Warburg be working for Pike? And why was she naked? Unless . . . No, not Warburg. He may be an unprincipled bastard, but I don't believe *that*.

Thesis 5

Person or persons unknown, having some connection with the White House. Either someone out to prevent another Pike sex scandal or someone out to stop Ellen's influence over Pike. Problem: nakedness again. Disposal of the body again.

All in all, the explanation with the fewest problems seems to be Thesis 1, despite the reservations of nakedness and the locked door. She actually wanted to die. But she was also strategic enough for a lot of other people to want her to die, and I am speaking as one of those people.

Leaving aside that question, something has been worrying me. We should have weighted Ellen's body when we threw it in the lake. I don't care what Warburg says about the lake being secret, it is still in Virginia, and that body is drifting about in it like the *Marie Celeste*. Sooner or later, someone is going to come along to catch sunfish and will instead catch an Ellen incompletely eaten by turtles. It's amazing it hasn't happened yet. At the moment, I presume her death is a secret. If Jimmy Ruggins is aware of it yet, he's keeping quiet about it. Actually, Ruggins is at this very moment having the time of his life at the Wocaluha Inquiry, summing up the evidence for the benefit of the Commission. I have a certain sick curiosity left over for such things.

'This is the way I see it, good people,' Commission of Inquiry Chairman Ruggins began his summing up. 'Can

141

you hear me? Great. I would not wish what I am going to say to you today to fall upon deaf ears, because as the Holy Bible says, preaching to deaf ears is a waste of time. I am fully conscious, I may say, of the great honor which my very good friend the President of the United States has done to me, by appointing me President of this very important Commission. I know that from the outset of our Inquiry, there were some people, there were maybe even some members of the Commission itself, although I don't want to name any names here, who thought that I would not be a suitable man for this task, because I am a Man of God and a former disc jockey. Well let me tell you, I am not ashamed to have been a disc jockey, and I am proud to be a Man of God, and I think President Warren Pike had his reasons for appointing me to this onerous task at this monumental stage in our history. I think the President felt that this terrible disaster we have been talking about for so many days may have been an Act of God, and that it takes a Man of God to explain it. Now you've all heard, I imagine, that God moves in a mysterious way, His wonders to perform. Have you all heard that? Good. Well when God starts moving in that mysterious way of His, that, my friends, is when you need a Man of God to explain the way He's moving this time. Because, after all, if God hasn't told one of His own men, then whom has He told?

Well, then, I said this terrible disaster at Wocaluha of which we speak may have been an Act of God, I said that the President may have thought that, but what exactly do we mean by an Act of God? We mean an accident, don't we? That's what we mean, an ACCIDENT. But what a crazy thing that is, brothers and sisters, to call the Acts of God, ACCIDENTS. Do you think God created the world in seven days as it says in the Holy Bible by ACCIDENT? Is that what you think? And do you think His only begotten son our Lord Jesus Christ came down to earth and died on the cross to save us from the fiery consequences of our sins, by ACCIDENT? Or that when the last trump sounds He shall separate the sheep and the goats by ACCIDENT? Well then. I tell you, my friends, there isn't the tiniest thing that happens in this whole universe, not the death of a sparrow, not even the death of a streptococcus, that happens by ACCIDENT. And we are not talking about the death of a sparrow or a streptococcus in this Inquiry, we are talking about the deaths of 7,000 people. Now if God didn't take the life of the smallest streptococcus in your larynx by ACCIDENT, you can bet your immortal soul (and you have to bet your immortal soul, you don't have much choice about that, my friends), you can bet your immortal soul that He didn't take the life of those people by ACCIDENT. God was planning something, my friends, when He caused that factory to blow up. We're here to find out what.'

Ruggins has been talking all day, and he hasn't even mentioned any evidence yet. It seems like at this rate he'll talk for a month. Fred Zolph believes Ruggins is planning a bigger and better cover-up than Senator Florian ever dreamed of.

'Guess the Blood of the Lamb washes whiter,' Zolph wrote me blasphemously today; but I just am not in the mood for current affairs. I stand and look out of my window at cherry trees (is that what they are?), I smoke cigarets, I drink coffee, I look at my computer terminal, time goes by, and at this very moment informers are being horribly murdered by Shamanist dissidents in the Saint-Sépulcre area of Lazar, a fact I can do nothing about, and which President Miraz denies. OK, OK, seven hours later than this very moment, that's not the point. Miraz continues to deny the murders, even though mutilated bodies are washed up in oildrums on the beach outside the Hotel Folio almost every day, making bathing unpopular. A corpse has been hanging from a giant crane high above the docks for several weeks because no one dares to cut it down. What can any of us do about things like that? The government is just as bad, if not worse, because they have professional torturers and real dungeons. Sometimes I think Ruggins is right, and this world is just so evil it deserves to be destroyed. I guess maybe I feel guilty about Ellen. I have to keep reminding myself it wasn't me that killed her.

Datastream 5; Fane, Robert

I escaped from the Saint-Sépulcre brothel with a swollen ankle and a grudge against Ravidan, who has since been to the brothel and discovered all the whores weeping and screaming accusations at each other. Fallela was weeping the loudest, and claiming that none of the others had moved a finger when I seemed about to kill her. Ravidan thought they should try to put it behind them and go on with business, but when they saw through their tears who he was, they flew at him and demanded to know my whereabouts. Naturally, Ravidan replied that he had only met me that day, and that I was a friend of Carlos and had flown back to England. The owner was too smart for him, though, and pointed out that no one could fly back to England at the moment because the destruction of the British plane had put the airport out of action. One of the brittle white-suited men pulled a knife on Ravidan.

'What?' I ask as I limp beside him towards the Department of Strangers, 'what did you tell them?'

'Ravidan very intelligent. I tell them British Embassy. I say you are here because of plane.'

The men said they would wait outside it and get me when I came out. So I am now an undesirable alien in a strange country, with no passport and no money, and men in white suits are waiting outside the British Embassy for me with a knife.

I am tempted by the smell of hot doughnuts from the US Bomber Pilots' Bakery, and spend my last riba.

'You have money, you spend,' Ravidan says encouragingly, holding out his hand for the doughnut he feels he is owed after not getting his share that day. I am hungry, however, and refuse to give in. When we arrive at the Department, I am picking crumbs of sugar off my T-shirt and eating them sadly. I notice that the door is open again. Maybe Ravidan really is a fixer.

'I get passport and papers. I get you nice job at Hotel Folio. Then you thank Ravidan. Much women, much doughnut. *Big man*,' he adds with heavy irony. Ravidan is the only friend I have, and knows it.

We walk in without knocking. A small bearded man with an air of great wisdom is sitting at the desk where the one-eyed boy formerly sat. Ravidan speaks to him, and the man waves a hand dismissively and speaks a few contemptuous words.

'He say where passport.'

'In that desk. A one-eyed boy put it there.'

When this is explained to him, the man begins looking through the desk in a curious way, as if he has never seen any of its contents before. It contains:

piles of index cards without any writing on them
pencils
ballpoint pens
rubbers
drawing pins
paperclips
a stapler
a box of staples
a broken plastic ruler
a large blank pad (ruled, narrow feint and right hand margin for writing on in Lazari)
a large blank pad (not ruled)
a rubber thimble for sorting through documents

However, there are no documents visible to sort through. None of the paper in the drawers is written on or printed.

'He must work very hard,' I say, via Ravidan. The man smiles and nods happily.

'He say no one-eye boy,' Ravidan says. 'Never in all Lazar history one-eye boy at Department of Strangers. On grave of St Paul, Lazarene martyrs, Blessed Virgin, father, grandfather, uncles.'

'How long has he worked here?'

'Almost one day.'

'I want to speak to his boss. Tell him that.'

'His boss President Miraz. New broom in Department of Strangers. Therefore empty desk. Destroy old records and start again. Very efficient, very ruthless.'

'Miraz has sacked the one-eyed boy?'

'No record one-eye boy at Department of Strangers.'

The bearded man makes basil tea with peanuts, and as I taste the flakes of skin on the surface, I feel a vivid short-term nostalgia for the day before that is now irrevocably and officially lost; the one-eyed boy, the passport, the moment when my identity was locked in the drawer. No record one-eye boy at Department of Strangers. No record Robert Fane anywhere, except in the unforgiving memories of white-suited stick-like brothel employees with knives.

'If they've sacked all the officials,' I say to Ravidan, 'perhaps he can give me a job.'

'He say yes, very good. Where papers?'

'He's supposed to give me the papers.'

'Very good, he give you papers – he is new here. Where passport?'

'A one-eyed boy took it.'

'Where one-eye boy?'

'I don't know. Anyway, it doesn't make very much difference now, because your friend with the beard has probably destroyed it in the name of Christian efficiency.'

'He say impossible you not have passport. Person no passport no exist. However, he overlook you this time.'

'Then he'll give me a job?'

'No, impossible give job no papers. Impossible give papers no passport. Therefore no job. However he overlook no passport.'

'What good does that do me?'

'You not in prison.'

Ravidan calls me into the corner beside the filing cabinet for a secret conference, although since the bearded man apparently speaks no English, this is unnecessary and only makes us look furtive.

'His name Hossip Maria. Give him money, he give you job.'

'I haven't got any, I spent my last riba on doughnuts.'

'Borrow,' Ravidan says.

'How much will you lend me?'

'Not me, stupid bastard, borrow Hossip Maria.'

'I don't follow.'

'Borrow 500 riba Hossip Maria. Give 500 riba Hossip Maria. Get job Hossip Maria. Get 500 riba Hossip Maria pay. Pay 500 riba Hossip Maria.'

'Don't tell me, tell him.'

Ravidan goes over to Hossip Maria and they wave their arms at each other. Hossip Maria proves incorruptible or uncomprehending, and threatens to have Ravidan shot. In the circumstances, I think it is time I got myself another passport. In the evening, we go to the Café Européen.

We find Carlos outside, looking romantic and bohemian in the last rays of the sun. He still has not shaved, and is wearing a broad-brimmed straw hat. Today he is not carrying his guitar but scribbling in the smallest notebook I have ever seen.

'I'm a fucking poet, man,' Carlos says as we sit down. 'Fuck you, fuck everybody. This is minimalism. You like?'

'Nobody fucking anybody today. Roberto beat up whore. Didn't even pay, so now they going to kill him,' Ravidan explains.

'I don't believe you,' says Carlos jealously.

'You don't have to believe it, Carlos,' I tell him, 'because it isn't true.'

'I don't care about fucking truth, man,' Carlos says savagely. 'My name not Carlos today. Stuff Carlos, you can call me Karl. Have some wine. Karl paying.'

'You have to pay,' Ravidan says as Carlos pours the wine. 'Him no money at all. Spend last riba on doughnut, greedy bastard.'

'I need a passport. I want to get a job at the Department of Strangers. You said you could get me one.'

'What kind of passport you want?' Karl asks, 'Italian very good, also Swedish. There are many Lazari, but no good because war coming, Shamanist, no wine, no screwing, very bad.'

'I tell him that already,' Ravidan says, nodding and smiling. Ravidan is younger than me, and I am younger than Karl. Karl, despite his broadbrimmed hat, unshavenness and minimalist notebook, has obviously lived. My turn to be jealous.

'What about British?'

'What for you want be British, man? British very unemotional, cold, no good bed. Also perverts. You be nice Swedish person, have saunas also large blonde woman. Volvo very reliable cars.'

'I don't want a Swedish passport, because I can't speak Swedish.'

'Is no difference. I speak Swedish neither, have Swedish passport. Is almost no Swedish in Lazar, British, French, Italian, also Greek, Arab. Besides British passport ugly, great big black bastard. I let you have Swedish passport special offer, 500 riba only.'

'Him no money,' Ravidan says.

'Not even tiny 500 riba.'

'Not even tiny one riba,' I say, irritated. 'Why does everyone want money from me before they give me anything?'

'Is life, man.' Ravidan pours some wine. Sententious little son of a bitch.

'Life is stinking capitalist conspiracy,' Carlos says. 'You are my friend, not capitalist, therefore I help. I get one Swedish passport for you, you get one job?'

'He get very good job at Department of Strangers,' Ravidan adds, 'chief assistant in charge of everything. Free car and women, expense account at Hotel Folio, king size salary also cigars.'

'I give you Swedish passport,' Karl says, 'therefore you get job, therefore you give me 500 riba.'

'Make it a British passport and you've got a deal.'

'British have no imagination, yes? All right, I get you nice excellent black pig of British passport, very ugly therefore you grateful.'

Ravidan and I sit outside the Café Européen, drinking wine as the sunlight vanishes unexpectedly and Carlos vanishes with it. A small owlish waiter hovers over us, and Ravidan, now almost completely invisible in the Mediterranean darkness, calls out, 'More wine. Karl paying.'

'Are you sure Carlos will come back?'

'Of course come back. Must pay for wine,' Ravidan says. 'Also is getting you passport.'

'How is he going to get the passport?' I say, but there is no answer. Some red and green electric light bulbs now light up on a bush next to Ravidan's chair. They make everything seem darker. I remember how I sat like this in the roof garden of the brothel, losing track of time and getting deeper into debt with the management. The one-eyed Shamanist boy was right; I am enchanted. I am under some kind of ancient Lazari spell from the pre-Christian days, a spell which has taken my identity and is now taking everything else, my sense of time, my ability to move, to think, to escape. Loup de Mer has a bad effect on me.

Carlos reappears eventually under the red and green electric light bulbs, clutching a passport. Relief! I take it from him and gaze at the familiar large black rectangular form, the two little oval windows on the front and the vague gleam of gold scrolling in the unearthly red and green light.

'Welcome,' I say, to Karl and the passport.

'Karl fucking brilliant, man. Karl get you fucking pig of black passport, no.'

It is warped and battered, but British. I cannot read the flowery writing which says, as I already know, that Her Britannic Majesty's government requests all persons to allow the bearer of this passport to pass without let or hindrance. I can tell, even in the mottled light, that it has a lot of visas. The name looks foreign.

'Where did you get it, Carlos?' I ask.

'Karl secret. Karl has method, fucking genius man. Live on street all his life.'

'Look at photo, man,' Ravidan says, 'see who you are now.'

'Will have to change photo anyway, or people not recognize you,' Carlos says.

I turn to the photograph.

'Carlos, you bastard, this is a woman!'

'So, you not like woman?'

'Carlos like woman very much,' Ravidan says, 'more than Ravidan even.'

'I don't want to be one.'

'Well, you are change photograph, like I say,' Carlos says.

Ravidan squints at the page. 'Can be a man's name also, Sandra?' he says.

'No. Look, she's a Systems Support Manager, whatever that is, she's blonde and she's got a birthmark on her neck.'

'She look nice,' Ravidan says, peering hard.

'What about the visa?' I ask, 'What does that say?'

Ravidan studies the visa, reading it intently as if it were a novel. 'It says you are whore.'

The bearer of the passport is Miss Sandra Elizabeth CASTELVETRO, accompanied by spouse blank and by blank children. Her national status is BRITISH CITIZEN. Number of passport is N 938787 D. Occupation is Systems Support Manager; place of birth: Surbiton; date of birth: 17 DEC 60. She is not a whore in Anglo-American terms. The Lazari immigration authorities automatically put this on the visa of any unaccompanied woman, since they cannot think of any other reason for her to travel alone.

Am I more enchanted now, or less? I have found an identity, but it belongs to someone else. I decide to postpone this question until I am feeling better. I have had a hard and confusing couple of days; my ankle still hurts, and I have been drinking too much and eating too little. I have started on the wrong foot.

'Perhaps I should leave the island altogether, and then come back again,' I say dreamily, 'then none of this would have happened.'

'Come back as woman,' Ravidan says, 'fucking crazy.'

Datastream 1; Telemann, Alb

What happened today, Alb? Something really spooky happened today, and I thought I was immune to spookiness by now. Wrong again. This morning, I was standing at the window, looking out over the White House lawn when the terminal on the desk behind me suddenly beeped. When I turned round, I saw the screen go blank.

You are saying, is that it? No, that isn't it. You have to see it in context, anyway. I was standing at the window, not thinking about the lake in Virginia where nobody ever goes. I was successfully not picturing the decomposing corpse of Ellen Axaxas, half-eaten by turtles, bumping gently against some poor guy's fishing boat. Ellen Axaxas, from elementary-school teacher to elementary biology, finishing as elementary particles. Except that she wasn't an elementary-school teacher – I forgot that. I was holding the knob of the blind cord between finger and thumb, and thinking maybe I ought to pull down the blind to keep the eyes of passing security men off my terminal and make a start when the terminal got tired of waiting and started without me. By rights, it should have continued displaying the word WHOM in bold green eyeball letters, each letter being composed of hundreds of normal size letters.

On the desk, beside the aberrant and menacing terminal, there were three paper cups, each containing a cold inch of opaque coffee from the personal coffee machine, and an in-tray stacked with unread memos and bulky newspapers. Outside, reflected in the blank screen, was the usual smoothly patrolled lawn, men in broad suits, dogs with muscular shoulders, sunshine. Beyond was Washington D.C., its white facades, its Georgian simplicities, its tunafish sandwich shops, its Greyhound station, its seven universities and 77,000 swimming pools. And beyond: Hillingdon Village D.C., its leaves, its birds that wheezed and rattled at night, its empty house where an elementary-school teacher had once lived, its pimps, prostitutes and respectability. And beyond: a lake in Virginia which no one ever goes to and which I was not thinking about.

When the terminal began behaving abnormally, I was finally jerked out of my paralysis. I let go of the cord and went over to the desk. The message:

Please enter identity

was displayed on the screen. I entered my identity:

Identity: SECAT
Password: EYES

The screen cleared again and displayed the regular main menu:

MENUMENUMENUMENUMENUMENUMENUMENUMENUME

Welcome to your first menu. Please select the option you require.

F1 What is WHOM

F2 WHOM News and Current Affairs Digest

F3 Application Procedures

F4 Staff Profile: R Entwhistle

F5 Electronic Mail

F6 Accounts Procedures

F7 Word Processing

F8 HELP

Enjoy your data.

MENUMENUMENUMENUMENUMENUMENUMENUMENUME

I stared at my reflection between these alternatives and thought about making a start. After all, I had a lot to do, reports to write and electronic meetings to attend. Maybe I was feeling better today.

Maybe everything had worked out for the best. Maybe after all the weeks of worry, I could at last begin to rest easy in my office, if not my bed.

I selected electronic mail and looked at the latest Sleeping Partner reports. There was nothing of interest there, just three screens with attractive green borders, a bold heading of doublewidth characters, and the cheerless message:

Subject has not related since preceding timewindow

That was all. No text, no names, no cross references to the partner file, no consummation forecasts. Just the single line in the center of the screen to commemorate the sexual aridity of the post-Ellen era. Pike is taking it badly. I sent off an electronic memo to Fred Zolph.

To:	Fred Zolph
From:	Alb Telemann
Subject:	Sleeping Partner

Hi, Fred. SP results continue negative. What gives? Hasn't subject met any nice girls recently? Please advise.

To:	Alb Telemann
From:	Fred Zolph
Subject:	Sleeping Partner

Hi, Alb. Subject unusually depressed and morbid at this time. Is seeking spiritual advice. EA has not been seen for some time, and subject shows no interest in substitutes. Why worry? In view of her religious associations, EA was becoming a major pain in the fundamentals. Besides, this way you get less work to do.

To:	Fred Zolph
From:	Alb Telemann
Subject:	Sleeping Partner

I'm supposed to worry. It's what they pay me for. Please indicate reason for subject's unsatisfactory emotional status. Spiritual advice from whom?

But there was no reply. Perhaps Fred had logged off the system. Anyway, I knew where Pike was getting his spiritual advice from, and I didn't want to hear it confirmed by someone else. I feel so helpless in this office sometimes, as if the screen in front of me is keeping reality out, not letting it in. I sat in front of the keyboard for several minutes, paralyzed (again), waiting without enthusiasm for a reply that didn't come.

That was when the really spooky thing happened, the reply did come. It was not, however, a message from Fred Zolph, but a message from someone I have been trying to forget, along with that lake in Virginia, a man I first saw rollerskating past my third official car on a spring evening in suburban Hillingdon Village. I knew, of course, that Warburg was a car thief, a pimp and a suspect in the murder (or suicide) of Ellen, but I didn't know what he was doing on the White House computer. He has no business there, no business at all.

To:	Alb Telemann
From:	USER?????
Subject:	???????????

Hi Alb – how R yr interpersonal relations these daze? seen any good interfaces recently?!? stay open. stay flexible. stay in touch. ETC. yr friend and mine
WARBURG

This is the kind of thing Ernest Hellbaum refers to as an incident. 'Always report any incident directly to me right away,' he said at my induction (he was not undergoing psychotherapy in those days), 'as once those gremlins get into the database, you would be amazed how quickly they can corrupt your data.' This intrusion by Warburg could not have been the sort of incident he had in mind, but I had an intuition that something had been or else was being corrupted, so for once I followed Hellbaum's advice and reported it – not that I expected a reply.

To:	Ernest Hellbaum
From:	Alb Telemann
Subject:	Incident Report

Wish to report a problem with my computer terminal. It apparently logged itself on at 11.30 this morning. Is this possible? Also I received a message from an unknown user called USER????? Could this be connected with the other incident? Thank you for your assistance in this matter.

The story goes that since Ernest Hellbaum sought psychiatric help, he has been taking blue capsules twice a day and writing down his dreams. They now say that instead of escapist fantasies about ranches in Omaha or wherever, he is applying himself to making a stable and fulfilled life for himself in the context of Washington, the White House, data processing etc. He has made passes at two data entry clerks, a typist and (unwisely) a systems programmer, so far without success, but he claims to be coping better with rejection all the time. Maybe he's coping better with work, too – at any rate, he replied almost immediately with a formal electronic memo he designed himself for such eventualities. He is supposed to fill in / delete the relevant details and send it off, but he apparently forgot this, and added a PS to the end.

To:	Alb Telemann
From:	Ernest Hellbaum
Subject:	Incident Report

Thank you for your bug report of # inst. This is being looked into, and we hope to have a resolution for you in the immediate / near / indeterminate future.
(DELETE AS APPLICABLE.)

P.S. The System Manager has the power to log users on to the system automatically. I certainly did not do this, or I would have remembered. There is no USER????? known to the system. It appears we may be dealing with a security violation here. Please report to me at once if there is any recurrence of the situation, and ensure that all confidential information is encrypted. I am taking appropriate steps.

P.P.S. Would you mind telling me the exact words of the message?

Yes, I would mind. As you will appreciate, I could not possibly tell him the exact words of the message, for the same reason I could never tell Roly Entwhistle what exactly I was doing in Hillingdon Village when my (his) (the nation's) cars were stolen. Actually, I could not tell Hellbaum for even more of the same reason, since Ellen is now dead, and I am implicated in the murder by virtue of having accessorized it after the fact. Also by virtue of having planned it before the fact. The only bit I left out was the middle, and nobody would believe I had been so careless. I could not tell Hellbaum any of this because that son of a bitch (Warburg, not Hellbaum) had somehow hacked his way on to WHOM and now my security, as well as that of the system, was violated. Because he was there that night and he knew all about it. Warburg took the hands and I took the feet. She was naked except for a blanket that was in the trunk of Warburg's car, and when we swung her, the blanket slid off and fell to the ground. By now, the turtles are eating Ellen Axaxas, and nobody is supposed to know it, except Warburg, who is an accessory himself. Of all the stupid places to bump into a man you never wanted to see again, a computer system.

So I just sat there. I sat in front of the screen, looking at the message from Hellbaum and trying to think of a reply that wouldn't incriminate me further, something on the lines of the Fifth Amendment, only digital. From time to time, the green letters twitched and blinked on the screen, as if they were getting ready for something, some new and terrible surprise.

At 4.00 pm, there were still only three paper cups in front of me, each containing a cold inch of opaque coffee, but now the coffee had developed floating oily islands of some obscure White House mineral deposit, an allotrope of non-dairy whitener. The sun no longer shone directly on the blind and the light which passed through it was not so yellow as previously. Beyond the blind, on the sloping lawns, men and dogs were casting lankier shadows. The terminal beeped again, forcing me to look up. The green letters drained away to some remote region of electronic memory, and more letters seeped in. The screen refreshed itself.

To: Alb Telemann
From: Ernest Hellbaum
Subject: Incident Report

Thank you for your bug report of # inst. This is being looked into, and we hope to have a resolution for you in the immediate / near / indeterminate future.
(DELETE AS APPLICABLE.)

P.S. Thank you very much for the bug. I haven't had such

an interesting problem for a long time. Could you answer the P.P.S. of my last note, please, about the exact words in which intruding message was couched? This could be useful. Also, are you sure it was USER????? with five queries? I am beginning to suspect a hole in the operating system, and in this case, a query more or less might be germane. Thank you again. Ernest H.

It looks as if Hellbaum, under the influence of blue capsules, analyzed dreams and a really interesting problem at last, is beginning to regain some of his zest for life. Damn it. I still could not pass on the message because, even though it was not significant in itself, it nevertheless would take some explaining, and explaining is an expensive hobby, one I cannot afford at this time. Even when I start to imagine an explanation, I feel like my soul is a wet rag that someone is wringing out. I feel really bad about everything. Poor Ellen, the woman may have been sloppy about the home, but she was still a Saint. There is something very wrong with a world in which she gets eaten by turtles and Warburg gets to live the life of an affluent pimp in Hillingdon Village.

To:	Ernest Hellbaum
From:	Alb Telemann
Subject:	Incident Report

Thanks for your interest. I'm afraid I cannot remember the exact words of the message. It was just some nonsense, have a nice day or some such. In reply to your question, the number of queries is six, like so: USER????? I'm sorry if I misled you about this.

But Hellbaum didn't reply to this right away. The memo I found in my electronic mailbox five minutes later was not from him.

To: Alb Telemann
From: USER?????
Subject: ??????????

POEM

by warburg

I remember I remember
a little honey blonde
we took her to Virginia
and threw her in the pond

I remember I remember
you use to walk the streets
and follow her to home at nights
upon your little feets

I remember I remember
how we found her in the john
curled up with your automatic
naked, with nothing on

You knew it was going to happen
1 hour before You said you knew,
I remember what you were doing when you told me,
Do you remember 2?

Alternative last line:

And ROSE remembers 2.

Dear Alb, sorry 4 keeping you in suspense all this pm man.
I've been penning this a4mentioned prosody. I hope you
like. it took me 3 hours, I guess it was harder knowing
what to send than WHOM. Don't go home 2 early tonight
alb, Im hoping I may get to visit with U. Strictly on a
digital basis, U understand.
WARBURG

I have to admit (bitterly) that Warburg has style. Well, he has *a*
style, anyway, which is halfway there. Of course, I'd guessed by
now that he wanted money, and was just wishing he'd get on
with it and tell me how much to send and how to send it. I
thought probably he had some special electronic way of debiting

my MasterCharge account. There is no doubt that, in addition to his other talents, he is some kind of computer whizzkid, one of the new generation of super-hackers we are all being warned about. In that case, it seemed to me terribly unfair that he should stoop to blackmail his friends, when he could probably rip off every finance company in the country. Besides, does Warburg really need money that much? He has his automobile business, and the pimping must be highly profitable. Rose is pure black gold, and Warburg is probably sitting on a fortune. OK, OK, *Rose* is sitting on a fortune. The point is that Warburg gets to spend it.

ROSE. It was strange to read that name in Warburg's loyal capitals so soon after abjuring Hillingdon Village forever. I have this thing about nostalgia. Things always look better to me when I'm looking back at them. Even the worry and the fear seem somehow innocent – if you try hard enough, you can actually find yourself missing the itch of earwig bites. So for a moment, I was lost in a reminiscent haze, thinking about the good old days when I used to follow Ellen Axaxas to home at nights upon my little feets, those evenings of leaves and rattling nightbirds. Only for a moment, however.

To:	USER???????
From:	Alb Telemann
Subject:	Incident Report

Warburg, what do you want, you bastard? You know I didn't do it.

To:	Alb Telemann
From:	Ernest Hellbaum
Subject:	Incident Report

Thank you for your bug report of # inst. This is being looked into, and we hope to have a resolution for you in the immediate / near / indeterminate future.
(DELETE AS APPLICABLE.)

P.S. We have an interesting new development in your bug. There appears to be a message addressed to USER???????, like so with seven queries in the electronic mailbox. Did you send this? The operating system cannot direct it because receiving ID is not registered with the master logger. Number of queries is causing great confusion. In your last report, you said six but wrote five, thus: ?????? I wish you people would realize that exact numbers are important to us people. It may be only a query, but there's a whole algorithm resting on it. Sincerely, E. Hellbaum

I continued to sit on my ergonomic chair after 5.30 pm, when the security guards and dogs had been changed for more security guards and dogs with post-five o'clock shadows that were longer and more intimidating. Fred Zolph must have been working late, too; he wrote me to say that the strange behavior of Warren Pike appeared to be due to the spiritual advice he was getting from Jimmy Ruggins, which I knew already. For once, I know a lot more than Fred Zolph about the reasons for Pike's strange behavior.

I wished Warburg were present, either in person or in the electronic sense, despite the fact that Warburg clearly had every intention of blackmailing me. Do you understand that? I really needed Warburg, because he was the only man who had shared that experience with me. Warburg and Warburg alone had been holding the other end of Ellen Axaxas (the hands) when the blanket slid quietly to the ground. It was only Warburg who knew what I was suffering and therefore only Warburg who could get close enough to the part that was hurting to put calamine lotion on it. Part of me still clung to the irrational hope that when Warburg finally turned up he would be bearing calamine lotion, irrational because Warburg was obviously a son of a bitch who would do anything for money, except help someone. Outside the office it was not yet dark; it would not be dark for another hour and yet, because the blind was not drawn, a little premature darkness was already seeping into the office. I got up to switch on the fluorescent light, and suddenly it was very dark indeed. In Hillingdon Village it was beginning to smell of night flowers and matured daylight. Soon, that nightbird I used to hear would probably shake itself and begin to rattle again, as it had done when I was following Ellen, when I stood under the dogwood tree in her front yard waiting for her and she gave me the shock of my life with that unexpected and saintly kiss. (It was only the shock of my life so far, of course. Since then, there have been others.) Insects, many of them poisonous, would be rising above the lake in Virginia like a mist.

I was staring at the green letters of Fred Zolph's memo, which I had not even bothered to erase from my screen. (Working late, Telemann? You must be real busy. Yes, sir, I am, I have a lot of data to catch up on. Well, keep up the good work.) They weren't actually twitching and blinking, it was just my overwrought imagination which was doing it. Suddenly, the letters faded, and the screen went blank. The word:

Alb

appeared in the middle of it, in eyeball letters, each letter being made up hundreds of smaller letters.

Alb

it said, and disappeared. Then it came back again.

Alb is that you?

I watched the letters flashing off and on.

Alb is that you? This is yr good friend warburg. Press F1 to get into talk mode over

I pressed the F1 key, and the screen cleared again. I typed rapidly.

Warburg what the hell do you think you're trying to do

I then sat staring dully at the screen. Nothing happened. After a couple of minutes, I typed a query at the end of the sentence. Then it disappeared, and another message took its place.

You press F1 to SEND the message 2, you asshole

Now I was in possession of this vital detail, I got into communication mode right away.

WHOM

What do you want Warburg, just tell me and get it over with

Alb Don't you like my shithot comms system??? Hey ALB?? You understand man you are not in WHOM anymore, this is a parasite operating system that lives inside it, that is Y you don't have to do that To: ALB from: WBG stuff any more, see. EYES, what kind of a password is that 4 an intelligent security man, hey? Also, this Ernest Hellbaum man who keeps writing 2 you knows nothing about computers. Some kind of system manager, ha ha. The point is that the number of queries is entirely irrelevant because the hole in the operating system is of VARIABLE SIZE! Takes M big, takes M small. Oh that reminds me, Rose sends her regards.

I dont know how youre doing this Warburg and I dont care. Just tell me what you want

Alb, you have no soul. An I wrote a poem 4 you, it took 3 hours, an you didn't know I had even been to Hi school. You remember you remember Alb because I was there 2 that Ellen Axes was a good woman an a Bible believing Christian an you deceased her. There was no doubt about it man otherwise I would never have agreed to throw her in the lake. Warburg has some scruples

Stop showing off Warburg, and tell me what you do want

Little help with my overdraft. earnings supplement 4 poor Rose, you know how hard she works. Also I want a new modem and some extra chips owing to my computer is not big enough 4 my brain

I know why you call it a parasite system, Warburg. I'll bet you don't even have an overdraft, anyway

Neither have you, Alb. I know exactly what you have and an overdraft is not it. Do you remember Alb how we found her in the john, curled up with yr automatic, naked with nothing on. You couldnt have gone through with it if it wasnt 4 me Alb, she wd still be lying there bleeding on the carpet tiles which was not a pretty sight 4 my young eyes Alb

*

162

It is late now. Eventually, Warburg withdrew from the hole in the operating system, leaving me alone with the jagged edges, that is, with the following message displayed on my screen:

E0E4C3B1 00A580A4 B4D3A380 C0B04020 D1B36080 E0E0E0A0
D9E10000 C4B4D280 E0E4C3B1 00A580A4 B4D3A381 80402080
80402080 C4B4D280 D1B36080 E0E0E0A0 D9E10000 00A580A4
B4D3A38 A00ọk, Alb

                                    you can have 7 daze I have every
confidence
            in U
00000000000000000000000000000000000000000000000000000

I don't know if the variable sized hole in the operating system will close itself. That is Warburg's problem, after all, not mine. My problem is to get hold of $20,000 and make sure my wife doesn't find out about it. I am less worried about being blackmailed than I might have expected to be, partly because Warburg has cleverly kept his demand down to a sum I can afford without resorting to extreme and suspicious measures, partly because I am not quite ready yet to be worried about blackmail, having been worried about so many other things recently. I am suffering from anxiety lag. It is difficult to worry about everything.

Datastream 5; Fane, Robert

'Hey wake up, Roberto,' Ravidan says in the Youth Hostel. 'You go to the Department of Strangers, get nice job, pay me money. You owe me forty-five riba, not including girl.'

'Girl?' I ask, thinking vaguely of Susan and the imaginary Sandra.

'Whore you not screw at brothel.'

'But I didn't screw her.'

'Is your choice, man. You could screw her if you wanted to. Now you get nice job at Department of Strangers to pay for not screwing her.'

'Anyway, I don't owe you anything. You left me to do the paying.'

'Yes, and you not pay, right? Run away like irresponsible bastard. Therefore you still owe for whore.'

We have coffee at the Café Européen, then go to the Hotel Folio so I can get my photograph taken in an automatic booth, but nothing comes out of the machine. I go to fetch the manager, while Ravidan hides in a corner of the lobby because this is his on-duty morning in the kitchen and he doesn't want his employer to notice he is not at work. The manager opens the machine with a key like that of a dungeon, and extracts a strip of four technicolour smudges which he proudly hands over. Ravidan emerges from his corner as soon as the manager has gone.

'Is colour, anyway,' Ravidan says.

'So what? They won't accept a photograph without any features. Look, I haven't even got a nose.'

'Why not? Is still picture of you, even without nose. Also, is war on.'

And Ravidan is right. Hossip Maria, the wise bearded Christian official at the Department gazes at the photograph, then flicks thoughtfully through the epic visa. If he notices that I am a system support manager, a woman and an alleged prostitute, he shows no interest. He frowns at nothing in particular, to point out the gravity of what he is about to do, and then produces my immigration papers. Filling these in is an imaginative exercise for him, rather like school creative writing practice. Every now and then he stops and stares at me, sucking the end of his pen. Then he turns back to the paper and continues writing his long paragraphs of jagged Lazari script. When this is over, he makes basil tea and Ravidan begins to negotiate with him about the job. The conversation takes place in very rapid Lazari, with a great deal of raising of eyebrows and shrugging of shoulders. After all, it is Hossip Maria who wants my services, and Carlos and Ravidan who want my salary for the foreseeable future, so my own opinions are irrelevant. After the third cup, Hossip Maria and Ravidan embrace each other and weep. Then they both laugh and pat me on the back, and Hossip Maria puts his stove on for more tea. While this is brewing, Ravidan tells me what they have agreed.

The main problem is language. Hossip Maria speaks no English and I speak no Lazari. There are no other employees to translate for us. The big point in my favour, on the other hand, is my piety; Ravidan has explained in vivid detail how I go to Mass every morning, tell beads in my lunch hour and refrain from sex on Sundays.

I last set foot in a church in 1976, and consider myself a freethinking Buddhist. I will give myself away after the first five minutes. However, Ravidan is convinced it will be all right as long as I don't learn any Lazari. I have been appointed the new UK assistant; my job is to screen all British and American applicants for immigration papers. Those that I accept will be placed in a YES tray (marked with a squiggle the shape of a frying pan), those that I refuse in a NO tray, whose squiggle is more like the tail of a pig. Then Hossip Maria will write his essays on the ones who have been accepted. Any journalists entering the country have to apply for a resident's permit, as must all foreign residents whose permits have been issued by Shamanist officials. President Miraz is concerned to prevent foreigners from leaving Lazar in large numbers, because this would be bad for the country's image. People who wish to leave the country must first produce their residents' permits to prove they had been entitled to stay there, and then give a valid reason for wishing to leave. There is a backlog of applications from people who are entitled neither to stay nor to leave. For this reason, the office is open only occasionally at arbitrarily-chosen times, so that the staff will not have to deal with embarrassing personal appeals.

Hossip Maria, in token of his good faith, and with tears still in his eyes, has advanced me thirty riba, of which Ravidan has left me ten for lunch. Now that Ravidan has departed, with more tears and handshakes, I sit down at Hossip Maria's desk.

In the course of the day, I have tried every biro in the top drawer of the desk; some went blobby, but most were unable to write at all after a line or two. Finally, I chose the antique dip pen and alchemical inkpot belonging to Hossip Maria. The forms are difficult to understand because the questions are in Lazari and the answers in English. The questions are not the same on every form, and I wasted the first hour trying to work out the rationale which determines who receives which version of the form. I have spent the rest of the time trying to visualize the people who wrote the replies: small conformist block capitals (au pair), a hand that consists almost entirely of one horizontal line, with minimal gestures in the direction of pothooks and hangers (journalist) etc. Then there is guess-the-question-from-the-answer. What, for example, has inspired this response? *No, I don't, and I resent that question.*

Hint: it is the same question that provoked someone else to write, *Once, at approx age fifteen. I do not remember the circumstances.* Most of the time, though, I have been bored. I don't really have to do anything, but I retain enough work ethic underneath the Buddhism to make me feel guilty and uncomfortable. I am not only clock-watching but clock-listening as well, counting the thousands of heavy ticks until 5.30 pm. I try to compose Zen rags in my head, find that I have lost the knack, hum the old ones to myself, remember Susan Gray (Brideshead) and feel more uncomfortable still. To reduce the discomfort to manageable proportions, I imitate Hossip Maria on the other side of the room, who is staring at a crack in the wall and moving his lips in a Lazarene mantra. There is serenity. Hossip Maria's spiritual ancestors probably stood on top of pillars in deserts in Asia Minor – they were not, of course, his corporeal ancestors, being too holy for procreation.

Hossip Maria rouses himself at about 4.00 pm when the YES or frying pan tray is becoming full. He approaches my (his) desk from the other side with his chair in his hand, and begins to write essays. Deprived of the dip pen, I am forced to shuffle papers. Hossip Maria writes these essays much more slowly than his character study of me, because in this case there is no Ravidan to keep him up to the task. I watch his hand moving backwards across the paper; a fly is moving in similar patterns on a picture of St Fleur (the original one) behind his head. At this moment (4.12 pm by the official clock), my eyes fall to one of the papers on his desk. I read the following name: Sandra Elizabeth Castelvetro.

I don't care that Sainte-Fleur is in a state of crisis; all I know is that I am in a state of terminal lust. Ravidan doesn't know of another brothel apart from the one where men in white suits are keeping their knives sharp for me. Carlos, who has plenty of women, is not as generous with them as he is with wine. Both of them are puzzled by this sudden change in my personality. I am flailing on the top bunk, punching the pillow and shouting 'I HAVE TO GET LAID', while Carlos hesitates in the doorway (Ravidan, bottom bunk, has told him to get a fire extinguisher).

'When can screw, don't,' Ravidan says, 'when don't screw, can.'

'I DIDN'T HAVE A PASSPORT THEN.'

'When do screw, can't,' Ravidan continues.

'Is dark everywhere, man,' Carlos says.

'FUCK THE CURFEW!' Ravidan is shocked; I am not usually like this.

'Usually good boy,' Ravidan says appeasingly, 'work hard, sleep early, cold showers.'

'GET STUFFED!' I punch the pillow off the bed, and Ravidan picks it up with a reproachful look and puts it back. Carlos in the doorway shrugs. Fuck the curfew.

Café Européen, closed and darkened. Hotel Folio bar, closed to non-residents. Carlos on the right arm, Ravidan on the left, they are leading me round the darkened streets, as if I were drunk. I feel as if I were, and several times they have to stop me from shouting out obscenities.

'You get arrested, man,' Carlos whispers, 'cut everything off with breadknife.'

It's pointless to search for women in the circumstances, so I suspect Carlos and Ravidan are really looking for a bottle of Loup de Mer, in the hope that this will put me to sleep. First, they have to find somewhere that doesn't acknowledge the authority of the President over Lazari alcohol consumption. Bar Sport, closed. Bougainvilea, closed. Le Public, closed. I stagger, Carlos and Ravidan creep.

Presently, we come to a small crossroads, where a narrow alley runs across the road. To the left, a lamp hangs over the alley, suspended between the houses on either side. I see the colourless shapes of flowers in big tubs beside the walls. I sniff the air, and detect the earthy scent of geranium leaves.

'Let's go down there,' I say.

'You don't want to go there, man,' Carlos says. 'Is Full Moon Street.'

'We could get a drink there, Carlos.'

'Carlos very bourgeois, I think,' Ravidan says. 'What's matter, Carlos? We might find girls.'

'I don't want girls. Want sleep. Anyway, there is no girls there.'

I listen; music from the direction of the geranium tubs, a buzzing stringed instrument, not a banjo but something more Eastern, older (veils, sequins, torchlight). I look, and see other lights further back in the alley, higher up the walls, bedrooms. The alley is narrower at the top than on the ground, like a drawing of a medieval village.

'Is nothing, man. Is no bar, no brothel, nothing.' Carlos says.

'Music,' I say, 'I think I can hear music.' I sniff again, trying to smell it. An Eastern spice of some kind, something Biblical, like cumin; fresh mint leaves; something resembling hot yoghurt; the rich, slightly nauseating smell of imported Turkish cigarettes; sweet black coffee. Finally, there is something overlaying or underlying all the others, in the thread of the air itself. It is a warm nectar smell, of the same order of being as honeysuckle. Carlos and Ravidan lead me trembling down the alley towards the East.

The leaning walls are crusted with dark, intricate leaves, so thickly that birds and small animals make their nests under the surface; tiny clawlike white flowers look out and exude. The growth has the look of a creature that is keeping still on purpose, holding its breath, waiting for the chance to move. Through the window, the bar looks like most of the others I have seen in Sainte-Fleur. Small round formica-topped tables and tattered canvas chairs, Lazari men in groups of two or three, drinking coffee. There are one or two differences, however. There is no bar visible, for one thing, and nobody is drinking wine or beer. All the occupants are wearing traditional robes. They are young, most of them less than thirty. They have nothing to say to each other, but stare into their coffee cups in silence, intent possibly on the music, which is coming from somewhere in the depths of the building.

'Should we go in?' I whisper.

'We are come here, don't we?' Ravidan says.

We do not move. The room is unnerving, its solemn coffee drinkers, its coils of cigarette smoke, its faltering, long-legged insects.

'Why don't we go home?' I say. 'We don't belong here.'

'You not belong anywhere on Lazar,' Ravidan says.

'Very gloomy religious bastards,' Carlos adds, 'too much coffee, no beer, no girls.'

Robed young men are arriving through a bead curtain at the far side of the room. The waiter moves among the tables, carrying coffee.

'We go now?' Ravidan says.

'Wait a bit, there's someone coming.' All the coffee drinkers are now staring at the curtain. The figure of a man is moving towards us through the striations, a shadow interspersed with beads, red yellow green red yellow green, like a crystalline structure forming on a watchglass.

'Shit man,' Carlos says, 'is Scorpion.'

We run. Our route takes us through alleyways full of open, spice-smelling dustbins, where scavenging animals, a lame dog, several cats, a couple of sinister white herring gulls, look suspiciously at us and at each other. Carlos leads, we attempt to keep up with him. Even when we reach the curfew zone again, Carlos does not slow down. He seems able to see the cobblestones in the dark.

Carlos is white and shaking when we arrive at the Youth Hostel.

'We keep from those bastards from now,' he says. 'If you want to be murdered, go to brothel and be murdered by nice harmless beater, OK? At least is not religious.'

Next day, Sandra Castelvetro phones the Department to find how her application for an exit visa is getting on. I take the call, breathing deeply in an attempt to make my heart beat more quietly.

'I'm afraid we can't find your application, Miss Castelvetro. There *is* a war on, you know, and we're extremely short-staffed. My advice would be to apply again. Naturally, we're very sorry for the inconvenience, but these are troubled times.'

'You bloody bureaucratic bastard.'

'I'm only doing my job.'

'Listen. What guarantee have I got that if I do another one, you won't go and lose that as well?'

'I'll deal with it personally. You have my word of honour.' I look at Hossip Maria, who is contemplating the Blessed Virgin. His eyes are without curiosity. 'Why don't we meet for lunch?' I ask, 'Café Européen, one o'clock. I'll bring the form and you can fill it in there and then.'

After a long and thoughtful pause, she says, 'How will I know you?'

'Don't worry, I'll know you.'

'How?'

'It's my business to know people,' I tell her mysteriously.

She is small and sturdy, with limp blonde hair, and acts warily when I order snapper.

'It's fish,' I explain, 'you get it all over the Mediterranean. I don't know what it looks like before it's cooked, though.'

'Oh, I like anything,' she says mournfully, 'I mean I like any fish. Even fish I haven't tasted. Oh God, I wish I could get out of this country.'

I pour her some wine, and she drinks her glass down in one, as if she hasn't tasted wine for a long time.

'Everything tastes like fish here, even the bloody wine tastes like fish.'

'It's an island,' I say.

'Britain's an island.' I cannot think of a reply to this. 'It's the terrible feeling of being in limbo,' she continues. 'I want my death to be reported in the papers.'

'We're not dead yet.'

Something chips a big flake of wood out of the table in front of my wine glass. The table does a little scuttling jump, shaking the plates and cutlery and knocking the bottle over. Loup de Mer spreads like an estuary. Confused cries spring up.

'Who did that?' I feel offended.

'Get down, you stupid sod!' Sandra replies. 'They're shooting at us!'

The guns cough remotely in the marketplace. The breaking glass and china, the thud of falling tables, clang of cutlery and gabble of Lazari prayers are all around. Sandra and I take refuge behind our own overturned table, although, as Sandra says, it won't save us from bullets. Thick pillars of smoke are rising from surrounding buildings; a window explodes in one of them. A man behind the next table has been hit in the hand. He curses bitterly under his breath as if he has hit himself with a hammer, which is exactly what the blow sounded like. Then he gets up shakily, in full view of the snipers across the road, and walks into the Café, to put something on the wound.

I hope the damp patch on my trousers is only the spilled wine, which is making the air brackish and stomach-turning. I study the grain of the wood on the underside of the table top; I am becoming expert in its cracks and knot-holes. Then we try to guess where the bullets are coming from and how close the snipers are. I claim they are getting further away, because the interval between flashes and bangs is getting longer, as with thunderstorms, but Sandra refuses to see the connexion. We cry for a while, quietly and companionably. After an hour, we are bored. We begin singing. Apart from my Zen rags, which have no words, I know only the beginnings of Bob Dylan songs.

I tell her some highlights from my life, omitting the passport, but including Susan Gray and the brothel. 'There are two men there who want to kill me,' I say.

'Why single them out? There are men all round us who want to kill you.'

I tell her that last night I defied the curfew and went to what was probably Full Moon Street, where I saw a man who was

171

probably the Scorpion probably planning all this. I do not explain what I was doing there.

When the shooting stops, it is nearly dark. Across the road, a thick cloud of smoke is rolling ponderously away. Sandra doesn't want food, or wine, or sleep now; she wants to get laid, and tells me so.

'I mean this is ridiculous, Robert,' she says. 'I suppose I shouldn't be talking like this, but, fuck it, we've nearly been killed together, haven't we?'

She changed her mind four times on the way back to the Youth Hostel, and changed it again when she saw where I was taking her. Now, in the entrance hall, half a dozen disconsolate young men are sitting on the floor staring in front of them or pretending to tighten their rucksack straps. Ever since I first arrived at the Sacred Heart, there have always been half a dozen disconsolate young men waiting for something on the floor of the entrance hall, but I'm not sure whether they are always the same ones, so cannot tell whether it has happened yet. There is no one in the caretaker's hut just inside the entrance, so I pull Sandra inside and kiss her aggressively, so that our front teeth clash and both of us feel bruised and shocked. Afterwards, Sandra touches her right temple with the tips of her fingers as if contemplating a migraine and giggles anxiously.

'You ought to know,' she says, 'I never intended to do this. Sex is bad for women, it's been proved.' Perhaps she is thinking that the last time she did it, she lost her passport.

Sandra waits outside in the corridor, pretending to be interested in the small piece of flame-lit skyline visible through the window. I fling open the door of my room and accost Ravidan, who is lying on the bottom bunk watching the mating dance of the flies in the middle of the room. 'Ravidan, you owe me a screw,' I say.

'I not screw boys. Also, you are ugly foreigner.'

'I don't want to screw you. It's a girl.'

'Is pretty?'

'I want you out of the room, just for an hour or two. You owe it to me, Ravidan, after that day at the brothel.'

'Was your turn to pay.'

'How could it have been my turn? We only went once.'

'So? Is your fault. If you pay nicely, we have gone every day.'

'I hadn't got any money.'

'Why you go to brothel if you not have money? Every day, every day,' Ravidan says, making faces at the flies. 'Complain, complain. You are an old woman, Roberto. You want to relax, have fun. Enjoy. Life is for living, you know.'

'I'm trying, Ravidan, that's why I want you to get out.'

'Get out? Where I go? Is fucking war on, you know, man. You want me get shot by Scorpion? Is not changing guards at Buckingham Palace, is proper Lazari war.'

'Go and stay with Carlos.'

'He probably got girl, too. You not the only man who fuck women. Carlos screw arse off twice every day, also after meals. Only Ravidan not screwing girl. You get stuffed, baby, I watching television.' He turns back to the flies, depressed.

'What's the matter, Ravidan?' I ask.

'Scorpion win fucking war, is what,' Ravidan says. 'No fucking, no brothels, no wine. I got to go, man.'

'It'll be all right. Wait a couple of years, and there'll be another war. Ravidan, this woman I've got.'

'What woman?'

'Her name is Sandra Castelvetro.'

Ravidan sits up and swings his legs over the bed.

'Roberto, you are fucking genius! You are fucking crazy, is what you are!' He laughs.

'Anyway, even if you don't owe me a screw, at least you owe me a favour.' The two flies Ravidan has been watching in the centre of the room now deviate a couple of feet and begin chasing each other around his head.

'We give you favour already. Passport is favour. We not know you want to screw it. Fucking flies crazy. Everybody fucking but Ravidan. Even fucking Scorpion fucking.'

'Wouldn't I do the same for you?' I say.

'How can you do same for me, man? I not fucking nobody. Do same for fucking flies. Why not we both go out and let flies have good time?' He is in a better mood now. 'She look nice,' he says, opening the door.

Sandra is still pretending interest in the Sainte-Fleur skyline, when Ravidan sidles barefoot into the corridor and calls to her,

'Hey, Roberto's girlfriend, I leave you now in nice room, you make passionate love with Roberto, yes, and not mind the flies, okay?'

'Flies.'

'Flies, yes, and afterwards you tell me all about Roberto, whether fuck nicely, has good body.'

'I think this is a mistake,' Sandra says, as I shut the door behind us, excluding Ravidan, who shrugs and sniffs as the door closes.

'No,' I say, gently, but putting as much urgency as I can into it. 'No, not a mistake. You were meant to come here.' I hang an arm carefully round her shoulders, and she looks at it as if it were a boa constrictor.

An imperfect moon stands outside the window of the room, and by its light I watch the woman in the bunk. She is underneath me, but not immediately so, since I moved back to the top bunk as soon as we had finished, realizing that she needed sleep and that both of us needed to be out of range of each others' elbows. She is asleep now, with the sheet pulled round her waist like a peasant skirt, and I am hanging over the edge of Ravidan's bunk, staring at her and thinking that one can tell that human beings came out of the sea. It may be the mermaid illusion caused by the sheet, or the moonlight, or the lingering smell of Loup de Mer, but I have a strong feeling that Sandra is really some kind of fish, smooth-skinned, glistening, breathing in a wave-rhythm. I can see my passport jutting out of the side pocket of my rucksack underneath the window. Why do I have this suicidal urge to lose my identity? Why am I sleeping with disaster?

Datastream 3; Prunewood, Kate

This morning, there is no man to interview me, whether wretched and Shamanist or urbane and Christian. Instead, there is a constant noise of jets booming overhead, and the vast and mournful apparition of the Matron in the room. The Shamanist army, the largest ever known in history, is only five hours' march away from the city. Their leader is a man called Tuli, a great general and widely believed to be the Antichrist from the Book of Revelation. The Government army has suffered a terrible defeat in the mountains; not a single man is left alive. There is no hope for Christian Lazar, and therefore, as St Paul promised, the world is about to end. The Matron is very moved, and breaks into muttered Lazari prayers and imprecations every now and then. When I ask her if she will be saved when the great Day comes, she shudders and crosses herself several times. I take all this with a pinch of salt, perhaps because it is impossible to take anything seriously against the background of theatrical wailing that has arisen in all parts of the hospital simultaneously.

I am beginning to feel hungry. It is now after 1.00 pm, and no fish in yoghurt or lamb and beans has appeared, so I leave my room and walk hopefully up and down in the passage. The wailing from invisible patients, nurses and doctors makes me feel that I am in a haunted house; in fact, as I pace about in my black nightdress, I wonder if it is haunted by me. The Matron is kneeling before an ornate crucifix in her office with the door open. I would be embarrassed to disturb her at prayer simply to ask for lunch, so instead I ask her what is going on and what I should do now.

'Do? Pray, like all Christians. Antichrist is now only one hour distant.'

Somehow, I am still not frightened of this Antichrist, who appears to be moving faster than time.

'I want to go.' I hadn't realized until now that this was true.

'Where go? Antichrist is coming. End of world at hand.'

'I thought I might go to the British Embassy. I know the Ambassador is dead, but there must be other officials there who will help me.'

'Antichrist will kill them. Antichrist killing everyone.'

'The Antichrist is not allowed to kill Embassy officials,' I explain, 'they have diplomatic immunity.'

'No? Then why Ambassador dead?'

'You mean he didn't just die? Somebody killed him?'

'Certainly. Antichrist killed him in rocket attack.'

'This Antichrist has powers I wouldn't have believed,' I say. 'How could he have killed the British Ambassador in Sainte-Fleur if he was busy defeating the government troops in the hills?'

'Antichrist is everywhere,' Matron replies, 'therefore no sense go anywhere.'

'But if you really think the end of the world is at hand, it won't make very much difference to you whether I stay or leave.'

'No,' Matron says, 'staying and leaving is same thing.'

I ask for my clothes, which, it turns out, have not been retrieved from the plane. Oh my God. I've just remembered what I was doing when the plane exploded. I am blushing suddenly, but the Matron, if she knows the story, has sins of her own to worry about. She offers me some of her own clothes (she is beyond such worldly vanities now), on condition that I go away and leave her to await the rapture in peace. There is something like the re-entry window used by astronauts, and if the Matron misses it, she may never get another chance. Any interruption to her prayers could be the fatal lapse which prevents her getting away in time (or from time).

Back in my room, I don't attempt to put on the thick and complicated undergarments, with their many straps, hooks, buttons and other projections, or the shoes which are far too big for me, but I feel reasonably secure and respectable in a voluminous dress (black, of course) and a headscarf. I might pass for a Lazarene woman at a pinch, though I have no way of knowing whether this is a safe thing to look like or not.

I leave the hospital at about 2.00 pm and set off on the Sainte-Fleur road, trying to think myself into the role of a peasant woman going to the market. The road burns my bare feet and the dress pulls me downwards, smothers me and trips me up, but I no longer care about comfort. What can happen to me that hasn't already happened?

I walk to Sainte-Fleur along the empty road. There is no sign of the Antichrist's army as yet. My greatest danger appears to come from the government planes, which shoot backwards and forwards above my head with great determination, as if trying to prove a point. They are solitary, like crows; there is seldom more than one in the sky at a time, and on the rare occasions when two of them share the same airspace, they ignore each other. They pass in different directions, crisscrossing the sky in an air display of panic, using the sonic boom as a substitute for gunfire. I wonder when I will come across the war itself, gunfire, blood, flames, corpses.

I am sitting with Andy, a photographer, on the balcony of the Hotel Folio bar. I am wearing a pastel T-shirt and jeans belonging to Andy's colleague Polly from the *Sun*, eating an orange, doodling on a thick pad of ruled A4 paper, watching the Mediterranean, light blue and dark blue. The noise of gunfire in the streets is almost festive, like fireworks, and if I turn my head to the right, I can see an occasional small flash, and the almost transparent flame of buildings burning in strong sunlight.

'Don't give your story to that cow,' Andy says, 'I'll write it for you.'

'I can write it myself, if it comes to that,' I say, 'I'm not entirely ignorant of the media world, you know. I've been in religious broadcasting for more than 18 months.'

'You could play up the Paradise Lost angle. From Songs of Praise to Sainte-Fleur Airport. "My Night of Sin with Terrorist".'

'There was no sin involved, actually. We went through this last night.'

Last night, I went to the British Embassy, was shot at by a Security Guard because I was in native costume, returned to the lobby of the Hotel Folio, and bumped into Polly (who complimented me on my disguise and asked if I was there for the war, too).

'Not for it, exactly,' I said, 'more because of it.' I decided to sell my story to Polly, who promised to interview me, and even let me sleep on the floor of her hotel bedroom, where I lay awake for hours planning my article and listening to the small snorting sounds Polly made in her sleep. She is such a forceful character, she even sleeps with determination: 'I'll sleep on it,' she told me about the article, and last night I thought I could almost hear her considering the options in her dreams. By this morning, I am beginning to wonder how interested Polly really is. I rather like Andy, on the other hand. He is vulnerable and diffident, despite his James Dean looks and shirts with an extraordinary number of pockets in them. There was obviously something between the two of them once. I am glad to be back in the comforting world of sexual intrigue and thwarted passion, so familiar from university and the BBC, so different from the outraged male Puritanism of Lazaris, Shamanist or Lazarene. At the end of that long, drunken and confusing evening (last night), Andy actually asked me to come up to his room for coffee, but I refused, not because he hadn't got any, which we both knew, but because I am married. And there was no sin involved.

Now, on the balcony at the Hotel Folio, I argue that my marriage is valid (at least from my husband's point of view) because he believes it is. Since he believes that my consent was irrelevant, I have to respect his belief that I am married to him, even though I reserve the right to believe that I'm not. Andy believes that the marriage is invalid because I didn't consent to it and wasn't even present at the ceremony, and incidentally because the government has declared Shamanist marriages to be illegal. A marriage, he feels, is either a marriage or it isn't. Admittedly, I felt a bit like that when I was shut up in the baking first class cabin of a hijacked 747 with Jalal unbuttoning his shirt. Now, however, I have had time to think, in the hospital, during the long walk into town, and for many sleepless hours last night on the floor of Polly's room.

Polly turns up in time for lunch, flicking with a comb at stray wisps of her timid-looking hair and complaining about having been shot at. She is formal today – dark stockings and high heels in the middle of a civil war. Also she is hot and irritated. 'There's a bloody war going on out there,' she says.

'I thought they were only fighting in the dockyard area,' Andy says.

'Don't believe what you read in the papers. For Christ's sake, I was nearly shot three times. And blown up. They're throwing handgrenades, in the market would you believe.'

A small waiter with big glasses comes to clear away my orange peel and take our orders for drinks.

'I met an incredible man in the market,' Polly says. 'He used to be with the Scorpion, training in the mountains. That was last year, before the war got started properly. You wouldn't believe the things they used to do, weeks without sleep, starvation, one hundred mile hikes without water, regular floggings.'

'How do you know it was true?' Andy asks.

'He was a really incredible man,' Polly repeats. Andy twitches slightly and stares at my A4 pad with the doodles, figures of eight and unmathematical Venn diagrams. I wonder if Polly is really as promiscuous as Andy thinks she is. But surely not in the market with handgrenades going off and bullets flying, no matter how incredible her ex-terrorist was? On the other hand, Truth is relative, so that it is in a sense irrelevant whether Polly has been making love to her interviewee in the middle of the street fighting, so long as Andy thinks she has. It follows from this that President Miraz is right to claim that he is in excellent health (blood pressure one hundred and twenty over eighty-five, pulse sixty-five to seventy, push-ups, pull-ups, three miles of jogging), even though Polly, like every other journalist in the Hotel Folio, insists that he suffers from severe angina, insomnia, depression and a duodenal ulcer, and that he has had two heart attacks already. Apparently, some of the more extreme Shamanists maintain that the President has been dead since 1965. The same goes for defeats in the mountains, and whether or not they are throwing handgrenades in the marketplace – it all depends on your point of view. As for Polly and her ex-terrorist, who is to say where the truth lies? Perhaps she is jealous of my machinegun wedding to Jalal in the hijacked 747 and has imagined something equally dramatic for herself.

Polly is apologizing for being late. 'I went back with Carlos. He lives in the Sacred Heart Youth Hostel, really sleazy, you should see his mattress. I expect to have fleas at the very least. Still,' she sips her beer by way of a dramatic pause, 'I'm seeing the world. Last week I'd hardly been anywhere more exotic than Camden Town, and now look at me.' She is a junior foreign correspondent, sent out to cover the hijacking and delighted to find herself covering a major war instead.

I do look at her. Anybody would think she'd never been to bed with a man before, and as for that name . . .

'Is he really called Carlos?' I ask. 'A terrorist called Carlos?'

'Karl, Carlos, depends what mood he's in. He's a *former* terrorist.'

Pitiful. She is jealous of me, so she has developed an imaginary lover, a sort of hysterical terrorist. Who is, of course, entirely real from her point of view. Which is as valid as anybody else's. Including mine. But to think I thought she was sophisticated.

'I can believe it of him, though,' Polly insists. 'You should have seen his back. He had great long scars across it from the beatings. And I mean endurance . . . He was really something.'

'Incredible,' Andy says. I continue, self-consciously, to draw Venn diagrams on my A4 pad. I don't label them, but I imagine labels for each one. This is Kate and this is Polly and Andy, with just a little bit of overlap. And this one is Polly and the Imaginary Terrorist in the Sacred Heart Youth Hostel. The terrorist has scars on his back, like so.

Return of waiter. 'Do you like inkfish?' Polly says.

'Is it the same as squid?' I ask.

'No, I think it's better. More garlicky, if you see what I· mean.' I lean my head back to let the sun fall on my face, and pretend to think about inkfish. This heat is from the sun. Perhaps also some of it is from those burning buildings in the marketplace, with their beautiful translucent flames. 'Is that the marketplace we can see from here, with the flames?'

'No, I think that's the Cathedral.'

The Mediterranean is beautiful, a huge vista of it, light blue and dark blue. Here is me, and this is Hugh, and this is Jalal in the first class cabin of a 747 at Sainte-Fleur Airport. Just a little intersection, because it was over very quickly. This dotted one is Andy. 'Is that really the Cathedral? How awful. Only it looks so beautiful burning like that.'

'It's only nineteenth century, I believe, the original Templar one was burned down. I suppose this one will be too. The Templars always built round churches for some reason. Did you say which university you were at? I must say, you don't seem very jealous about my terrorist.'

'Well, I had one of my own, didn't I? And I was married to mine.'

'We are going to have a long talk about that,' Polly says, 'after the inkfish. My masters have empowered me to offer you £10,000 for the whole story, plus photographs taken by my dear friend Andy, so it will be inkfish first and ink afterwards if that's OK.'

'That's wonderful,' I say, 'because I have to tell you. I have to tell everybody. It's important to make people understand. I've been *involved*, if you know what I mean, and I don't think that's something that happens to many of us.'

'Us?' Andy asks.

'English people. Europeans.'

The inkfish is exactly the same as squid, small pink rubber rings on a plate of rice surrounded by lemon segments. 'It was a lot better than this in Earl's Court,' Polly says. 'It came in a sort of dark sauce made from the ink, and it was more – '

'Garlicky,' Andy says.

I eat the circles with enthusiasm, thinking this one is Polly and this is Andy, and this is Hugh, Jalal, me. You are what you eat. What a shame we're all so tough, though.

'What the hell makes you think you're married?' Andy asks again.

'You don't give up, do you? I told you last night, I don't think I'm married. My husband thinks I'm married, and all I'm saying is that he has a point.'

'But you still refer to him as your husband. Do you love him?'

'Listen,' Polly interrupts, 'we aren't ready to talk about this yet. Inkfish first.'

'Screw the inkfish. What I'm saying is, do you love him?' Andy says.

'It isn't a question of love,' I answer. 'It's a question of understanding.'

After lunch, exhausted by my walk yesterday and my sleepless night, I must have fallen asleep on the balcony despite the noise of gunfire. Now I am awake again, and in the presence of a splendidly dressed sunset. The Scorpion's offensive is apparently over for the day; at least, the gunfire has stopped. There are still a few flames twisting round the struts and beams of the nineteenth century

Templar Cathedral away to the right. Every now and then, one of these gives way with a decisive crack and falls with a more tentative noise into the ashes. As the sun gets dimmer, the Cathedral is getting brighter. There is a scared silence in the air.

Polly comes out on the balcony behind me. 'You're up, then,' she says, as if I had been in bed.

'Yes.'

'Only I'm sorry I had to leave you. You were dead to the world anyway, and you looked reasonably comfortable under the circumstances, so I thought you would be all right. We got called away in a hurry. A lot going on, you wouldn't believe it. Andy's out taking photographs of the town burning. Actually, it isn't burning all that much, but there's still enough fire to look good against the evening sky, that sort of thing. Do you feel up to being interviewed tonight? I don't want to push you, but tomorrow I'll really have to get down and start talking to the women who've been raped and so on, and I suppose we ought to get this story out while it's still topical. Actually, when you think about it, it's a bloody nuisance the war ending so quickly because now everyone will forget about the hijack. Thank God you're British, anyway, otherwise we wouldn't have a story at all.'

'Are you going to get me out of the country?'

'Well, of course I am. I told you I would, didn't I? Listen, why don't we have a drink? It might make you feel better, and then we can get on with the story. I really want to get the whole lot over with tonight so that tomorrow I can catch up with news. God, I wish there were two of me sometimes.'

'I thought I was news.' I clutch the balcony, watching the last drops of sun spill into the sea.

'No, of course you're not news, you're human interest.'

News has been made while I was asleep. The Scorpion is completely in charge of Sainte-Fleur. Discipline is good among the urban guerrillas and the expected looting and violence have not taken place. Lazarene citizens are lying low, adopting a wait and see posture. Rumours are spreading thick and fast through the deserted streets. Many believe that President Miraz will not give up the struggle so easily as he appears to have done, and that he is contemplating a deal with his former government colleague General Tuli, regarded by the more informed members of the Lazarene community as the acceptable face of Shamanism. Others claim that he has crowned a lifetime of clandestine activity by disappearing altogether. Tuli is now very close to the Sarrasine gate in the North-West of the city, leading an army of some 20,000 Lazarene and Shamanist troops with a tank and several APC's. Fresh from its victory in the mountains over Miraz's demoralized and reluctant warriors, Tuli's army is the most powerful force in Lazar.

Nobody wants the Scorpion, Polly claims, except the Russians. The Scorpion represents only a tiny minority of Lazar's large, highly educated and Westernized community. Shamanism is, after all, essentially a conservative religion, and it is therefore not surprising that the Scorpion is seen by most Lazaris as an undesirable influence. There is the legacy of British rule to consider, the Hotel Folio itself, the tourist industry, the Sainte-Fleur cricket club (one of the strongest in the Mediterranean).

Polly and I are sitting on the bed in Polly's room at the Hotel Folio, drinking gin from the bottle. Polly says this may be our last opportunity for some time, since no one knows how long the Scorpion will be in charge of the town, and he is bound to ban alcohol for the duration. There will be plenty of time for tonic later.

'The point is,' Polly says, 'you're making these hijackers sound too human, if you take my meaning. Of course, I don't mean they weren't human. It's just that in a newspaper article there isn't the room to spare for nice cosy touches. As far as my readers are concerned, they were just a bunch of Communist thugs. Full stop.'

'All I said was that Haq was frightened of the red headed stewardess,' I say. And then the gunfire starts again.

I wake in Polly's room at the Hotel Folio; the sun is shining in my eyes and a noise like enraged bees is seeping in through the door. I pick up the pen I dropped last night and consider the sentence I had been writing. 'Despite all that I have been through in the last few weeks, the one thing I have never lost sight of . . .' What was it? Also, what is that noise? It is a bright, irritating music that seems to be being played with comb and tissue paper but magnified 1,000 times. It is coming from inside the hotel somewhere, not from outside in the direction of the beach. I get up and stretch, noticing the headache that has been lurking at the back of my eyes, waiting for a chance to announce its presence.

WHOM

When I open the door, the music definitely gets louder. There is a voice in it somewhere, too. I look up and down the corridor, which is empty and has that surreptitious look characteristic of empty hotel corridors. The door of the room opposite is open; the bed is still unmade, and some towels are lying screwed up on the floor. It must be early, and the hotel staff haven't had time to clean up and make the beds. I remember the instrument now. It is called a khabkha, and it is like a banjo, though it sounds more like a kazoo at this distance. I go to the window.

On the balcony of the Hotel Folio, overlooking the Esplanade Touristique, the beach where mutilated corpses are occasionally washed up in oildrums, and the charred and still smoking remnants of the nineteenth century Lazarene Templar Cathedral, the Hotel Folio Khabkha Band is playing optimistic songs.

> Sun is shining
> I am a happy man,
> and you a happy woman,
> I am a happy man,
> Bird is singing,
> upon the happy trees,
> It must be happy too,
> So let be happy please
> Sun is shining,
> I am a happy man
> we got a happy life
> we got a happiness plan

I take the key from the wall and lock the bedroom behind me. I have to go downstairs if only to find out what time it is. I take with me the dozen or so A4 pages I wrote before falling asleep. When Polly excused herself and set off for the gate to get the story, I felt quite relieved. Clearly I was not going to get the article I wanted by collaborating with a professional. Polly insisted that, for news purposes, Jalal must have raped me, and wanted the hijackers' dialogue to consist of nothing but 'Get down!', 'We shoot', and other terse interjections. Alone, I could write the article Jalal deserved. I wish I could remember what it was I never lost sight of . . . well, never mind. The music is beginning to get on my nerves.

184

If it were not for the noise of the Hotel Folio Khabkha Band
twanging optimistically in the background, I could believe myself
in an empty building. Most of the bedroom doors are open, and
clothes and suitcases lying around suggest that people have left in
a hurry. In one room, a window is open, and a small, finch-like bird
has got in. It is slamming itself against the other, closed windows
in fury, but I am too timid to rescue it, feeling somehow averse
to going into someone else's room, even if they aren't there any
more to resent it. As I wind my way through the corridors to the
staircase, unwilling to use the lift during a national emergency,
the khabkha band plays:

> Is a great day coming,
> Is a golden day,
> We got a saviour coming
> he is on his way.
> We got happy sunshine,
> good for you and me.
> In the ultraviolet
> we cook endlessly.

'Thank you ladies and gentlemen,' a voice says from the bottom of
the stairs. 'Thank you, thank you, that was Ultraviolet Khabkhaba,
and you know this is a great day because we really do having a
saviour come. Thank you thank you.'

Who is he thanking, and for what? There is no sound of applause.
And besides, who is the saviour he was singing about? Jesus? The
Scorpion? General Tuli?

There is no audience. The band is five men in white dinner
jackets with slick moustaches and khabkhas of various sizes, and
a lead singer in a red dinner jacket. There is also a waiter, leaning
on the door of the bar.

'Thank you, thank you,' the singer says, thanking me for walking
in. 'Now we are playing requests for your pleasure, please.'

I sit down at a table. Perhaps I am dead. Hugh always said
that the one thing we really know of heaven is that it's going to
be unexpected. 'Of course,' he said, 'for myself, I hope it has a
high tranquillity quotient, but I wouldn't be arrogant enough to
assume that it has, just because that's what suits me. We are told,

are we not, that we shall be changed? You may or may not believe what you read in the Book of Revelation, but it is important to remember that that is only a vision, and a vision comprehensible to a man of the first century. What, I wonder, would St John say if he saw our own age, with its compact discs, computers and religious broadcasting? That is, assuming he didn't see it, which I would not wish for a moment to imply. We must each of us expect some personal revelation after death, some revelation appropriate to the sort of life we have led and the sort of person that we are, and that after all, is why I hope for some kind of heaven-haven as it were, a seaside resort out of season, where one can stroll and listen to the waves, contemplating the hiss and roar of eternity.'

That is all very well for Hugh, but possibly I have gone to someone else's heaven by mistake. The tranquillity quotient here is alarmingly high. Clearly, it is not a dream; I am not still asleep at the desk in Polly's room because I have the A4 sheets with my story on them still clutched in my left hand. Yes, I recognize my own handwriting, which I probably wouldn't do in a dream.

'Yes please, thank you,' the man in the red dinner jacket says.

I look up and see he is looking at me. His eyes are brown and have a cringing bewilderment, like those of a bloodhound.

'I beg your pardon?'

'We are playing requests now.'

'I see.' The other members of the band all look at me with bloodhound eyes, dangling impotent khabkhas. They want me to make a request. I am the only guest here.

'Have you got the time, please?' I ask.

'Naturally, we are here for your express entertainment, madam.'

'I'm sorry, I just wondered if you knew what time it was. Before you play the request. I mean this is a request, really. It just isn't a musical one.'

'Time is 1.00 pm, madam,' the vocalist says proudly, 'lunch hour at Hotel Folio, therefore Hotel Folio Khabkha Band perform khabkhaba on bar terrace for your pleasure, this day as every Monday, Wednesday, Friday. *Especially* as every Monday, Wednesday, Friday. Request, please.'

'I don't know any khabkhabas. Perhaps I'll just sit here and have a drink and you can play whatever you feel like. By the way, do you happen to know who won the war?'

'Not necessary khabkhaba,' the vocalist says, 'we play whatever you wish, including Lennon and McCartney. Drink available tonic water, soda water, Pepsi Cola, orange juice.'

How tactful. Now at least I know it wasn't Miraz who won. Perhaps the man doesn't even know whether it was the Scorpion or General Tuli, and is just being joyful indiscriminately, a wise move.

I sit in the sunshine of the first day of the new era, drinking orange juice, listening to the Hotel Folio Khabkha Band playing 'A Hard Day's Night', 'With Love From Me to You', 'Money Can't Buy Me Love', waiting for developments, or the return of Polly, or lunch. The waiter has told me that normal service in the kitchen will be resumed as soon as possible, and I presume the kitchen hands have all run away and are expected back when the new and stable political situation is known. The khabkha band plays 'She Loves You', 'I Wanna Hold Your Hand' and 'Please Please Me' (strangely melancholy on the khabkha).

An hour later. I am still sitting with the sun in my eyes, hungry and dizzy, contemplating the smoking remains of the Cathedral, and the dregs of my second orange juice, for which no one has asked for payment. The first noise I have heard from the extra-Folio world today has suddenly appeared in the distance. It coughs and says something in a faint tinny voice, but I cannot catch it. It is coming closer, however, as if someone is turning it up slowly. It is like the vocal equivalent of an aeroplane, an aeroplane powered by a voice instead of an engine. The Khabkha Band are playing 'Listen, Do you want to know a secret?'. I call the waiter over to ask him what is going on.

Five men in white dinner jackets are plucking, grinning and rolling their eyes at me in an attempt to be flirtatious, the lead singer is twitching and flexing his legs, in time to the distant noise as much as to the music. He is asking me, in a Mediterranean parody of a Liverpool accent, if I want to know a secret. He yodels his love to me as the khabkhas throb to a climax. Well, yes, I suppose I do want to know a secret, but not the one he wants to tell me.

'What is that noise?' I ask.

'What noise is, madam?'

'The noise in the distance. Do you hear it? Like an engine.'

'Is government announcement madam. Band will cease when close enough to hear. Very important news for all. Great days, madam,' he says sadly. 'Besides, is almost two o'clock, at which time lunch over. It has been great pleasure to serve, madam.'

Loudspeakers. The new government explaining who it is.

Datastream 1; Telemann, Alb

Being blackmailed is a full time job. Oh, the financial aspect was no problem. I dealt with that easily enough. The bank knows that I am a White House employee, and was not, therefore, too surprised when I suddenly asked it to make $20,000 available on two days' notice. White House employees often do things like this. I'm good at the practical side of being a victim of electronic blackmail. What I find harder is to come to terms with the emotional aspect, my surges of hatred for Warburg, my surges of guilt about Ellen (even though I didn't murder her), my surges of fear about being found out. I have been having some serious surges. They keep me standing at the window day after day, staring at the lawn and the trees, trying to preserve my equanimity, trying not to think about the lake in Virginia. Now that I'm feeling so guilty about so many things, I've started feeling guilty about a whole lot besides: all those people I followed in my earlier career, who undoubtedly thought they had developed a persecution complex when they had merely developed a private detective, all those silent evenings with my father by a different lake (in Maine), when I might have said something meaningful if only I could have thought of something meaningful to say. I even feel guilty about having taken a job spying on the President's love life. Somehow, you have to admire a man who can make love to 279 women and still be so innocent about it. Pike always seemed to me like a little first grade kid having a biology lesson. (This is a biological high, Warren. How can you tell that, Miss? Well, because you see, the blood vessels are distended here and here, and the muscles contract, and . . .) If only I hadn't been so cynical in those days. Then, perhaps, I might have realized that the reason Pike had never yet fallen in love with any of these women had nothing to do with Don Juanism, he just wasn't old enough yet. His knowledge was still at the theoretical stage, or, at any rate, he was only practising. We should have seen the potential for love in his personality right away, then none of this need ever have happened. The whole business with Ellen was my fault, mine and Roly Entwhistle's and Fred Zolph's. We were just obsessed with arranging Pike's sexlife for him in the hope of occupying his mind. A mind can be too occupied.

Electronic memo from Fred Zolph this morning.

To:	Alb Telemann
From:	Fred Zolph
Subject:	Current Affairs

Greetings. Have you seen Ruggins's amazing Wocaluha allegations in the news digest today? Hot off the daisy-wheel – he only just announced it a few minutes ago. A hell of a shock, Alb. Even I was surprised. Now everyone is waiting for a statement from subject, and I will keep you informed just as soon as I hear anything.

It goes without saying that JR's allegations of political sabotage are completely unfounded. The methods used for manufacturing the stuff in bulk were never one hundred percent reliable from the safety angle, which is why they put the factory in Wocaluha in the first place. Ruggins still doesn't know shit about chemistry, so nothing is going to come out of the second inquiry per se, except maybe the potassium divinylchloramine blues, at least so long as Pike doesn't believe it. On the other hand, with the news from Lazar as bad as it is, there would be cause for concern anyway, Ruggins or no Ruggins. It's probably premature to start praying, but not that premature.

You may wonder why I'm confiding my fears to you like this, Alb. The fact is, there is nobody else I can trust. I don't know anybody in this building, all I see is the godforsaken terminal, day in, day out. I've never been as

overworked as I am at the moment, and it is getting to me, the loneliness and so on, I guess. I work like you, Alb, I get
E0E5C3B1 00A580A4 B4D3A380 C0B04020 D1B36080
E0E0E0A0 80402080 D0E10010 C4B4D280 E0E4C3B1
00A580A4 B4D3A381 D9E10000 80402080 80402080
D4B4D280 D1B3A080 E0E3E0A0 D9E10030 E0E4C3B1
00A580A4 B4D3A38 A00Hi, Alb, just a reminder that if U do not like our product U may return it to us within 2 daze and O us nothing. On the other hand, Alb, if you want to take advantage of our SPECIAL offer, hurry hurry hurry. Rose sends her Best Wishes & regards. Includes postage and packing. WBG. 0000000000000
000000000000000000000000000000000000000000000
000000000000000000000000000000000000000000000
00000000000 both eyes on things.

By the way, Alb, I hope you delete this document and all my others as soon as you've read them. I got a memo this morning from Hellbaum. He claims there are hackers loose in WHOM these days.

I deleted this message from the screen, experiencing a perverse and morbid satisfaction at causing the green garbled letters to be swallowed up by meaningless blackness. I know now what it is like to be insane. It is like having thoughts in your head which you know for a fact that you are not thinking. It is as if the English language itself has caught a disease. WHOM has contracted Warburg like a virus.

While I was stretching, yawning, standing up and sitting down again, the green letters on the screen recouped their energies, regrouped and returned.

To:	Alb Telemann
From:	Ernest Hellbaum
Subject:	Incident Report

Thank you for your bug report of # inst. This is being looked into, and we hope to have a resolution for you in the immediate / near / indeterminate future.

P.S. I hope you were not too offended by the tone of my communication of a few days ago with reference to the number of queries in USER???? I do not see many people in the course of a normal working day, and tend to get overwrapped up in my work. As it happens, the whole query question has become more or less irrelevant, because USER?, as I hope I may call him for short, has become more sophisticated of late. He no longer has to rely on using the electronic mail, and can break directly into the user interface. Have you received any more communications today, notably about five minutes ago? It seems to me, from the data I have to hand, exceedingly likely that you did. Maybe you didn't notice it? Anyhow, whether you did or not, the good news is that I believe I have traced ? to an address in Hillingdon Village D.C., with a little help from the Phone Company. Of course, the thing to do now is to contact Security and get them to sort it out in physical mode. As you probably know, my responsibilities are at the logical end.

It is too bad about our friend #? He must be one smart cookie. I don't mind telling you I could never hack like that, not even if I tried. Do you happen to know whom I should contact in Security, since I understand it is your department? I feel rather ashamed of not knowing this, but I have never had a hacker before and they are not really in my job description. I mainly do a great deal of housekeeping and debugging.

Thank you again for your bug. I really enjoyed it. Five days is quite an acceptable turnaround, if I may say so. I don't think you put a priority on the initial report. You can have Low, Medium or High. May I suggest you put High? If I solve Low priority bugs too quickly, it looks as though I haven't enough work to do.

P.P.S. The hole in the operating system is healing nicely.

To:	Ernest Hellbaum
From:	Alb Telemann
Subject:	Security

I am in charge of computer security. That is my personal responsibility. I'm glad the operating system is feeling better. Please send address from which intrusion took place. Thank you. A.T.

To: Alb Telemann
From: Ernest Hellbaum
Subject: Security

Are you sure? Naturally, you can have the address if you want it, but I understood you worked on the Sleeping Partner project. It sounds absorbing work to me. At least there is a certain human interest in it. I sometimes wonder if computing is a rather cold and impersonal thing. Of course, it has its compensations, such as when I solved your problem just now. It's good to get right in there among the bits and find out what the machine is really thinking. However, I often wish I had more to do with the analogue forms of life. Do you enjoy your work?

To: Ernest Hellbaum
From: Alb Telemann
Subject: Security

I was on Sleeping Partner project, but now no longer. (By the way, this is supposed to be top secret. How did you know about it?) Research has shown that this kind of work is psychologically harmful when protracted beyond two years, leading to voyeurism and other sexual perversions. I have recently been transferred to the area of computer security, as no doubt the intruder was aware. I think we can take it that he was only playing a practical joke of a non-severe variety. However, if you will send me the address, I will follow it up personally.

To: Alb Telemann
From: Ernest Hellbaum
Subject: Security

Of course you can have the address. It is intriguing, though, I wouldn't have thought the task of ensuring system integrity was really appropriate for someone with no programming experience. I hope you don't take this personally. I like you a lot, really I do, insofar as one can like a person on

193

a purely electronic basis. Maybe we can arrange a meeting soon. I think we should, as there is considerable overlay between my work and yours. I am currently trying to get in touch with the child in myself and would like to tell you about it. If you have any similar problems you would like to share with me, that would be good, too. My psychoanalyst has suggested to me that I should explore the world of human relationships and take more initiative in trying to achieve intimacy with people. Did I ever tell you my theory about the OM in WHOM? I think it stands for universal harmony.

I should be very interested to hear what action you decide to take with ? The address is as follows:

2054 South Roseberry Avenue,
Hillingdon Village D.C.

P.P.S. I was considered for the Sleeping Partner job myself when the idea was first mooted, but Mr Entwhistle said I was not ideally suited for the work. I have often wondered why.

That address? Ellen herself? I refuse to believe this. Alb officially opts out of this belief system.

Shortly afterwards, I arrive at a place I had never intended to see again on a warm night just as it is getting dark and familiar night noises are beginning in the dogwood and redbud trees. I am standing now in front of the door whose bell I rang unsuccessfully that evening. Surely there must be some mistake, that interference on the computer must have come from Warburg's address, not Ellen's. It said it was Warburg, of course it was Warburg, since it was written in unmistakeable Warburgese, but somehow, it seems to have been from Ellen at the same time. It is as if I am being haunted. Ellen Axaxas, high technology ghost. I glare defiantly at the front door.

'I didn't do it, you know!' I tell it. It opens suddenly.

'What the fuck are you doing, Alb?' Warburg says. 'You are talking to a door, is that right? And it isn't even the door of a normal human being, it is the door of a deceased lady. Now if

I didn't know that you were the only person foolish enough to do a thing like that, I wouldn't even answer it, I would just leave you on the doorstep like the stranded fish you are. What are you doing here anyway, Alb? You were supposed to be in Hillingdon Park the day after tomorrow.'

'Let me in, Warburg.'

'Do you at least have the money, man? Tell me, Alb, tell me at least you have managed to do that without screwing up. You may not be able to manage a murder, but I have some hope you can manage to be blackmailed.'

'Of course I don't have the money, Warburg, you said yourself I don't bring that until the day after tomorrow. Now let me in, I look suspicious standing in the doorway. Everybody in the area must know there's a dead woman living here.'

'Now that is where you are mistaken, Alb,' Warburg stands aside and lets me through, 'everybody in the area knows almost nothing about almost anything. Nobody even knew this Axes woman.'

'She told me she was just passing through,' I say.

Warburg squeals. 'She lived like it, too, Alb. It was like the subway in this house, I don't know why she didn't paint Jesus Saves on the walls. Took Rose three days to clear up this mess, in between customers of course. I live in the bedroom, now. I presume you remember where that is, Alb.'

'I feel sick.'

'I'm just passing through, too, Alb,' Warburg says, showing me up the stairs, 'this place is just a temporary stopover on my way to fame, fortune, riches and glory. I have my computer in the bedroom, because that's where the phone is. In fact, just about everything was in the bedroom, if you remember, before Rose cleaned it up. All except the deceased lady herself and she was in the bathroom.'

'You're crazy to come here, Warburg.'

'Yes, Alb. I guess you were crazy to come here too. And she was crazy in the first place. That makes this quite a crazy house, doesn't it? When I moved in here,' he continues, 'this room was not even congruous.'

'Why did you move in, Warburg?' The transformation of Ellen's bedroom is remarkable, even down to a kitschy painting of a naked black girl in a kneeling position on the wall. Most of the room is taken up by Warburg's computer equipment, the PC on a dressing table weirdly reflected in the mirror, a printer and disk drive unit on the carpet under the window, the telephone cradled in the arms of a modem.

'You like my chocolate box, Alb?' Warburg says, pointing to the picture.

'Rose is prettier. Why did you move in?'

'Rose needs a lot of privacy for her work. I feel I have to respect that. Of course, I can always go out on the skates, I enjoy that, it gets me out of the house, and gives me a chance to meet people. But you can't spend every evening on wheels, can you, Alb? Besides, it just wouldn't be right with poor Rose working so hard. She works flat out, you know, man. I needed somewhere for my studies, and I thought I would take advantage of the new vacancy that has opened up in the neighborhood.'

'What about the police?'

'What about them?' Warburg asks. 'I'm just a PC freak, man, I mind my own nose, they mind theirs.'

'When they find out about Ellen,' I say, feeling that there is something irreverent about using her Christian name in the circumstances, 'they'll be swarming round this house like vultures.'

'Vultures do not swarm, Alb,' Warburg points out, 'they congregate.'

'I don't care what they do, you're taking an insane risk, and not just on your own behalf either. If they catch you in here, Warburg, I take it I will get shopped. I don't suppose you would be noble enough to keep your mouth shut if you could get your sentence reduced by talking.'

'You're right there, Alb,' Warburg says, squealing, 'you did the chopping so I do the shopping. And there is almost nothing I cannot get by talking, even though I say so myself. However there is no reason why they should ever find me out. I checked up very carefully on Eleanor Axes. There was no one of that name anywhere in the neighborhood, man. No one in this street knew anything about her. None of them had ever been inside this house. One suspicious woman, Alb.'

I sit down on Ellen's bed, now cluttered with Warburg's manuals on ADA LISP, Pick and Unix, demons and debugging techniques.

'Listen, Warburg. You aren't safe. They're on to you at the White House. They know where you've been hacking from.'

*

Just before I leave the office, the phone rings. A long beep first, indicating an outside line. I naturally assume it is my wife since no one else knows my work telephone number. Instead, it is Warburg, who knows a lot more about me than that.

'Are you out of the house yet?' I ask.

'No.'

'Well hurry up, Warburg. I want you to know, I did you a favor, warning you off like this. Get out quick before you get caught. I can stall Hellbaum for a while, but not for ever. Sooner or later he's going to want to know what I did about you. He keeps asking me to share things with him.'

'Alb, listen.'

'It isn't easy, Warburg,' I tell him, 'I've had four more memos this afternoon. He's accusing me of not being open. He says I live too much inside myself, and I should learn to reach out to people. Only Connect, he says. This is the man who taught me about encryption and the importance of preserving data integrity. He never used to believe in connecting anything, he said it was inviting corruption.'

'Alb, will you shut up?'

'What is it, Warburg? Are you packed yet?'

'No, I am not packed. I was packing, Alb, and then I found something.'

'Yes?'

'I found. No . . . just get over here.'

'What?'

'You heard me, Alb. Get over here right away. I have to see you. This is urgent.'

'Oh, Warburg, you know how I hate that house, it makes me nauseous. Can't I meet you in Hillingdon Park or back at Rose's place?'

'Negative, Alb. Definitively not. Be here.'

Warburg is still packing. To be precise, he is running round the room waving his arms and disconnecting things, looking like an agitated maid in a French farce. As he rips his chocolate box pin-up off the wall, I remark, 'This is the first time I've ever seen you really worried, Warburg. You weren't nearly this worried when we found poor Ellen in this very house. You look as if you're about to wet yourself.'

'I tell you, Alb, if I ever get out of here alive I'm going to enjoy wetting myself. I am attached to my bodily functions, Alb, I want to keep them, man. Do you see that box under the table?'

'This one?'

'Well how many boxes are there under the table for Christ's sake? Hand it to me, will you? Oh God.'

'How are you going to lose your bodily functions, Warburg?' I ask. 'They might put you in prison, but you'd be running the place inside a month.'

'How long, Alb,' Warburg says, lowering the PC monitor into the box, 'how long have you worked in the White House?'

'Two years.'

'What's your security ranking?'

'What? I can't tell you a thing like that!'

'Oh come on, man. You are talking to a person whose bodily functions are on the line. Don't shit such a person, Alb, he may not have time to shit back. What's your ranking, S60.A, S60.B?'

'S60.B.'

'Practically nothing. You hardly have clearance to go to the john. You don't even know where the coffee machine is. You get a certain electronic insight into the whereabouts of the Presidential prick, that's all.'

'I have my own washroom and my own coffee machine,' I say. He has hurt my feelings.

'Oh man,' Warburg says insensitively, 'don't just stand there treading carpet, help me with this CPU.'

'I see, you did the hacking so I do the packing,' I tell him bitterly.

'Listen, baby, my point is that you know nothing of the kind of thing that goes on in the White House, you have not even scraped the surface man.'

'And you do know,' I say, 'I suppose you're some kind of agent, right?'

'You know me, Alb, I'm just a hacker. But I have a brain which is moderately functional, and I am trying to keep bullets away from it. I know who killed Ellen Axaxas, Alb, and if they get to know I know, and they get to know where I am, then I won't be anywhere any more.'

'But,' I say, 'you were blackmailing me. You knew I didn't do it, and you were going to get $20,000 out of me, because I couldn't prove I didn't. You dirty black bastard.'

'Alb, this is not the time for personal recriminations. I'm just a businessman, I saw a gap in the market, and I filled it. I was trading in guilts, you might say. Besides, Alb, I really thought you did it, until half an hour ago.'

'You stole my car, too.'

'Yes, Alb, both cars. It's just a sideline, it wasn't anything personal. Look, man, if we are not out of here before somebody finds out that we're in here, we are going to be zeroized.'

'Who are we running from?'

'Look, Alb,' Warburg says, holding something up, 'I found a key while I was packing. I like keys, they often unlock interesting items such as banknotes and jewelry, so I invested a few minutes trying which drawer it would fit. I found the drawer, Alb. And this item is what I found in the drawer. This is what changes everything.'

'It's a gun.'

'No, Alb,' Warburg says, 'it's *your* gun.'

Warburg takes me to his new car, which is parked outside the other house, the one where Rose habitually does business. 'Aren't we going inside?' I ask.

'You do not appreciate the scope of this incident,' Warburg says. 'This is a major glitch in my résumé, man. It could lead to premature termination. Were you followed here?'

'Followed? Why should I be?'

'Come on, Alb, you're a detective, aren't you? Were you followed or not?'

'I wasn't followed.' I load the PC into the trunk. 'Where are you going?'

'Where are *we* going, Alb? We are going to a small lake in Virginia where no one ever goes.'

'I don't want to go there.' The mist will rise over the blank lake, there will be rustling bushes, insects, memories, bloodstains on the ground.

'It is a mandatory option,' Warburg says. 'Nobody ever goes there. Listen, man, I know a safe lake when I see one.'

'Why? Me, too? What about Rose? Warburg, what is going on here?'

'Just get in the car, Alb. I'll drive, it releases my frustrations.'

We sit eating hamburgers and fries in the car and watching mist and insects rise over the grave of Ellen Axaxas. Warburg's panic is infectious, and I objected at first to the stop-off for hamburgers on the road to the lake.

'Listen,' Warburg told me, 'don't you trust me? This is a secret hamburger shop, no one ever goes there. It is like the lake in that respect.'

'There are no secret hamburger shops.' But my misgivings were overruled by my stomach. Fear makes me hungry. When I was on someone's trail I used to eat hotdog after hotdog. When the wind was behind me, paranoid suspects probably believed they were being followed by the smell of onions and mustard.

'How do you know I didn't kill Ellen?'

'I got some bourbon in the glove compartment,' he says, lowering a fry into his mouth. 'This is going to be a long night.'

'Do you have ice?'

'Do I *look* perfect?' Warburg produces bourbon and paper cups from the glove compartment.

'So how did you know?' I ask again.

'I didn't know. Not till I found your gun. We threw Ellen in the lake, plus gun, didn't we, Alb, on account of murder weapons are always highly suspicious. You told me you gave her your gun that night, and I didn't believe it. Then I found a WH38 in the drawer, and found out you were telling the truth. Therefore . . .'

'Therefore, I was right, and she killed herself.'

'With an identical gun to yours, Alb? With a WH38? Where is a humble elementary-school teacher going to get such an item?'

'Maybe the President gave it to her.'

'Yeah, maybe she was into arms control. Why would the President give her a gun? So that she could knock herself off, thus rendering herself nonfunctional from the fornication angle? No, logically speaking, she must have gotten the gun from Jimmy Ruggins.'

'They give theology advisers guns?'

'Maybe. Maybe he has friends in high places. Anyway, he killed her, or persuaded her to kill herself – she was screwy enough to do it. You should know that, you talked to her. Maybe he was in the house when we came along. He could actually have seen us doing the Lord's work for him by disposing of the body.'

'But why? What was his motive?'

'Maybe you didn't see the TV news today,' Warburg says.

Datastream 6

And I saw a sea of glass, mingled with fire. And in the midst of that sea there arose a land, and its name was called Lazar. And the land was beautiful, for in the north of that land were mountains and scrub pine, myrtle, olive and aromatic shrubs. In the centre of that land were orange orchards and rich fields for planting. But in the south, I beheld the long shore with fishing boats. And all around the island were fishes.

And the inhabitants of the land were ignorant people, and knew not God. For they considered and said to themselves, how shall we know a god? Surely such a one must come out of the sea, for we know of no dry land he may come out of. So they had many gods, like unto fishes, and they believed on them. Also they believed this: that a man should come out of the sea and be king over them, and should reign for one thousand years, and that they should become fishes and the sea would return over the dry land, and there should be no more land, for they loved it not, and longed for the sea. And each man among them loved a fish, and ate it not, for they worshipped them. But their meat was fish, which they savoured, but each man ate not that fish which he worshipped. And the fishes which they worshipped were the gurnard and the wrasse, the conger eel and the rock eel, the red mullet and the red snapper. For they said, surely a man hath kinsmen which are fishes, and shall a man devour his proper kinsmen?

And I saw a man come to this land, the servant of God, whose name was Paul. He was cast on the shore in a storm, and there were with him two hundred threescore and sixteen souls. And they were all cast on the shore, and none among them was injured. And when the people of Lazar saw Paul, they said, surely, it is a god come among us? And they took Paul and cast him in an hut, and they said, he shall be our king, and rule over us until the sea returns, but Paul was their prisoner and might not escape. And they gave Paul a slave boy to serve him, and Paul suffered it not, but said, Let the boy go free. And Paul made a broom of leaves and branches and did sweep the hut with it, into the which they had cast him.

And they believed Paul was their king, for that he had a distemper. For he was seized with a fit, and might not move his limbs, but fell down. And his body was not still, but moved as it were a vessel of liquid, and his eyes were white. And when they saw this, they marvelled and said, He is a fish, for behold his body is like unto a fish, moving.

And Paul stood before the people, and they acclaimed him. The virgins were bedecked with white flowers, and the women with purple flowers, which they wore in their hair. And every man had a spear, and every man a bow, with arrows. And the people said with one voice, Vaskha-viskh, which in that tongue is Behold, the fish cometh. And I saw two priests, and they gave him one a crown of silver, and one a fishing net. And Paul walked among them as their king, but he liked it not, for he was the servant of the Lord. And he knelt on the ground.

But the people of that country would offer Paul a woman, and this he liked not, although she was comely. And he said, This is not lawful. Ye would defile me with wreaths and crowns and with a maiden, but it is not lawful. And he escaped, and Luke was with him also, and others. And the boy that he freed was his friend and prepared a boat, and he escaped in it. And they all escaped from that place on the sea.

Then I saw the boy return to the island, and he carried in his hand a seed, which he planted. And from the seed, there sprung a tree, and the name of the tree was Holy. And the Lord stood by Paul while he slept, and said Behold the tree is planted, but the battle is not yet. Woe to the inhabiters of the earth because of the battle which is to come. And Paul wrote it down, for that he was an holy man.

And I saw the land of Lazar was holy and loved God, and I saw a great beast came out of the sea. And the beast stood on the mountains, and its eyes were as coals of fire, and the smell of the beast was like olives when they are crushed, and like oranges, and dill. And the beast struggled with the tree one thousand years and did not prevail, and neither side prevailed for one thousand years.

And I saw when they were fighting, there was a city, and there were in it flowers and high streets. And in the city was the noise of fornication and the smell of unclean things. But also the voice of God was heard in the high streets, beside the voice of the beast, and they struggled also in the city as on the mountains. The Temple of God was builded in the city, and its walls were round like the sun. And there was the smell of cakes and sweetmeats. And I heard a voice saying, woe to this city and to its people, for no man shall aid them when the beast cometh, and they shall feast no more, neither on fish nor on olives, nor goat's cheese, nor red peppers, nor spices, nor oranges. And I saw a great marvel, for I beheld a maid child, whose voice was sweet, and her hair was as honey, but her eyes were as glass, and the sun did not rest on them. And the child stood by the oilpress and an angel stood beside her. And the angel said, Child, the Lord hath work for thy hands. And the child said, even so shall it be, and her heart was joyful.

And I saw a city still greater than the first, and its walls were as white marble, and its trees brought forth flowers and every rich thing. The king of this city was king over a third part of the earth and his power was great over the nations. But I saw he was an whoremonger and a doer of evil and no thing which he touched was pure, and his kingdom was defiled because of his fornication. And many women were fed to the king to satisfy his lust, and it was not satisfied, neither with purple flowers nor with white. And the name of the king was Pike, for he was as the fish king which was worshipped in the former place. And the organs of the king were free, and his blood ran freely in his body, for that his deeds were natural, but the land was sick for that his deeds were evil.

And a woman was brought before the king which had an angel in her stomach and in her breasts, and the king knew it not, but loved the woman. And the woman was a virgin, and the king knew her. And Pike said to the woman, Behold, thou art beautiful, thy skin is as silk or as velvet, it giveth forth radiance. But she said,

I am a woman. And the king saw the angel in the woman, which had stood by her at the oilpress, for she was the same, and he loved her and called her Incandescent. But she spoke to the king and reproved him, for that he took the name of the Lord in vain and that he was a tyrant and loved not his people. And he was afraid.

And I saw a beast standing on the former island, and its name was Scorpion, and many men died from its sting. And the king rose up against the Scorpion and said, It is evil. And the armies of the king were standing by. But the Scorpion was king in Lazar and prevailed, and the tree that was called Holy was torn up by the roots.

And another angel came and stood at the altar, having a golden censer; and there was given unto him much incense, that he should offer it with the prayers of all saints upon the golden altar which was before the throne. And the smoke of the incense, which came with the prayers of the saints, ascended up before God out of the angel's hand. And the angel took the censer and filled it with fire of the altar, and cast it into the earth: and there were voices, and thunderings, and lightnings, and an earthquake. And I saw smoke in the heavens and a glow as of fire, and the smell of the air was as dill, and a voice said, It is another island. And the name of the island was Wocaluha, and there died there seven thousand because of the smoke. And men were sick and blind because of the smoke, and they were tormented in the head and in the body.

Then I saw a man arise with the mark of the Lord on his brow, and a lyre in his hand, and he was clad in white. And the song that he sang was pure, for that it was the song of the Lord. And the man stood beside the king, and sang to him, and the king was amazed. And the man sang, There is hellfire and damnation in the bedclothes of the lewd. And his song was, Babylon the great is fallen, is fallen, and is become the habitation of devils, and the hold of every foul spirit, and a cage of every unclean and hateful bird. And he told him, The time may not be long in which to repent of your sins, notably fornication.

And this man was glad of the woman, for that she was godly and gave good counsel, but he was sad for that she was an whore. And he knew that the woman was the servant of the Lord and the Lord would take her up to him.

And the man went to the woman and counselled her, saying,

thy time has come to go up to the Lord. And she said, Jimmy, you're so late. I was just going to bed. And she opened the door.

'Are you all right?' Ruggins said. Ellen showed him into the living room, but he didn't sit down.

'It's late,' she said. 'I almost gave up on you and went to bed. I don't like to be up this late, but I'm kind of getting used to late visitors.' She sat on the carpet in her usual position with her legs drawn up beside her. Ruggins still didn't sit down. He was never comfortable in this room. Ellen passed a hand over her forehead a couple of times as if to say how tired she was, and for once she didn't look him in the eyes, but stared at the carpet.

'What visitors?'

'Oh nothing, just neighbors. I try to, you know, help them.'

'I didn't know you knew any neighbors here.'

'No one really. I mean, I don't know them well.' Another light summer dress, too flimsy for the time of year, at least, too flimsy for most women in this weather, for it was still quite cool late at night. There was no heating on in the house, of course, and Ruggins felt suddenly cold in his lightweight suit. The dress was white, like the suit, and he saw she wasn't wearing a bra. She almost never did, and Ruggins was ashamed of himself for noticing, and for having noticed on other occasions. He saw himself and her from a great distance, as if from heaven, and realized at that moment that Ellen was like a blank page in a book. What you read in Ellen depended entirely on what you had been reading before when looking at the other women, at the rest of the world. As Ernest Hellbaum used to say about software, she was context-dependent. Ruggins recognized in himself the carnal lust which he had experienced occasionally as a DJ in Portland (not as often or as spectacularly as he claimed at his prayer meetings, however), and understood that this was something he brought to her, that for her there was no concupiscence in semi-nakedness. She wore her body with the carelessness of a child, and the lust came from others, from Pike, and even, God help him, from himself.

'Ellen,' he said gently, 'do you know why I've come?'

'Oh shit,' she said.

When he handed her the gun, she was still apologizing for it. 'I never said anything like that in my whole life,' she said, 'I'm really sorry, Jimmy, really. I thought I was ready, but I guess you never know, do you, until it's time?'

'Do you trust me, Ellen?' he said.

'Yes, you know I do.'

'And you believe it's really time to go?'

'Yes.'

'And that Jesus loves you? And that He died for you? And that you are now going to die for Him? And that you will be saved and go to a far better and happier place, where you will be forgiven for your sins because you committed them for Him?' She seemed to have lost concentration during this speech, and her mouth had dropped open. She looked like a bored and fidgety schoolgirl.

'I guess so,' she said, 'it's just . . .'

'What?'

'I mean, what a terrible thing to say! On the very night that I'm going to meet the Lord. Do you think He'll forgive me for it, Jimmy? I'm not sure I've had time to repent properly.'

'Ellen, you've done worse things than that, you know you have. This very night, you've committed sins far greater. Now I think we ought to kneel down and pray together, and then I'll show you how to use the gun.'

Dear Father in Heaven, we ask You to accept the soul of our dear sister Ellen, a sinner. We ask You to believe that she loves You and Your Son Jesus Christ, and that the sins she has committed have been for Your sake. We ask that You have mercy on her, for she is truly penitent.

He took the safety catch off for her, because her hand was shaking. 'The bathroom would be a good place.'

'OK,' she said dully. 'I thought I'd take my clothes off.'

'Why?'

'I want to leave the world as I came into it. It seems purer somehow. Clothes are just an encumbrance, you know, worldly. Don't come in.'

'What?'

'Don't come in when I do it. I don't want you to see me. I always have loved you, Jimmy, you know. I don't mean in a sinful way.' She kissed him and went upstairs. The stairs creaked. Every single stair creaked. And then there was a silence, during which he held his breath. And then she called out, suddenly:

'Jimmy, do you think He'll forgive me for taking His name in vain?'

'He forgives everything,' Jimmy Ruggins called back automatically. Then the gun went off with a gentle pop like a paper bag exploding, and his first thought was, take that back at once, you stupid woman. You can't die saying a thing like that. You didn't take His name in vain, you said shit, and I didn't have time to correct you.

Ten minutes later, he was still standing in the same spot, brooding over Ellen's mistake and hoping the Lord would understand, when he heard voices outside.

'Alb, fuck your human integrity. Just open the goddamn door.'

And he gave her a weapon, which she took, and she hid herself and took off her robe so that she was naked, for she would go to the Lord as she left Him, and die as she had lived, which was naked, and she took the gun and let out her life at the head.

And the man beheld the island of the smoke (which is Wocaluha), and he saw that the Scorpion had destroyed it. And he said, I told you, good people, that whatever it was that happened in Wocaluha on that fateful day, was the will of God, and that in that case, the verdict of this Inquiry had to be that the catastrophe itself was an Act of God. But I also told you that an Act of God is not the same thing as an accident. I told you God does not do things by accident. I told you God does not make mistakes, and whatever He does, He does for a good reason. If you needed me to tell you that, my friends, well, I just hope you were listening, because it is time and high time that you understood that. Now what we are here to do, and what my very good friend the President has asked me to do, is to determine exactly how the will of God allowed this terrible catastrophe to take place. Now I'm not a technical man, as I've told you before, I can't tell you what a molecule of potassium divinylchloramine looks like or how to make one. That's a technical problem, and it needs a chemist to tell you. We've had some chemists here to talk about it, and they were darn good ones too. I won't repeat what they had to say except for one thing. Potassium divinylchloramine is a form of nerve gas. It hasn't any purpose in the whole world except to kill people. I have evidence which I have not brought forward so far for security reasons, which proves conclusively that the

Wocaluha factory was blown up by Communist terrorists from Lazar, acting under orders from a man known as the Scorpion. I can prove that this evil action is part of an international terrorist campaign to undermine the military foundations of the Christian religion.

And the President looked for the woman and found her not. And he said, Where the hell is she, Jimmy? Has she got another man? If she's got another man, I'll kill him, so help me.

And Ruggins said, She's gone. These are very special times, Mr President. No other man has ever had such a great responsibility as you have at this moment.

'What do you mean, gone? You mean she's dead.'

'No, Mr President, that's the glory and the wonder of it. She isn't dead, she's just vanished. You always said she was an angel, didn't you, Sir?'

'Well for Christ's sake, Jimmy, bring her back, can't you? Find her! I need that woman. It shouldn't be beyond you to seek her out. She's been kidnapped or something.'

'Yes, Mr President, in a way she has been. She has been kidnapped for Christ's sake, Sir, and I'm not taking the Lord's name in vain when I say that.'

And Jimmy Ruggins stood before the Wocaluha Inquiry. And there were of that number, seven senators and thirteen congressmen and two score of representatives of the press. And he said: 'I want to tell you today, good people, about something which you may not think is that relevant to this Inquiry. I want to tell you about a woman I know. No one very special, just a plain ordinary woman, though I don't mean plain in the sense of homely. In fact, if you'll glance at this photograph, I think you'll agree she's quite a looker.' He handed her photograph round, and the members of the Commission, the world's press and, eventually, the world itself, gazed at the photograph of a grim-faced, honey blonde elementary-school teacher. Ruggins smiled; he looked, briefly, like a kindly country doctor. 'Apart from her looks, there's only one thing you might consider special about this woman, and that is her surname: Axaxas. Ladies and gentlemen, dear brothers and sisters, Axaxas is a Lazari name. Now you all know that there is a critical struggle going on in Lazar at this very moment between the forces of good and the forces of evil, and I have brought evidence to show you that the forces of evil were responsible for this great disaster we are here to investigate. I said that Lazari terrorists were responsible for this explosion in Wocaluha, and that means we are involved in this war. And we are all involved in a war anyway, brothers and sisters, the war between good and evil. We can't escape that war, we can't sit it out, we can only choose sides. Ellen Axaxas chose sides, she didn't sit it out, she was on the side of good. And she was a very special person on the side of good, because she was the first person in the army, the leading warrior. Now you probably haven't heard of St Paul's Epistle to the Lazarenes, have you brothers and sisters? Well you're going to hear about it, and not just from me, either. You're going to hear about it from the President himself, because . . . Because Ellen Axaxas was a good friend of his, and he can bear witness that what I am going to tell you is true. Ellen Axaxas is not on the earth any longer. She has gone to meet the Lord in the air. Oh what a joyful day this is for all of us, brothers and sisters, because . . .'

'Because,' Warburg says, 'the rapture is now official. Ruggins declared it at the Wocaluha Inquiry and Pike ratified it a couple of hours later in a special Press Conference. Ellen has been officially rapt. You and I are the only people who know she was only rapt as far as this lake. Apart from Ruggins, that is, who was probably pleasantly surprised when we cleared up his mess for him. I imagine if she did show up on the shoreline somewhere, he was able to hush it up without much trouble. A powerful man, Alb. And when I think of the hours poor Rose put in, scrubbing that bathroom.'

'Oh Jesus.'

'Jesus is the whole point, Alb. So, OK, probably Ruggins regards Ellen's death as a sort of home-made rapture. I assume he would rather Pike didn't find out about the home-made part.'

'But the whole thing's stupid, Warburg. Nobody's going to believe a thing like that. I'll bet the President doesn't even have the right to declare the rapture anyway. It can't be in the Constitution.'

'I guess you're right, Alb,' Warburg takes a slug of bourbon, 'leastways, I have always considered myself a believing individual, and I don't believe it. Maybe rapture is one of these issues you only believe theoretically, like relativity. We shall see, man, we shall see.'

'Anyway,' I say argumentatively, 'one woman has disappeared. One swallow doesn't make a summer. Does Ruggins claim that

DATASTREAM 1

other believers are vanishing, too? What's he going to do, start
kidnapping people all round the country?'

'Ruggins says that the rapture is happening gradually, starting
with the best people first. Hence Ellen. Naturally Pike is only
too ready to believe that, owing to where he thought the sun
shone out of. Also, he is in a state of shock. It doesn't really
matter whether he still believes it in a month's time, or whether
the American people believe it at all. Soon it will be too late.
Ruggins has gotten the lever he wanted to start the war against
the Antichrist. They are going to send the fleet into Lazar, man,
and that is only the beginning. Nicaragua, Cuba, Poland. Ruggins
feels that once he gets Armageddon under way the Lord will take
care of the rest of it.'

'Then we're dead.' I whimper slightly. 'Roxanne was right. We're
all finished. We are not saved, Warburg.'

'Speak for yourself, man. I have wrestled with the Lord these
many nights, I can tell you, in between earning my living, and if
I was not exactly victorious, He gave me good marks for trying.
Besides, Alb, if we tell the world where Ellen is, we can prevent the
whole thing. Armageddon will be forestalled. We have a wonderful
constitution, Alb, it has a system of checks and balances that
ensures the sincere guys never win, thank God. I tell you, Alb,
today Lazar, tomorrow . . . Well, maybe the world, but probably
Lazargate.'

'This is comforting.'

'Well it's the only comfort you got, man,' Warburg says, 'especially as you are in a danger somewhat more imminent than
Armageddon. You may reflect, Alb, that you are not at home
at this instant. That is suspicious to anyone who may or may
not be watching your house. A lot of your behavior has been
suspicious recently, staying out late at nights following people,
losing official cars in mysterious circumstances at regular intervals,
sending out worried memos about Presidential mistresses which are
undoubtedly preserved on the system somewhere. So to that extent,
Alb, we are both in trouble, you because Ruggins will soon know
who you are, and me because Hellbaum debugged my hacking, and
there will shortly be colleagues of yours asking questions all over
our tiny suburban community. In short, Alb, this beautiful lake
which harbors so many precious memories (not, unfortunately,
our own) is our personal Shit Creek. You want to jump in?'

211

I shake my head and reach for the bourbon. 'What do we do, Warburg? Do we go public?'

'I'll think of something, I usually do. Maybe we could go somewhere else, somewhere real remote, like Tierra del Fuego. I always liked the sound of that. Anyway, if we stay too long by this lake, one thing is certain, and that is that our hamburger fund will run out eventually. Likewise the whiskey.'

We finish the bottle of bourbon by dawn, and settle down to get some sleep.

'I've been thinking,' Sandra says from somewhere underneath. I realize I am awake. It is daylight but feels early because the sun is not yet hot. I feel as if I had suddenly woken up in my childhood. I look out of the window half-expecting to see a lawn, suburban houses and a quiet road haunted by Jaguars. What I see is Sacred Heart Street as it has been ever since the beginning of the Scorpion era, which is to say that the architecture is still picturesque, but there is no smell of frying doughnuts, and the orange and olive stalls are empty.

'Yes?' I say cautiously.

'Yes,' Sandra says with an air of finality. I hang over the side of the bunk and stare at her, as I have done every night since our relationship began. My alter ego. She has pulled the sheet up around her, and is using it to cover her breasts, exactly like a character in a television play. I am intrigued to find that women actually do that. Why should she want to be suitable for family viewing? A bad sign.

'I mean, here we are, aren't we?' Sandra lies down and rolls over to face the wall. 'I know nothing about you, you know nothing about me, and the whole country could go up in flames at any moment. Probably is going up in flames. I think we ought to get to know each other.'

'We haven't done badly,' I say, with a slightly nervous laugh.

I am not sure that I really want to get to know anyone. I have enough trouble knowing myself. Did I know Susan? Probably not. She is nothing to me now, only a vignette (guitar, RF Rag VII, Brideshead).

'All we do is fuck,' Sandra says to the wall, 'I don't mean fucking, anyone can fuck. That's just biology. I mean what kind of people we are, understanding each other and all that shit. You talked about love the first night, didn't you?'

'I didn't mean it.'

'Of course not, nobody's blaming you, I didn't think you did. But the point is, we have some kind of relationship here, haven't we? We have to find out what it is.'

'Well, what is it?'

'It's easier to say what it isn't.' Sandra speaks to the wall with great earnestness, as if she has some kind of relationship with that. 'We're not in love, are we? I mean neither of us is young and innocent. I'm not contemplating marriage or anything like that, so you can sleep easy. On the other hand, we have a certain background of shared experience, as it were. We've been stuck in a war. We've been shot at. We've made love. OK, so maybe we owe each other something. Not everlasting love or whatever, but at least honesty, loyalty of a sort. So I think you ought to know, you're a very nice person, I like you a lot, but I'm in love with someone else.'

'In Surbiton?'

'No, here.'

'Here? Who do you know here? The man that stole your passport, I suppose.'

'He's a bastard,' Sandra says, 'a typical exploitative male bloody bastard, but I can't help it. This always happens to me, every time.' She sniffs noisily, although without tears as yet. 'I didn't want to come here that night, it's just that I didn't have anywhere else to go, and I owed it to you, somehow, because you'd been nice to me, even though I was in love with him because he hadn't been. Ironic, isn't it?' she asks angrily, sitting up with the sheet.

'Do you want to tell me about it?' I feel oddly smug, possibly because she has waited so long to tell me.

'He just assumed. He saw me at the Hotel Folio and just sat down at my table without asking me or anything. It was my first evening here, and naturally I told him to fuck off, and he gave me just about every opening line I've ever heard in quick succession. Did I have a light, was I English, did I know the time, would I like to be shown round the city, wasn't the weather beautiful in this country, wasn't I beautiful, wasn't he beautiful, all so quickly I hardly had time to answer one of them before he got onto the next. Was I married, did I have brothers and sisters, did I go to many parties, did I enjoy love. It was just so funny I couldn't stop laughing. He got very offended, then, and said if I was going to laugh at him, he would find some other girl to talk to. So then I thought I was on holiday, and it might be fun to sort of play along, just for laughs, you know. And then he's so good looking. Creep.'

'Do you always go on holiday on your own?'

'Oh I wasn't on my own, I was with my fiancé.'

'Fiancé?' My God. 'This is a new angle, isn't it? What fiancé? Where is he now, anyway? Couldn't you have gone back to him when you were stuck in Lazar without your passport?'

'Don't be ridiculous,' Sandra says, 'how could I possibly go back to him after what I've done? I always seem to get myself into these positions, God only knows how. First Carlos and now you. Besides, I don't think I miss him very much. It was a strictly Surbiton relationship, if you know what I mean.'

'Yes. I knew it was Carlos.'

'It's almost funny, isn't it? He pretends not to know me, now. I could report him to the police, I suppose, if there were any police to report him to. I don't want to get him into trouble, he's in enough trouble already. Did you know he was a terrorist?'

'Carlos?'

'Yes, he was with the Scorpion on intensive training before the Sainte-Fleur campaign began. Really. He showed me the scars where they used to beat him.'

'Carlos? Don't be stupid.'

'That's probably why he acts so scared these days. It isn't just that he's afraid of me, he's afraid the men in black will knock on the door. Poor bastard. What do you think the son of a bitch did with my passport? Sold it, I suppose.'

'Yes, I expect he did.'

Ravidan charges into the room, where Sandra is still lying face down on the lower bunk. 'Hey Roberto,' he says, grinning, 'you better get out now. All Westerners been given twenty-four hours to leave the country. Executions of Lazarenes beginning already. That poor fucker Carlos is in Shit Street, too. He say he getting out on a fucking fishing boat, or he going to be oildrummed. I told him he was stupid to get involved with bloody religion. In the end they always put you in oildrum. Bastards!'

'Do you mind?' I say.

'Of course, you would mind being in oildrum, too. Fucking English, think you know everything. You going to be oildrummed, too, if you don't leave country at once. I heard it on radio. You, too, Roberto's girlfriend.' He grabs her abruptly by the big toe, which is protruding from under the blanket.

'Fuck off.' Sandra's voice is muffled and unenthusiastic.

'I know all about you, English girlfriend,' Ravidan says slyly, 'Sandra Castelvetro, system support manager, Surbiton. Carlos says you fuck quite nice for your age.'

'He's a bastard, too. Tell the arrogant son of a bitch to give me back my fucking passport.'

'You better get it soon,' Ravidan says, 'you got twenty-four hours to leave country, otherwise you get drummed out.'

'He hasn't got the passport,' I admit, 'I have.'

Datastream 3; Prunewood, Kate

'Don't you notice anything?' Polly says, throwing clothes into a suitcase as I sit on the bed with the A4 pad clutched to my bosom. 'Do you even know who's in charge here?'

'The Scorpion, although the radio keeps calling him Wol something.'

'His real name is Wallalla,' Polly says, 'I don't know why you're being so calm about it. Nobody knew the Scorpion was going to win . . . nobody! I mean, everyone thought it would be Tuli. He had the army, after all, or we assumed he had, till the buggers all deserted. We thought the Scorpion was just some jumped up little terrorist taking pot shots at policemen in the dockyard. Sod it.'

'Well, it's all news,' I say cautiously.

'To hell with the news, I'll think about news when I'm back in London. They keep shooting at me.'

'We've both been shot at before. Are you getting shell-shock or something? You ought to be used to it by now.'

'That was different,' Polly says, 'there was a war on then, and I was just caught in the crossfire. This time they mean it. Listen, the Scorpion is not a man of the world like Tuli. He's not going to play safe and diplomatic and try to be recognized by other governments. He doesn't even believe in governments. Practically the first thing he announced was that the state was going to wither away at the earliest possible opportunity.'

'Why?'

'Marxist theory. The state is supposed to wither away when the workers have taken over.'

'Politics.' I lean further back on the bed. 'It's just the usual revolutionary jargon. He'll get used to it. Hugh always said . . .'

'I am not interested in your bloody guru. We are not reading comparative religion now. He won't get used to it. He believes we're evil, and so do most of his men. They will shoot on sight, believe me. You remember it was him who had the British ambassador killed. Well, he's given every British and American citizen twenty-four hours to get out of the country. God knows what it will be like at the airport. Now are you coming or aren't you?'

Datastream 5; Fane, Robert

At Sainte-Fleur airport, crowds of English people are sitting on huge piles of baggage, looking like Robinson Crusoes on tiny islands. I can understand the Scorpion's point of view when I see them, smug among rucksacks with pots and pans dangling from the struts, leather suitcases, handbags, flight bags with the names of exotic airlines all over them, and all pretending to be so martyred by the weight of it all. The English are all exactly the same, old or young, right wing or left wing, male or female.

'How do two people get out of the country on only one passport, that's all I want to know,' Sandra says.

'You just explain,' I tell her, 'you just say it was stolen, that's all, and now you've got it back again.'

'The picture isn't even right. It's my name and your picture. I was really wrong about you, wasn't I? I thought you were different. I thought you were gentle and considerate and all that kind of crap.'

'I am,' I say, 'I gave the passport back, didn't I? Anyway, I'm not leaving.'

'Oh come on, come on. It's ridiculous, of course you have to leave; you're English, aren't you? Of course you've got to go back; you can't live in a dictatorship, especially without papers, especially when they're going to shoot you as soon as you open your mouth. You don't even speak Lazari. The Embassy officials are bound to let you on to the plane, they can tell you've been to Cambridge, and if they let you on, the Lazaris won't stop you, they'll be only too glad to get rid of you. Only there is no future for an English person in this country, none at all: only the oildrum, that's all. It was all right for a holiday, at least it would have been, but that's all over now. You belong in England.'

'And what do I do in England, get a job?'

'You told me you loved me, didn't you? That proves it. What you really want is a stable family life.'

'What I really want,' I say, 'is to find myself.'

'You haven't lost yourself, you stupid bastard. You're just scared shitless of getting a decent job and being like anyone else.'

'I can go with Carlos. I can go with him to that fishing village up the coast and stow away somewhere.'

'He hasn't got any choice. You have. All you're doing is running away from yourself.'

'How can you tell me I've got a choice, and then tell me I have to go back?'

'Well I think you're crazy. You're just being immature.'

'Oh yes? Weren't you being crazy and immature when you left your fiancé and went off and screwed Carlos instead?'

'At least,' Sandra says, 'I didn't go off in a fishing boat with him.'

As we arrive at the front of the queue, they are making an announcement over the tannoy.

'I wonder what that's about,' I say.

'I can't even tell what language it's in,' Polly says, 'I suggest we ignore it.'

'It might be something useful for my article.'

'Forget the article. It'll be old news by the time we get to England anyway.'

'Kate,' Andy says, 'what if it's Jalal?'

'Don't be stupid.'

'No, I mean it, what if it is? It could be Jalal pleading with you to come back. Actually asking you this time. Kate Prunewood, you are my wife, if you have any respect for the sacred values of Shamanism, come back to me. Would you do it?'

'Of course it isn't,' I say. 'They probably killed him long before Tuli's army arrived.'

'Maybe. Maybe they did. What I'm saying is, would you go back? Forget all this relativism and liberalism and tolerance, would you, Kate Prunewood, actually go back?'

'I am what I am. I'm conditioned by the cultural norms I was brought up in.'

'Such as?'

'Such as the C of E, the BBC etc.'

'So the answer is no.'

'Of course the answer is no. I tolerate his beliefs; it doesn't mean he tolerates mine.'

'But the belief you tolerate allows him to take away your right to believe anything.'

'Yes.'

'So if you tolerate him, you end up not being tolerant because he refuses to tolerate it. How do you get out of this paradox?' Andy is the only person present who looks cool. He is wearing a many-pocketed short-sleeved shirt with three cameras around his neck, which he constantly uses while smoking a cigarette and arguing philosophy with me.

'You don't get out of it,' Polly says, 'you get out of the country.'

Datastream 6

And there were jet planes in the darkness, and in the dawn. And the crack of the planes was overhead like gunfire. And there were thunderings, lightnings and an earthquake. And men were crushed under the bricks and under fallen girders, and stones and rubble. And they were burned with fire. And their bones were broken. And many died. And their wives and children died also. And there was smoke and ash in the sunshine, there were tears and lamentations and the scratching of birds.

Datastream 5; Fane, Robert

Ravidan leaps off the bunk without waking up as soon as the walls begin to shake and the explosions to resound from the direction of Saint-Sépulcre. 'Shit, man, another war.'

'Don't be stupid,' I mutter from the top bunk, 'there can't be another war, there's no one left to fight it.'

'What that noise?' Ravidan says. 'Fucking stomach rumbling? I tell you man, maybe Scorpion decided whole city is evil. He going to blow us all up overnight.'

'God, the walls are shaking. Is it an earthquake?'

'Is a fucking war, man. We better get Carlos, and find that fishing boat.'

'You mean there really is a fishing boat?' I ask. 'I thought it was only a figure of speech.'

'It better be real fishing boat,' Ravidan says. And the walls shake.

Datastream 1; Telemann, Alb

Vans drive through the early morning streets announcing the rapture, announcing the action the US has taken against Lazar, announcing the actions it intends to take in the days, weeks and months to come. Even Warburg and I, waking in the car beside a lake even blanker and mistier than it was last night, hear the announcement faintly somewhere behind the bushes, probably coming from the main Roanoke highway. And there is the scratching of birds.

'People of the world, rejoice! President Pike has announced . . .'

'Do you hear what I hear?' Warburg says.

'What?' I am temporarily unable to move any of my limbs, having fallen asleep in a posture so uncomfortable I am stuck in it.

'Shit,' Warburg says. 'Now we slept on it and it is thoroughly crumpled. What do we do, Alb? Do we tell the world what happened to Ellen or do we go somewhere safe and hope for the best?'

I look at the lake. Insects are fading above the water. I imagine that Ellen Axaxas is steaming quietly beneath the surface.

Datastream 2; Luke, Saint

'I go away for a few weeks, Paul, and when I come back this is what happens!' I was pacing the deck of the ship in a rage. Paul sat calmly and unorthodoxly crosslegged in the middle of the deck, where sailors walked round him without complaining as they coiled and uncoiled ropes, and did whatever else it is that sailors do before a voyage.

'You talk as if you were distressed that I am free, Luke,' Paul said. 'I am sorry if this is the case, but I must admit that I cannot understand it. All the saints knew that I was not guilty. I constantly affirmed it, and it is not surprising that the Emperor finally saw the justice of my cause. I am, as I keep telling everybody, a Roman citizen, and I have a right to Roman justice.'

'Roman justice!' I fumed. 'Do I have to remind you, Paul, you of all people, that it was Roman justice which put our Lord to death?'

'Nonsense, man. It was the Jews that put our Lord to death. Pilate wanted to save him. Besides, if our Lord had not been put to death, he would not have redeemed us from our sins. He moves in a mysterious way, as I believe I have pointed out before, and he is not above using Roman justice for his own purposes.'

'But everything was so perfect, Paul.' I heard the pleading note coming into my voice despite myself. You could not browbeat this man.

'Nothing is perfect in this life,' Paul said infuriatingly.

'The fact that you were under arrest was neither here nor there. We all knew that you were in the best possible position to preach the Gospel. For two years, you were in Rome, preaching to all who would listen, no man forbidding you. And now what?'

'And now,' Paul said, 'my task is done, and others will preach instead of me. I am free to go, and that is what the Lord instructs me to do.'

'Sometimes, Paul, I wonder if the Lord gives you quite as many instructions as you claim he does.'

'Well, that is for you to wonder, and for me to know. Let us not part enemies, Luke.' He was standing suddenly. We embraced, and I turned to go. The sun on the water was like the Holy Ghost, but, despite the bright day, and the sea breeze, I could not feel joyful.

'A fishing boat,' I said. 'Of all the means to choose. And you are a Roman citizen from a good family. It smells of fish even when empty.'

'There is nothing contemptible about fish. That is the gentile and the doctor in you speaking. I don't know where the Church would be today without the fishing industry. Ask Peter, or any of them.'

'Where are you going, anyway?' I asked as I stepped on to the shore.

'A fine time to ask me,' Paul said, 'the boat only goes as far as Gaul, but that is further West than I have ever been in my life. I shall stop there for a month or two and do what I can to sow the seed. And then on again. Iberia. And beyond if needs be.'

'There isn't anything beyond.'

'Well if there isn't, I trust the Lord will warn me before I fall off the edge. I am a fortunate man, Luke, to have such good communications with the Lord. And to serve him in such a way. Goodbye.'

'God be with you, Paul.'

I stood on the wharf and watched the boat out of sight. My eyes were full of dazzling tears, for I loved the man, and it was sunny. Perhaps I shall never see him again, I thought. If he can, he will go to the end of the world.